COMPLETION

ANDRÉA FEHSENFELD

Copyright © 2018 by Free Form Productions

All rights reserved.

No part of this book may be reproduced in any form or by any electronic or mechanical means, including information storage and retrieval systems, without written permission from the author, except for the use of brief quotations in a book review.

For the spirit, the state and the people of New Mexico.
And for JY.

My story is about love and gasoline.
It might not be what you expect.

PREFACE

It came to me at the worst possible moment, when there was sweet fuck all I could do about it and memories of a hundred fires raged clear and bright. I was standing and wanted to lie but couldn't and closing my eyes didn't help. I could see the piles of ashes I left behind, powdered scars, pieces of me, dusted in the breeze from Ventura to San Bernardino.

I've been lighting fires since I was ten and it might've gone on like that forever - eat, sleep, work, light fires - but eventually the universe bends and cracks and where there was no way, suddenly there is one and boom, just like that, I'm pushed through and everything's different.

But that doesn't mean everything's better.

The fears and doubts that threatened to swallow me didn't disappear. I was holding on tight when I needed to let go. I just didn't know how. Or, truthfully, I knew. What I didn't know was what would be there when I let go.

So I never did.

But it's never too late, right?

In a weird way, change is exactly like lighting a fire: there's anticipation and nerves, a lot of questions that can't be answered, and once it starts, it's impossible it stop.

PART ONE

ONE

DAMIEN

CERTAIN PLACES RESONATE deep inside you as if you were always meant to be there. It's like they know what your soul is missing and promise to fill that space if you just give them enough time.

New Mexico isn't one of those places.

I've only been here a few hours and can't wait to get the hell out.

There's a twinge in my gut I can't explain and if I believed in angels or fate or the Easter Bunny I might call this a sign, except I don't trust anything I can't control. In my world it's about numbers and facts, things I can rely on. But there's a million miles in between what I can rely on and here, and that twinge is telling me I need at least a million more. Places can be like people – good or bad – and New Mexico is empty in a ghost town way, a way that feels like trouble.

I don't need any more trouble.

Today is Thursday and I've broken several laws in the past forty-eight hours. Being a lawbreaker might sound badass, as if I'm some kind of outlaw, when it's just another thing I'd like to forget and can't, like the faint scent of gas in my Lexus or the headache that won't away. It's hard to even think straight right now, and as shadows lengthen in the early evening sun, my mind drifts.

Tuesday now feels like a lifetime ago when I was squirming in my desk chair and trying to focus. The fifth-floor offices of Crayton & Brown Tax Services was muted. Everyone except me had Independence Day hangovers, or skin burnt red from too much sun. At 11:53 a.m., when the income statements on my screen started to blur, I leaned back and rubbed my eyes. Behind the maze of cubicle walls, hundreds of fingers click-clacked on keyboards, voices droned like zombies. It was another day, blending into all the other days, until the sound of my cell phone cracked the tedium like a gunshot. One of my cardinal rules is never answer a call from a blocked number, but I hoped it was Lorelei.

"Hello?"

"Is this Damien Hester, son of Gwendolyn Hester?"

Right away, my blood froze. When someone says your full name, it's always bad. "Who's this?"

"My name is Joseph Salberg. I'm a lawyer."

I ducked down and lowered my voice. "What's this about?"

"I'd like to meet with you. The matter is sensitive. Nothing I can discuss over the phone." And as if he could read my mind, *"You're not in any trouble."*

Not yet, he should have said.

There are a lot of reasons not to meet with a lawyer who calls you out of the blue: fear, guilt, dread. But there aren't many mysteries left in this world, and being involved in one seemed impossible. Joseph's office was down the street from mine in Century City so I cut out at lunch. I'm sure my boss, Hannah, is still wondering what happened to me, why I never came back. After everything she'd done I regret not saying goodbye, but regret is the least of my concerns right now.

I've got enough on my mind.

The fuel gauge hovers near empty and up ahead, a gas station shimmers in the lingering heat waves. I've been careful so far, filling up only at night, but the road sign I just passed said Santa Fe was eighty three miles away. If the rest of the highway is this deserted, I'm never going to make it.

And I don't want to get stuck here.

The landscape has shifted from rolling hills to a valley streaked with moody layers of light. Red rock cliffs loom like soldiers on either side. Gusts of wind rock the Lexus as if its a toy and after one blast nearly blows me off the road, my already frayed nerves snap. Ignoring the fact its still daylight, I gear down.

The gas station is one of those old school, middle of nowhere independents and looks deserted. But a rusted out Ford Fiesta is camped near the entrance, and a neon OPEN sign sputters in the window, so I park at the only pump, tug my baseball cap lower and head inside.

When the door chimes open, a cashier - fat, goth - looks up from her magazine and bag of chips. "Howdy," she says, sitting up to brush crumbs off her shirt. "What can I do for y'all?"

"Hi there," I say, scanning the store for anyone else. "Just need some gas. I'm paying cash."

"You don't need to pay first," she says, waving away my wallet. "That pump is as old as Moses. Go on and fill up. Pay after." She wags a finger stacked with rings and smiles. "But I'll be watching you."

It's not really what I want to hear.

At the pump, I try to keep things under control. Even when it's not a fire night, filling up the car is awkward. The smell. The anticipation. This is the worst it's ever been. I can still feel the heat, see the flames roar higher than I've ever made them go. My hand shakes the entire time and it's a reminder to check the news feeds once more.

Back inside, the cashier's eyes lock onto mine in a weird way.

"Do you have a phone I can use?" I ask. "Mine's died and I need to check my email."

"I wish. Mine died too." She holds up the magazine. "That's why I'm reading."

"Is there a computer here? I'll pay to use it."

She leans on the counter with a flirty smile. With the strain, a bead pops off her t-shirt. "Must be some important email."

"Is that a yes?"

Her face clouds. "It's a no."

"How much further to the next town?"

"Nothing 'til Abiquiu, assuming you're heading south?" She waits for my nod, then, "'Cept Bode's won't be open by the time you get there. After that, Espanola is another thirty minutes."

Even with the heat outside, the store is musty with mold. It's crammed with junk tourists buy, except no one's buying anything here. Cans of mystery food look weeks past best-before dates. Red bags of Doritos are faded pink from sun.

"Anything good to eat in here?"

"If y'all mean fresh, then no, but the burritos in the cooler came in a few days ago," she says, nodding to the back of the store. "Restroom's there too if you need it."

In the restroom, the air is funkier – warm, with a hint of refried beans – and how is it possible to feel dirtier after washing my hands? Drying them on my jeans, I survey the half empty cooler with sinking enthusiasm. The burritos are shrink wrapped like torpedoes and probably as tasty, but whatever. Beggars can't be choosers.

At the register, the cashier is applying lip gloss and quickly tucks it away when I return. She's chatty with the kind of small talk I don't do well with and rings up the burritos, a six pack of beer and asks for ID.

"Beverly Hills, huh?" she says, her eyes now very interested. "You staying around here?"

"Just driving through," I say and hand her a twenty.

"Mmmm," she says, batting heavily mascaraed lashes. "I close up in half an hour. If you want something more than burritos for dinner..."

Be careful, I tell myself. This is another one of those situations. After Lorelei, I'm not taking any more chances.

"Thanks, but I'm heading south. I'm on a deadline."

Her face flushes and she turns away to count out my change, her voice less friendly. "You better not to be planning on drinkin' any of those beer. Police are down the road aways, cleaning up some kind of accident."

Hold on.

"On the highway?"

"What other road you think I'm talking about?" She bangs the register closed with her hip and hands me back a few coins.

"You owe me another ten dollars."

"You gave me ten," she says.

"I gave you a twenty."

"No you didn't."

There's a momentary stare-down and I'd like to say I handled the situation with tact and diplomacy. When I finish giving her shit, she opens the register and fishes out the extra bills.

"Y'all need to take a chill pill," she says. "I said I was sorry."

Her bruised look almost shakes an apology out of me, but saying sorry has never fixed anything. "Any side roads you'd recommend instead of the highway?" I ask.

"Going south? Highway's more direct."

"What if I'm interested in some scenery?"

"Scenery," she says, like it's the first time she's heard the word.

"Yeah. Scenery."

She cocks her head. "You're never going to get in. People have tried. It's Fort Knox up there."

"In where?"

"You're not a reporter?"

"I'm an accountant."

"What's an accountant from Beverly Hills doing all the way up here?"

"It's a long story."

"Uh, huh. I bet it is," she says, and her black-rimmed eyes narrow as if she's just noticed my dress shirt, rumpled and dirty, hair disheveled, all of me in need of a shower. "Y'all really don't know about those people?"

"I have no idea what you're talking about."

"So much for California being the center of the universe, huh?" she says with a smirk. "I figured anything involving voodoo would get attention out there."

"Voodoo? Isn't that New Orleans?"

"We have it here. Bunch of crazy Natives."

"Natives like Indian natives?"

"Native Americans," she corrects.

"Crazy Natives practicing voodoo. Sounds like a bad horror movie."

Taking a hefty pull off her vaporizer, she blows fruity smoke into my face. "Don't make light of what you don't know. One of them died a couple months ago down in Espanola. They brought her in all bloody, out of her mind. Rumor has it they're doing all kinds of weird stuff up there. Black Magic."

I glance at her copy of *Scientific American*. "You believe in that stuff?"

"I believe we don't know everything of this world," she says and tilts her head at me in the way people do when they think they've figured you out. "Now, I don't know you, and we started off on the wrong foot and all, but you sure look like you could use some belief."

Before she starts going off about some new-age crap, I cut in. "And these crazy people...they live out there...where you're talking about?"

"In that direction. It's a spider's web of roads out there. Easy to get lost."

"How much time does it add to the trip?"

"An hour or so, if you know where you're going. You have GPS, right?"

I shake my head. "It's busted."

"Well, I'd stay away then if I was you. 'Specially with night coming and you not being from around here. Might be worth hunkering down."

With a raised eyebrow, her original offer is back on the table. On the wall behind her, a plastic cactus clock ticks out the passing seconds.

"I guess I'll take my chances."

"Fine," she says, and sits back on the stool with a huff. "Y'all do what you wanna do. Outta here, turn left back up the road and in a half mile or so take your first left. After that, if you go another two miles, you'll hit a T intersection. Go left again and follow that south. The road breaks off here and there and there's no lights. Like I said, it's easy to get lost."

She crosses her arms, defying me to remember everything she just rattled off. I can tell she's used to calling the shots, people listening to her. Two hundred and fifty pounds can give a person a false sense of authority, but I can't take anyone with a pink mohawk seriously.

"Thanks. Appreciate the directions," I say, and reach for the bag on the counter, just as she does. Her hand is sticky and warm. She doesn't notice me flinch.

"With your car, you might not want to be on those roads. They're pretty rough."

"I'll be careful."

I try to pull my hand away but her grip tightens. "I'm warning you. They say he sold his soul to the Devil."

"Who's 'he'?"

"Their leader," she says, whispering in a way I wish she wouldn't. "Promise me you won't go looking for trouble. Just stick to the main road, okay?"

"I'm not looking for anything. I'm driving straight through," I say, yanking my hand away. "I promise."

The need to get outside is overwhelming, but as the door bangs closed behind me my feet stop moving. In less than ten minutes everything's changed. The sun is big and red in the distance and casts a strange glow. Heat still rises from the gravel but the air has cooled and I shake off a shiver at the car. Yanking the door open, I dump the beer on the passenger seat, slump behind the wheel and slam the door. My hands tremble and I don't want to admit maybe she got under my skin. I'm tempted to crack a beer until I see her hovering at the window. She might be admiring the Lexus. Or she's waiting to see which way I go.

It's 6:52 p.m.

"Fuck it," I mutter and start the car.

Despite the cashier's warning, I pull out of the lot and turn left.

That's how easily everything can change.

At 7:31 p.m., after four beers, I'm a little drunk and not sure where I am anymore. There were a couple of unmarked forks in the road where I just guessed and something tells me I guessed wrong. The sun, slipping lower, flares in my eyes. I flip down the visor at the exact wrong time.

It's one of those out of body experiences where everything is magnified: the crunch of the chassis as it bottoms out, the steering wheel spinning under my hands. When I ease the Lexus onto the dirt shoulder, my face is pale and sweaty in the rearview mirror. Behind me, dusk approaches behind the dust plume that's settling. My phone clattered to the floor in the chaos and I power it on for the first time in two days.

No service.

The wind starts to blow and ripples of red dust flutter across the windshield. Turning the phone off, I step outside. In either direction, the road dwindles into infinity. Tumbleweed bounces across the asphalt, wedging against the tire like it's trying to make a point. I kick it away, staring at the flattened rubber with disbelief. A few yards back up the road, I find the culprit: a pothole so deep it could be a shallow grave.

As the sun ticks lower, a trickle of uncertainty creeps up my spine. I haven't seen a single car this whole time and in twenty, maybe thirty minutes, I won't be able to see anything.

Great. Freaking great.

Walking back to the car, the silence threatens to stretch forever. It's been years since I changed a tire, let alone half cut, and I'd laugh, if the situation were remotely funny. It's like I'm in one of those lame, Hollywood movies: a feel good, cautionary tale of not driving drunk, where a lesson is learned and everyone lives happily ever after. Except real life never works out that way. Not the way I know it. There's usually more bad than good and if I needed anymore proof, when I pop the trunk, the only good thing is I don't have to worry about being drunk anymore.

What's left of my buzz dies instantly.

TWO

THIS CAN'T BE HAPPENING.

I lean against the car dizzy, ready to puke.

In the closet of my apartment, back in LA, is the spare tire. I'd forgotten about it, like I'd tried to forget Lorelei.

Social entanglements are something I've managed to avoid, and since I have trouble saying things the way people want to hear them, these entanglements tend to avoid me too. But Lorelei staked me out, invaded my space. (Not that it was difficult: same coffee shop, same day, same time.) She refused to give up, even when I ignored her. She told me social awkwardness was part of my charm, and no one ever says I'm charming, no one that pretty. I let my guard down.

Having her around broke up the monotony of talking to myself, and it turned out we liked the same movies. So that's what we did, once a week. (That's about all the socializing I could handle.) Two months in, after a midnight double bill of blood and gore, it was late and she asked to stay over at my place. I agreed on the condition that she sleep on the couch and be gone in the morning. I kept my bedroom door locked.

Then she started to stay over after every movie. Since there was none of *that* stuff going on I let it slide, until she ambushed me one morning in the hallway. My t-shirt – the evidence – was balled tight in her fist. She blinked back tears and asked why I had snuck out late, why my shirt smelled like gasoline, why, why, why, and she kept saying 'gasoline' accusatorially like it was the perfume of a bikini model and not the only thing holding my life together. She said relationships require communication and commitment, and I'll never forget how her face crumpled when I asked how she thought we were in a relationship when she was sleeping on the couch.

Things went downhill from there.

Convinced there was someone else, she followed me the next time and what she saw was almost worse: I was intimate with fire in ways I never was, or could be, with her.

There were a lot of things I could've told her. She didn't want to hear any of them.

I'm not sure how she had smuggled so much of her stuff into my apartment, but it required every inch of space in the trunk to move it back out. That was the end of Lorelei. The memory still hurts.

Dismissing her from my thoughts, I slam the trunk closed, the pit in my stomach officially a chasm.

I'm screwed.

At 11:51 p.m., I'm still screwed.

No cars have come by. It's deep space dark and just as cold. The quiet isn't peaceful anymore; it's nerve wracking. When I can't hold it any longer, I take the fastest, most scared piss ever, eyes scanning the endless dark. Halfway back in the car is when I hear it: a faint rumble.

Sweet Jesus. It's a car. It's *something*.

The noise gets louder and the pitch-black night starts to diffuse. I shift from foot to foot, anticipation rushing through me. Somehow I don't get run over when darkness explodes into daylight and I'm like a zombie, arms outstretched, waving *stop*.

Tires squeal. The smell of smoking brakes cuts the air. Behind the wall of lights, an idling engine sounds like a jetliner. I swallow hard and move a little closer, hand above my eyes. A monster truck, straight out of redneck heaven, hovers several feet above huge tires and is plastered with more lights than any vehicle legally requires. The passenger door opens and a man with a weightlifter's body slides out. He swaggers over in cowboy boots.

"Evenin'," he says. "What's yer trouble?"

Up close, his rodent face twitches as if he's wired on some drug. Immediately I don't trust him.

"Hey. Thanks for stopping. It's just a flat," I say, pointing at the tire, "no spare, believe it or not. Any chance I could grab a lift?"

He takes a few steps backwards to look at my license plate. "California, huh? You're far from home. Where you headin'?"

"Santa Fe. But if you're not going that far, I'll take what I can get."

"Sure thing partner," he says, and looks over his shoulder, giving a nod to the driver, who kills the engine, but not the lights. The driver gets out and walks over funny, like one leg is shorter than the other. He strokes his wiry beard like it's a pet.

Just my freaking luck. The Backwood Brothers: Rodent and Beard.

"Our friend here has a flat and needs a lift to Santa Fe," Rodent says.

Beard glances at the tire without interest. "Do you even know how to change a tire, pretty boy?"

My eyes dart back and forth between them. "Yeah, but I don't have my spare. There's no cell reception and, ah, my girlfriend's waiting for me."

"Why isn't she here with you?" Rodent asks, peering into the Lexus.

"She's back at the hotel."

"What hotel?" Beard asks.

"Uh, the Radisson."

"There ain't no Radisson in Santa Fe."

How the hell does he know?

"I dunno. One of those chain places. I forget. We pulled in late last night."

Beard steps within inches of me, and my every muscle tenses. He reeks like sweat, and under the wife-beater scrawny arms are littered with jailhouse tattoos. "Any reason why you'd feel the need to be lyin' to us?"

"I'm not lying."

He spits a thick stream of goo out the side of his mouth. "A ride into town says you are."

"Listen, be cool, okay?" I say, taking a step back, my hands up. "I just need a lift."

"Doesn't sound like there's a girlfriend," Beard says, eyes flicking to Rodent. "What do you think? Should we help pretty boy out, even though he's a liar?"

Rodent slips out of my peripheral vision and I start to do the math. These two inbreeds are first place in the crazy department. The odds of taking both in a fight are slim. Behind me, Rodent's breathing is asthmatic, labored. Beard drums his fingers on the side of one leg. Trigger fingers. Itchy.

Three. Two. One.

I turn, shove a surprised Rodent to the ground, and bolt.

"You fucker!" Rodent screams.

"Let's get him," Beard shouts back.

The pavement blurs under my feet and behind me, the sound of Rodent's boots loud and gaining ground. When the truck roars back to life a sick sense of failure takes over.

Get off the road.

I swerve hard and hit the shoulder at full speed, skidding out in the dirt. Off balance, stumbling, my right foot plunges into a hole. Something snaps. I crash, face first. Dazed, out of breath, I push myself up, spit out dirt.

Move!

I stagger up, but my right ankle collapses and the ground rushes to meet me again. Then Rodent's fingers are clamped around one calf. I lash at him with my other leg, frantic. "Fuck you."

But his fingers only dig deeper, and the other hand joins the first. He scrapes me along the ground towards him. For a little guy he's strong. On the road, the truck screeches into position. Beams of light slice through the dark, putting a spotlight on a scene I don't want to be starring in. Rodent's only an outline against the light, fury pulsing off him like invisible solar blasts. He's holding onto my legs like he's deciding which one to snap off first.

"Nice try shithead," he says, panting hard. "Looks like your luck has run out."

Even if I had a response, he wouldn't hear me. I wouldn't hear me. Sounds muffle and everything starts to slow down, like I'm in a dream. All I can see is the black sky thick with stars, a sliver moon.

Then more stars.

After that, I don't see anything.

THREE

IT WAS dark and now it's bright. Why is it so bright?

Above me, thick wooden beams run across the ceiling and they shift in and out of focus. Beams? I don't remember beams...or this blanket. It's heavy and hot, smells like detergent I don't use. I try to push it off, but can't. It's like I have an entirely different body. Nothing works like I'm used to.

"Be careful. Go slow."

I spin hard towards the voice. Bad idea. Fireworks explode in my head.

"Men," a woman chuckles over my groan, "you never listen. I said *go slow*. You might have a concussion."

I struggle upright, needing both hands to steady myself as waves of nausea and faintness rip through me. Everything's fuzzy, including my memory. Something happened. Fire. Yes, but then I was driving. Where? Good question. Beside me, the woman sits on a chair watching me with curiosity. Sunlight streams through the huge bay window and lights her skin in a way that reminds me of the Mona Lisa, although this girl's smile is way more mysterious.

"Hiya," she says.

I unstick my tongue from the roof of my mouth. "Where am I?"

"Well, hello to you too, mister. My name's Addy."

"Yeah, hi," I say, trying to focus both eyes. "Uh, what day is it?"

"July 8th. Friday," she says, and watches me pad the swell around my left eye. "You'll have a bit of a shiner but it'll heal. How are you feeling?"

"Like shit."

Her laugh is smoky and sexy, matches her voice. "If it's any consolation, you don't look *that* bad," she says, and smiles, dimples on both cheeks. "And your name is...?"

"Damien." At least I remember my name.

"That's a cool name," she says. "Different. What does it mean?"

"My name? I don't know. Why?" I ask, confused.

"You should know. Names are important."

"What does Addy mean?"

"Wouldn't you like to know?" She smiles again and leans forward, a lowcut t-shirt barely containing her. "You're kinda cute, even after being beat up. They found you last night, beside the road. What happened? We're all kinds of curious."

Her eyes drift onto my nakedness where the blanket has slipped to my waist. I yank it back up.

What happened? Think.

Slowly the fog lifts. I stiffen and move back.

"What?" she asks.

"Do those guys live here?"

She follows my nervous glance around the room. "What guys?"

"The guys that did this to me."

After a long look, like I'm the one who's crazy, she gets up and plunks down right beside me. I pull the blanket up to my chin. Hasn't she heard of personal space?

"Woah, relax. No one here did anything to you." She reaches over and hands me a glass from the bedside table. "Here, you could probably use this," she says, and off my skeptical look, "It's only water, I swear."

I sniff it anyway, then guzzle, surprised at how thirsty I am.

"More?" she asks, but I shake my head and hand her back the glass. "What else do you remember from last night?"

"Ah, I got a flat, and didn't have a spare and then these two guys came by, pretended to help." I stop, the memory of Rodent giving me chills. "You sure they don't live here?"

She feels around on the top of the blanket for my leg, gives it a squeeze. "Positive."

"Is this your house?" I ask.

"I wish. No one gets to use it."

That's the second time she's said that, only now there's a slight edge in her voice. "What do you mean 'no one'?"

"You're from California?" she asks, as if she hasn't heard me.

"Yeah. LA."

"You heading back there?"

I pause. "Probably not."

"Probably not," she repeats, and glances at my hands. "Nothing to go back to?"

The way she brushes her thumb back and forth across her lower lip is distracting and the sweetness in the air, definitely coming from her, reminds me of something tasty and bad, like cotton candy. She's older than me but everything about her feels illegal.

"Do you know what happened to my car?"

She makes a sad face. "It's kind of smashed up."

"Are you kidding?" My stomach drops. "Really? How bad?"

"You've got nothing but questions, huh? I guess I would too. I don't know much about cars, all the engine stuff, but the windows are all smashed out. They pulled it up here last night to get it off the road."

"Did anyone find my phone or wallet?"

"Not that I know. Hopefully you can replace them." But she says this like she hopes I can't, and we stare blankly at each other before she reaches for a pile of clothes at the foot of the bed. My dress shirt is folded neatly on top and she touches it like it's something rare. "I washed your stuff. All the blood came out. Were you on your way somewhere fancy?"

"Those are my work clothes."

"You want a t-shirt?" she asks. "Something more comfortable?"

"I'm good, thanks," I say, my head still dull but almost clear, bearings coming back. "I should probably look at my car, see how bad it is. Do you have a phone I can use?"

A slip of shadow darkens her face. "Well, if you're feeling okay you need to shower and get cleaned up first. He wants to meet with you." She points behind me. "The bathroom's right there."

Déjà vu washes over me. "Who's 'he'?"

Her voice drops and something else lurks just behind her eyes. "Don't believe anything he says, okay?"

"What? Why?"

Before she can answer, heavy footsteps echo louder and louder outside the bedroom and we both flinch as the door bangs open. A freight train of a body, covered in orangutang-red hair comes to an abrupt halt. Addy leaps up from the bed, my clothes flying.

"What the hell is going on?" he demands, eyes slitting at Addy. "You're supposed to let me know when he's awake."

The levels of douchebaggery going on with this guy are so off the charts I don't even know where to start. Diamond stud earrings, a head tattoo, three-quarter length Dickie's like Mexican gangsters wear in LA. I don't like his looks or his rudeness. And I don't like gingers.

"Hey, cut her some slack. I just woke up."

He ignores me, growls at Addy. "I can't even leave you alone for an hour. Go home. I'll deal with it from here."

"I was just..." she starts.

He grabs her arm, the crackle between them fierce. "You hear me? Home. Now."

She yanks out of his grip, all the lightness in her vanishing. Without a goodbye she storms out and he kicks the door closed behind her.

"Don't even think about it," he says, turning to me with a smug smile. "She's out of your league."

"You have no idea what my league is."

"Your league is you got what you deserved. Too pussy to fight back I'd say."

"You don't even know what happened," I say, annoyed.

"Don't need to," he says, puffing out his barrel chest. "California. Long hair. You're probably a doper."

"I don't do drugs."

"Sure Mr. Drink and Drive, you're a regular fucking saint. Believe your own press if you want, but you ain't fooling me. Beer cans all over your car," he grumbles. His eyes are steely, testing me, like he knows there's only so much confidence I can bring to this argument in my underwear.

"I didn't ask for this to happen, okay? I don't even know where I am or who all you people are so just lay off."

"Yeah, well, if it was up to me, we wouldn't have even stopped. Almost one in the morning and I gotta drag your ass back here? Who the fuck drives without a spare?" He gives me a dirty look. "You probably couldn't change a tire anyway. Pussy. These are for you," he says and tosses the flips flops he's been holding beside the bed. "We couldn't find your shoes last night. Get ready. I'll meet you outside. Twenty minutes." He sniffs the air and makes a funny face. "And make sure you shower because you stink."

He slams the door and the room vibrates with lingering tension. Not that there's much to vibrate. The bedroom is as empty as my LA apartment. There's a king-size bed, a chair and two bedside tables covered in dust, nothing in the drawers. On one table, a clock radio blinks 12:00, and static crackles when I turn it on. I have no idea what time it actually is, although the angle of the sun, low enough to glint off the crystals hanging in the window, looks like late afternoon.

I feel like I've been run over. I could sleep for another twelve hours at least. Instead, I've got twenty minutes...until what?

Three days ago, I swore I hit rock bottom. It's hard to believe things have gotten worse.

FOUR

THE IRONY? I've been waiting for days to shower and now can't even enjoy it. Like a last meal in prison, my mind is focused on what's coming next. As thin trails of blood swirl down the drain, different images of this guy I'm supposed to meet flash in my mind, none of them good. I keep thinking of the cashier's story, but she said the crazy people were all native; Addy and Douchebag were white. It's small relief, but I'll take it, considering the rest of the circumstances.

Little bruises bloom on my body like a rash. My ankle is swollen to twice its normal size. Getting dressed is a challenge. Every muscle screams as if I've bypassed death and went straight to rigor mortis.

Before heading out, I do a quick lap of the room and find nothing. A few wire hangers dangle in the closet. French doors leading to a neglected yard are screwed shut. Out the bay window, a tall fence blocks any view, nothing but blue sky above it. I spin one of the crystals, the dust dry and slippery under my fingers. As the kaleidoscope of colors flash across the room, a low-grade hum starts to reverberate underneath me. I move my feet and look down, confused. It's definitely there. Goosebumps on both arms prove it.

But it's not a normal sound.

It's a frequency I've never heard.

The vibrations strengthen and wane, then disappear altogether. If the soles of my feet weren't still tingling, I'd swear I imagined it. My eyes skirt the room, not sure what I'm looking for. Even seeing a spider would help, anything to justify the black crawling up my spine.

What was that?

Being alone with that hum, even the threat of it coming back, creeps me out. Being in the company of Douchebag isn't much of an improvement, but someone is better than no one. Still, it requires a mental pep talk to open the bedroom door. The two possible outcomes to my situation - life or death – suddenly feel very real. It takes walking the entire length of the narrow hallway outside the bedroom before my mind can focus on anything else.

In the foyer, I find the front door ajar. Hot air pushes inside. From here, another hallway branches left into the rest of the house, everything filtered through a museum-like dimness. The thick layer of dust everywhere tells a story, but what is it?

"That's right. Who's your daddy? Who's your daddy?"

The sing-song voice drifts in from outside and I step onto the porch thinking its Addy, but Douchebag rocks on a wooden porch bench, scratching the chin of a grey cat lounging beside him.

"Yeah. You like that don't you? Of course you do. Yeah. Yeah."

The transformation from jerk to pile of mush is almost unbelievable. Lorelei encouraged me to get a cat, said it would it help my nerves. If cats had this much power, maybe she was right after all. I clear my throat extra loud.

He whirls around, the dirty look on his face dissolving into surprise. "Where do you think you're going?" he laughs. "A job interview? Jesus. It's a hundred degrees out here."

It is hot. Furnace hot. Even in the shade of the covered porch, my skin prickles from the heat. Red dirt stretches as far as I can see in every direction. It's like I've landed on Mars.

"Is that your cat?"

"No," he says, and stands abruptly. The cat stretches and blinks at me with dopey eyes, meows.

"What's its name?"

"Diesel."

"Really?"

"No, I just made it up. Yes, really." I move forward to pet it, but he chest bumps me away. His deep-set eyes are bloodshot and haven't gotten any friendlier. "It's not play time, bud. Let's go." He stomps past me, down the porch steps, and I've barely made it down the first one when he turns around and frowns.

"Christ," he says, hands on his hips. "You can't walk? We're heading up there."

He points left to a hill that slopes steeply upward. Paving stones are wedged into it like a staircase. On top of the hill, a low-slung house commands the landscape like an army general. Even at a distance it's imposing.

"I twisted my ankle. I don't know if I can make it that far. Can this guy come down here instead?"

A small puff of noise comes out of his mouth. "He doesn't come to you."

"Is there a car?"

"Are you that much of a wuss?"

"Fine. Whatever," I say and limp down the last three steps.

With a look of disdain, he sighs theatrically. "You can hold onto me going up. Just keep your hands away from the prize zones."

Right. As if.

We shuffle up the hill, and it's awkward on every level. Hot wind whips past us, and he smells like unwashed clothes, grunts whenever I lean onto him.

"Who am I meeting? Does he have a name?" I ask when we're halfway up and taking a breather.

"He'll tell you if he wants you to know."

"Is he pissed off about all this?"

"You can ask him."

Higher up the hill, I see nothing but land, flat on one side, stretching into the horizon, soaring red cliffs on the other. "How far away are we from Santa Fe?"

"Don't ask so many questions," he snaps.

On the plateau, the path diverts into two and leads to opposite ends of a U-shaped house. The clean lines of concrete remind me of a bunker and it's so integrated with the surrounding shrubs and grasses it looks like it sprouted out of the ground. He leads us left, away from what looks like the main entrance. The air up here is heavy and we're both slick with sweat. I'm happy to move away from him when we finally stop in front of a serious looking door. He jingles through a wad of keys from his pocket, using three different ones to open three different locks.

"Inside," he says. "And shoes off."

I slip out of the flipflops and stutter over the threshold.

"Don't touch anything," he warns, and closes the door behind me.

Click. Click. Click.

The locks fall into position.

My eyeball is slow to adjust from the brightness outside. At first glance, it's just an average room you'd find in an average house where nothing crazy is going on - *like killing people* - but the hint of pine, clean and antiseptic, hangs cold like a guillotine. Two couches face each other in the far corner and in front of me an Ikea-grade dining table is bare except for a pitcher of water, two glasses and a plate of cookies. Something about the set up reminds me of an interrogation, and my hand tightens on the doorknob. It's the only connection to outside, a world that now seems light years away.

Don't think about that.

Instead, a vision of a torture chamber enters my mind, and I'm so pre-occupied trying to get rid of it that I don't see the door on the far wall until it opens and I almost have a heart attack at the age of twenty-one.

FIVE

THE FIRST THING I notice about him?

Everything.

But whatever I thought he might be, it never added up to this.

His piercing look skewers me against the wall, a contrast to his respectful, almost formal, tone. "Damien."

He closes the door behind him and strides in, the air in the room shifting. Every hair left on my body stiffens. I forget to breathe until he towers in front of me. "It is Damien, right?" he asks, extending his hand.

How does he know my name?

"Yeah," I say.

His hand is still there and some instinct, some memory of what to do, kicks in. Although his hands are rough - outdoor hands - they're gentle when they clasp mine. Beneath his loose t-shirt, both biceps are ripped.

"Are you feeling nauseous? Headache?" he asks, his eyes drifting from the wound on my head to my eye, black and purple, like someone scribbled on it with markers.

"I'm sore, but okay, I think."

"That's good news." His hands slip off mine, taking their heat with them. "We didn't know how badly you were concussed. I had Cassius watch you while you slept last night just in case."

"Is he the guy that brought me up here?"

He raises an eyebrow. "Was everything okay?"

"Uh, yeah. But he wasn't exactly a ray of sunshine."

A faint smile drifts onto his face. "In fairness, he did have a long night. He is a bit of a bear with no sleep. Please, let's sit." He moves to the table and pulls out two chairs, his expression shifting to one of concern when I start to limp over. He comes towards me to help, but I raise my hand, not sure I want him so close again.

"I'm good, thanks."

But I'm not good. We sit facing each other and butterflies go ballistic in my stomach. All I can think about is angles: the ones on his face. There's a definite purpose in his gaze. Even the heat pouring off his body is formidable.

"First of all, welcome," he says, tucking his long, blonde hair behind his ears, "although it's unfortunate about the circumstances. Do you remember what happened?"

I give my best recollection and make it sound like I put up more of a fight.

When I'm done, he asks, "Did you see the license plates?"

"No. I don't know, it all happened so fast. It was dark. Those guys were crazy. Do they sound like anyone you know?"

He shakes his head. "Sounds like a random incident. We don't see a lot of people up here."

I think of how empty the road was yesterday. How lucky I am to be alive. How I want to *remain* alive.

"And thank you, by the way. I mean, thank you isn't close to being enough. Who knows what would have happened if you hadn't found me. You probably saved my life."

"You're welcome," he says, like it's no big deal, saving a life. He flicks a piece of fluff off his jeans and glances down at his trim, clean fingernails. "What brought you to New Mexico?"

"Oh, I'm, ah, on a road trip. You know, driving Route 66 and stuff."

"I see. Is there anyone you need to call?"

"For what?"

"Anyone who might be worried about you," he says, cocking his head. "Girlfriend? Roommate? Parents?"

"Oh. No."

"You're on holiday then."

Something about the way he says it, a statement instead of a question, unsettles me. "Sort of."

"How old are you?"

"Twenty-one," I say, and then, before I can stop myself, "Why? How old are *you*?"

His eyebrows arch in surprise and my face flushes.

Smooth, you idiot.

"Sorry," I say, and cough. "Sometimes I don't think and..."

He waves away my concern. "Would you like some water?"

"Yes, please," I say, avoiding his eyes. Something's weird with his eyes.

He pours two glasses with slow, measured movements, sets one beside me. A thick, white scar snakes down the inside of his left arm, the knotted line ending in his palm. "I'm thirty-two, since you asked." And after watching me drain the water, "You're nervous."

"A little," I admit. I'm not used to being watched so closely. "This whole thing has kind of freaked me out, you know."

"Of course. Puts a dampener on the road trip."

The smile I'm expecting never comes, and I'm unsure if he's trying to be funny. "Uh, that girl, Addy, she said my car was destroyed. How bad is it?"

His body language stills. "When did you meet her?"

"She was in the room when I woke up."

"What else did she tell you?"

"Nothing," I lie, aware of the slight edge in his voice. "She wanted to know what happened to me and I asked her about my car."

"Yes, your car," he says after a pause. "I don't know about *destroyed.* The windows are smashed. A few dents in the body. We pulled it up here after putting on a spare. We can donate that to you, since you need it."

His tanned skin creases briefly with a half smile and I can tell he'd never be caught without a spare. He oozes confidence, *ability*. Maybe he'll take pity on me.

"I know you've already done enough, but it sounds like those guys stole my wallet and ..."

"You need some assistance," he finishes. I nod, relieved, and he gives me a curious once over. "I imagine there must be someone you'd like to contact then? You're welcome to use the phone."

"Yeah, okay. For sure. There's someone I can call."

My heart starts to pound, my mind cycling through new levels of disaster. Maybe it's my imagination but the blood red walls of the room seem to pulse in unison with my heart. Creep closer. It's like I'm in the belly of some strange beast that swallowed me.

He leans back and pulls out a flip-style cell phone from the front pocket of his jeans, placing it on the table between us.

"You want me to call right now?" I ask, my eyes flicking from the phone back to him.

"Given the situation, I assume the sooner the better?"

"Uh, what time is it?"

"6:30. 5:30 in California. That's where you live, right?"

At the first mention of time, my mind drifts. 5:30 pm. I'd be leaving the office. Pending traffic, home at 6:20. Dinner at 7:00. In bed at 11:00, except on a fire night. Hundreds of miles away, nothing feels real about my old schedule, like I'm remembering someone else's life and not mine.

He waves his hand in front me - 'hello?' - and snaps my attention back.

"Ah, my friend who could help is at work right now. He can't take any calls. Or texts. Maybe later?"

Like, never.

"Okay," he shrugs, but the way he sees right through me, I know he knows I'm lying.

I glance at the cookies. "Do you mind if I eat those?"

"Go ahead. They're for you."

He watches me in silence, crossing one leg over another, snapping the grey flipflop dangling from his foot with small, rhythmic circles of his ankle. I force myself to eat slow, not look like a starved animal. When I'm done, I look around for something I can talk about, something about *him*, but there's nothing, not even art on the wall.

"So what's your deal then?"

"Deal?"

"Who are you?"

"Yes, of course, introductions," he says, and straightens in the chair. "I'm Garrett. Garrett Kaller." He pauses as if waiting for a reaction. I don't recognize him, but I've heard of Hollywood types moving to the middle of nowhere and the dude is seriously good looking.

"Are you a movie star?"

"God no," he says, chuckling. He tips back and rocks on the back legs of the chair, interweaving his fingers behind his head. "I try to stay *out* of the spotlight."

"I guess you chose the right place. Doesn't look like much is going on."

"There's enough going on."

"How long have you lived out here?"

"A few years."

"Do you know anything about the crazy natives?"

He stops rocking. "Natives?"

"Some cashier told me a bunch of stuff. I figured she was full of it."

"Did she know you were coming this way?"

"No."

"What did she tell you?"

"Some bullshit about voodoo, black magic."

Behind him, a blind covering one of the windows ripples as if a door opened. Or something invisible walked past it.

"You don't believe in any of that do you?" he asks.

"No way. Religion, voodoo, whatever. It's all garbage."

It looks like he's about to say something, then doesn't. The silence extends until it's weird. Finally, I clear my throat. "Can I take a look at my car if we're done?"

The chair legs creak as he starts to rocks back and forth again. "We're not done."

It's his tone. The imperceptible shift of energy. The moment becomes delicate and unpredictable, like propane, which is why I don't use it. It takes all my effort just to swallow.

"I don't have any money."

"Who said anything about money?"

"Uh, you didn't, but..."

"Do you think you've been kidnapped instead of rescued?" he asks, and the fact that he looks the tiniest bit amused bugs me.

"I know you helped me and I'm grateful, really, but I should look at my car. I've got stuff to do and..."

The chair legs crash to the ground and like a cobra he darts forward right into my space. Pinned to the chair, I'm shitting bricks he's so close and only now do I understand what was throwing me off about him. His eyes. One is blue, the other an unnatural emerald green.

"I think the question is what are we going to do with *you*, Damien?" he asks, and just like that, all the air gets sucked out of the room.

"What do you mean?"

"Do you expect me to tell you the truth?"

"About?"

He waves his hand in front of him. "Anything."

"Well...yeah," I hedge.

He leans back, pulls a piece of paper out of his back pocket and unfolds it so I can read. Something cold and black blooms in my chest. I thought I knew what it meant to be screwed, but this is a whole new definition.

"This is where you tell me what's really going on," he says, dropping it on the table when I don't take it.

My face boils with shame. And fear. "I'm not really on a road trip."

"I figured. Right now, I'm aiding and abetting a criminal. You better start from the top."

SIX

THERE HAVE BEEN times in my life when I knew I could wiggle out of something. This isn't one of them. After reading the LA Times article Garrett printed out, I start to feel green. It was posted this morning. My photo and license plate number are online for all of America, the world, to see. Garrett watches me, every bit of my reaction, and the temptation to weave more half truths into something believable dies. I'm deep in the no-bullshit zone and he doesn't look happy.

"I'm sorry," I say, barely able to make eye contact. "I didn't mean to lie."

He breathes deep and crosses his arms. "I want the whole story. No short cuts."

It's impossible to get comfortable in the chair now, and after watching me squirm for a bit he says, "Let's sit on the couches," and holds out his hand. He pulls me up with no effort, his arm solid, like metal.

Somehow I'm not surprised when he sits on the couch opposite me; it's a familiar arrangement, and not in a good way. All the offices I have sat in, the merry-go-round of shrinks offering useless advice (mostly the pharmaceutical kind). A stranger wanting me to talk never amounted to anything, but Garrett isn't taking notes on an iPad, or interrupting with annoying questions. He looks like he actually gives a shit when I tell him about the call from Joseph Salberg, the probate lawyer, what his news set in motion.

Reliving it's a jumble of emotions and when I'm done, it takes all my effort to stop my chin trembling.

Jesus Christ, don't cry like a baby.

The lean silence extends and our eyes flicker from each other to the floor.

Finally, he exhales. "I don't know what to say."

"TMI," I mumble, and he gives me a quizzical look. "Too much information."

"Ah, got it." He pauses, rubs his mouth. "Your stepfather paid your real father a half million dollars to walk away from you?" His tone is incredulous, as if he needs to hear it again to believe it.

I nod, almost not believing it myself. All I remember is how Joseph's office started to blur when I read the letter my real dad, Curtis, wrote to me before he died. The letter I jammed in my stepdad's mailbox with 'fuck you' scrawled on it.

"And your father needed the money," he says.

In the letter, Curtis said he hated himself for what he did. On the verge of bankruptcy, he was desperate. He needed cash, and I could almost forgive him. At least he had a conscious, could actually feel bad about something. My stepdad was another story. Even though it was a one-night stand and Curtis wanted to be part of my life, my stepdad tried to force mom into an abortion. She refused. He was in the middle of some deal with bible thumpers and couldn't risk a scandal.

So he went to Curtis.

The money was one part of the deal; no contact with me was the other. Convinced bone cancer was his payback, Curtis left me a bunch of money in his will. Money I don't ever want to touch.

The worst thing was seeing his photo. How I looked just like him.

"The lawyer confirmed what the letter said?" Garrett asks.

"He showed me the agreement they both signed for the money," I say, and a sour taste rises in my throat; I was referred to as the 'property' in that agreement.

"Did you ever suspect he wasn't your real father?"

"There were a few things that didn't make sense," I say. *A lot of things*.

He's careful with the next question. "Your mother never told you?"

Curtis' letter explained a lot, but I'll never know why mom didn't say anything, although I can guess. She grew up in poverty and the pain of having nothing outweighed the pain my stepdad inflicted on her. My last visit consisted of her staring out the window while a dark puddle of piss spread under her wheelchair.

"He threatened her. He was an asshole. Still is."

Garrett points to the article. "This development you burnt down, Virginia Hills. It's serious. Millions of dollars in damage."

"I know. It was three quarters finished. Don't worry, he's insured. It just means delays and pissed off investors."

"He knew it was you. Knew about your..." he trails off.

"Yeah."

"Wasn't there security guards on site?"

"Those guys sleep half the time. Maybe walk around once an hour. I timed it right."

A thin line creases his forehead. "You have no remorse."

"Why should I?" I ask, a swell of anger rising. "He never gave a shit about me. He deserves all of it, and more. Way more."

"Someone could have died."

There's no judgment in his look, only brutal truthfulness. He's right, but he can't understand what it's like. The pressure. Fire the only way out. No one can understand. I wipe at the corners of my eyes, but it's too late. Tears start to slide down my face. It's an awkward moment made worse when he gets up, pushes the coffee table aside and crouches in front of me.

"Hey. It's okay," he says, putting his hand on my leg.

"No, it's not okay," I say, my voice cracking as I shove his hand away. "It's not fucking okay. My whole life could've been different."

He sits back on his heels and raises both hands in retreat, but if he's fazed by my anger, he doesn't show it. After a beat he asks, "Is there more to the story?"

"What more do you want?"

"Pyromania is a reaction, triggered by something."

"You don't think what happened is a trigger?"

"It's not a one-off disorder is what I'm getting at. Pyromaniacs light fires to regulate emotions, tension. You've been doing this for a while."

"What," I scoff, "you know other pyromaniacs?"

"I know a few things."

I cross my arms, stare glumly at the wall. "I don't need a new shrink."

"What happened to your old one?"

Dr. T with her orange office, bearskin rug and clove cigarettes; she was more whack job than shrink. "I walked out. She asked me if I thought 'fire was my destiny' because I'm a fire sign," I say, rolling my eyes.

He tilts his head with a curious look. "Sagittarius?"

His poker face throws me off. Then his mouth starts to twitch and he bursts out laughing. His laugh is so wild and crazy, so unexpected, it makes me laugh, and in a weird way, that's how the ice finally breaks.

"Nice one," I tell him, still chuckling when he wedges himself into the corner of the couch I'm sitting on. "Seriously. What the hell does being an Aries even mean anyway?"

"I'm Sagittarius," he shrugs. "Apparently that means we're going to get along."

"You're not into that stuff are you?"

"Of course not," he says, smiling. "But I made you laugh."

I look down, now sheepish for being so rude. None of this is his fault. "Thanks."

The first comfortable silence sinks around us and he lets it linger. My toes flex into the thick pile of the rug. I relax into the couch cushions. Even the red walls aren't as threatening.

"If you don't mind me asking, what was your original plan? Before all this," he asks.

"South America. Colombia."

He looks impressed. "That's ambitious," he says and after a beat, "How did you end up in New Mexico?"

"I just started driving. Needed to clear my head. Took a couple wrong turns," I admit.

"Hablas Espanol?" he asks.

"Si," I say, surprised at his perfect accent. "Estoy con casi fluidez." I wiggle my hand back and forth. "Mas o menos."

"Impresionante. Yo tambien. Que harás ahi?"

"No sé. Maybe become a fisherman."

"That's a long way to go without a plan."

"I know," I say, bristling. "Once I'm in Mexico I'll figure it out from there."

He frowns. "You can't cross the border now. You can't even walk properly."

"It's too risky to stay in the states."

"Northern Mexico is cartel country. It's too dangerous to drive alone. And they're calling your fire arson. That's a felon. It means jail time if you're convicted. Trying to flee the country is a bad idea."

"So, what then?" I ask stupidly, like he has any clue.

"You could stay here."

"Uh..." He looks *serious.* "I guess. But if they find me here, you'll be in trouble for sure."

"Who knows you're here?"

I hesitate. "No one."

He shrugs - *see, there you go.*

"I mean, I appreciate your sympathy but..."

"I'm not offering sympathy. Or charity," he interrupts, squaring his body towards me, one arm stretched along the top of the couch. "Let me put it a different way. You're fucked. You have no ID, no money. You can see for yourself what your car looks like. Getting to Colombia's a wing and a prayer at best. The only rational choice is to stay here until we figure something out."

"We?"

"You're not in much of a position to help yourself."

That he's offering to help me skirt the law is intriguing. And confusing.

"Okay," I say slowly, "but what is this place?"

"It's private land. I own five thousand acres. We're very remote."

"Five thousand? That sounds huge."

"It is," he says, and stands up, starts to stretch. "I don't know about you, but I'm getting hungry. Why don't we have dinner and talk after? Your car isn't getting fixed tonight so let's assume you're here one more night."

Let's assume. He isn't really going out on a limb. What choice do I have? He's helped me, saved my life, and right now he's my only ally.

Maybe.

Even though I say dinner sounds great, I feel anything but. I'm not sure if it's a good or bad thing no one knows I'm here. He sounds casual about everything, but his eyes are still watchful, assessing me, and the ripples of intensity coming off of him tell a different story.

Still, something about him intrigues me, and that almost never happens.

What's one more night?

SEVEN

ADDY

"HEY!" Cassius shouts.

"What?" I yell back.

"You comin'?"

I take a long sip of the whiskey in front of me before I answer. "I'll be there in a minute."

We're back home, although I'm hard pressed to call the cabin we've been living in for the past six months home. It's a sentencing. A jail cell. (Both of which I'm already familiar with.) The cabin can't contain the volume of anger overflowing from me, but even the Taj Mahal would be claustrophobic right now.

In the darkness of the kitchen, the stove clock flashes 12:00 and neither of us bothers to change it. Cassius doesn't care, and me, well, I'd rather not know how long it's been since I had a glimmer of hope.

Desperation is a slow killer. It's what got me into this mess, *another* mess, and now I need to focus.

My real name is Vera Walby. No one here knows this, not even Cassius. He thinks I fell down from blowjob heaven and couldn't care less what my name is as long as I keep sucking. Besides, trying to find Vera is a fool's game. I've made sure of that. In between, I've been Dionne, Isis and now Addy. A new name every time, but so far, the same bad result.

"C'mon, Addy. Water's getting cold."

"I'm coming," I yell, and under my breath, "keep your pants on."

I slam what's left of the whiskey and the amber burn cooks my insides, gives rise to all sorts of negligent thoughts. My bones are heavy when I push up from the chair. The cabins were originally designed for rich people playing weekend cowboy (or so we were told) and they're too small for real living, although the bathroom finishes are like a fancy spa. The big soaker tub is the only thing I'm going to miss about this place.

Cassius watches my every move as I strip, my fingers fumbling from the whiskey as I pin up my hair with barrettes. I lower myself into the tub, and normally Cassius would ogle my breasts bobbing in the water and say something real romantic like 'you've got great tits,' but tonight he's silent. I cross my legs tight, pressing against the back of the tub.

"You must be tired," he finally says.

"You were up late too. All night."

"I have no idea why he wanted to bring that kid here."

"He could have died out there."

"Yeah," he admits, no concern in his voice, "but it's too risky. Especially now."

"It's riskier to leave a mess like that so close and have someone else find it," I remind him.

"Whatever. I don't like him."

"You don't even know him. You might try being a bit nicer."

He spreads his hairy arms along the rim of the tub like a Mafia Don and looks at me suspiciously. "I don't want any trouble, Addy."

"Who said anything about trouble?"

"You have a way of complicating things."

"Like when?"

"Are we really going to get into this?"

"You started it."

Usually this kind of back talk doesn't serve me well but surprisingly, he lets it slide. "He better get rid of that kid soon. We don't need someone else snooping around and causing trouble."

"Garrett will make the right decision. Doesn't he always?"

His eyes narrow at my snippy tone. "What's that all about?"

"Nothing."

"Don't bullshit me. I know how uppity you get when you think you're in the right."

"You know it's not right. Taking lives."

"There's lots of things in life that aren't right and you can't control. You of all people should know that."

"But he can control it?"

"Don't start," he warns. "I'm getting tired of going down the same path. I'm alive because of him."

You're alive because of me you dumb shit.

Cassius scratches his matted chest hair. "I know you wanted a kid more than anything," he continues, "but this is how it worked out."

His words, meant to soothe, have the opposite effect. They slice deep into my soft belly, a barren belly, and I swallow back the thin trail of bile creeping up my throat. He lets the silence build, then,

"You haven't done a session in a while," he says.

"No one has."

"But even before."

"I don't need them."

"I think if anyone does it's you."

"Well," I say, my eyes snapping onto his, "maybe you should stop thinking."

The vein on the side of his head pulses, never a good sign. "I'm not stupid," he says. "I know you, Addy. More than you wish I did. What's going on? He's got his eye on you lately."

"Why don't you ask him?" I sauce back. "He can't do anything wrong in your books. If you think everything he says is the truth, ask him."

"I know there's some kind of funny business going on with you two. If I find out, you know it won't be good for you."

I wish it were the truth, the funny business I've dreamed of anyway. Even if I lived four more lives, I'd never set eyes on anyone as fine as Mr. Kaller. That man is finger lickin' good looking, and he still fills my head something awful, even when Cassius, poor slob, tries his horrible best. I've never wanted a man as bad as I do Garrett, and my female wily ways have always gotten me what I wanted (or turned out not to want, in most cases), but he's a goddamn enigma. A dinosaur in the tar sands. Not budging.

"You told me I was pretty once, maybe he thinks so too."

Cassius smirks. "Rylan's just as pretty, and I don't think you're Garrett's type."

"What the hell is that supposed to mean?" I grumble, grabbing the yellowed bar of soap from the holder.

"You know what I mean."

He won't come right out and say it, knows I'm sensitive about it, but he doesn't mind flirting in the general area, just to stir the pot. "You feeling okay these days?" he asks, all innocent as his eyes follow the soap moving along my parts.

"I'm feeling just fine."

"She used to talk in her sleep. Before things got bad. That's what you told me," he says, egging me on. "You've been a motormouth as of late. I can hardly sleep."

"Oh yeah? What am I saying?"

He shakes his head. "I can't understand you. I've tried, but it's all gibberish. The other night you said something about ISIS. If you're dreaming of terrorists, no wonder you're..." He lets the sentence hang, knowing full well how it ends.

Crazy is as crazy does. That was Gramma's way of describing, in polite terms, the disaster known as my mother. After daddy left and before Mother went batshit with drugs, there was the slow death spiral of her mind, a condition no one ever described to me save for 'one of those things that tend not to skip a generation.'

When I don't reply, Cassius leans close, his voice low and full of accusation. "And your hallucinations. You're seeing shit that's not even there. Making stuff up. I'm worried. *You* should be worried." He pauses. Blinks like a dumb cow. "You haven't told anybody else have you?"

"No."

"Don't be lying to me."

"I haven't said nothing." Now it's my turn to pause. "What about you? Have you said anything?"

He flashes the crooked smile I once liked, and reaches out his hand in a peace offering. "Of course not. I wouldn't do that to you," he says like he's placating a child. "This is a good place. Good for both of us. Let's keep it that way, okay?" He wiggles his fingers until I put my hand into his. He squeezes gently. "I love you, Addy. Don't forget that."

"I love you too," I lie.

We're both quiet, the first whiff of a truce settling over us. It's not usually like this, this easy, and when his grip starts to tighten and tighten, crushing my hand, I know I've misjudged the situation again. He rises onto his knees in one swift motion and my head snaps sideways as he backhands me with so much force he slips a little in the tub trying to steady himself after the fact. A furious burn spreads across my cheek. I'm still, like I've learned to be, not knowing if he's finished. My tongue pokes at a metallic stream of blood.

"I don't want you near that kid again until he leaves, okay?" he says, his smile long gone. "I saw how you looked at him. Say you're sorry."

"I didn't look at him in any way."

(Oh, but I did. That kid, Cutie Pie, is ripe for picking.)

His fingers curl tight into the bun at the nape of my neck and he yanks down hard, bones crunching.

"You're never been very good at apologies, have you? You need to remember how I saved your ass," he says, his forehead inches away from mine, the stink of whiskey on his breath. He lets go of my hair and the water in the tub splashes around as he maneuvers so his half stiff dink dangles right in my face.

"Why don't you get busy and we can try and forget all about this."

His hand pushes on the back of my head and I slip him in my mouth, like I've done a hundred times. Thankfully, tonight he's quick. I still dream of clamping down, hard and vicious so I'll never have to do this again, but that won't solve my problem. Cassius would still be alive. Dick-less, but alive.

Later in bed, cool air snakes in through the window and does jack shit to stop the heat boiling inside me. Cassius snores while I'm wide awake with thoughts.

Cassius thinks I'm stupid. Thinks I don't see. But I'm the only one here who does see. I've ignored things for too long but not this time. The Good Lord has finally answered my prayers.

In a way I feel bad because there's something a little lost about Cutie Pie (takes one to know one, I suppose) and he's really an innocent in all of this, but as the saying goes, shit happens, and I've waited long enough.

Shoulda packed a spare, asshole.

EIGHT

DAMIEN

AFTER THE INTENSE conversation and stuffy room it's a relief to be back outside. The wind has disappeared. The sky is purple. With the hush of dusk, everything feels less intimidating, including him.

He locks the door behind us and asks, "You want some help over?"

"Sure, thanks."

He offers me his arm and his warmth is a buffer against the cool night air. He walks slowly to keep his steps in sync with mine. Warm light spills out from windows on the other side of the house.

"Do Cassius and Addy live here with you?" I ask.

"No, just Rylan. She's my girlfriend," he adds, almost as an afterthought.

"Does she know about me? What I did?"

He stops abruptly. "For now, let's stick with you're on holiday." His eyes flick to mine. "That alright?"

"Sure. I'm cool." I mean, what else am I going to say? And who am I to judge? But still, it's a signal he's not on the up and up.

"So why Colombia?" he asks, shifting gears as we start moving again.

"I saw a documentary on the west coast. It looks wild and beautiful, totally empty. You ever been?"

"I've read about it."

"I think you'd like it," I say, and he looks surprised that I'd offer an opinion on what he might like. "It's like here. Lots of space, super remote, but with the ocean. I couldn't live anywhere where there wasn't any ocean."

"You're a swimmer?"

"I can swim, but it's not that. The ocean is unpredictable. Powerful. I love it."

"You don't strike me as someone who's unpredictable."

I smile back, just a small one. "Maybe that's why I like it."

At the front door, a slab of wood so huge it belongs on a castle, I follow his lead inside and slip off the flipflops. The tiles are warm under my bare feet and a savory smell, like stew, fills the air.

"Hey," he calls out, closing the door.

"Is he with you?" a female voice answers back from the second floor.

"Yeah. We're coming up." He points to a staircase leading up to the second floor with an apologetic shrug. "Last hurdle, I promise."

I wish there was something more profound to say than 'wow' once we make it to the landing. Garrett looks normal sized in the soaring, open space, totally not what I was expecting. Thick rugs line the floorboards and I've been around enough high-end furniture to know everything in here is expensive.

A petite woman in tight jeans and a t-shirt comes out of the kitchen area, wiping her hand on her leg.

"Hi. Rylan." She shakes my hand once, firm. No smile.

"Damien. Uh, thanks for having me."

She scans my face. "What does the other guy look like?"

"It was two on one," Garrett explains.

"I think he's capable of telling me himself," she says, eyes on mine. "Would you like a beer or glass of wine?"

"A beer. Thanks."

Rylan heads back into the kitchen and Garrett tilts his head indicating we should follow.

"Miller or Bud?" she asks, rummaging behind the fridge door.

"Miller."

"I'll have one too," Garrett says, and to me, "be right back."

He wanders through the kitchen, down a hallway and under her breath, Rylan mutters, "*Please.*" With authority, she cracks two bottles on a deer head opener bolted to the wall and asks, "Glass?"

"Yes. Please."

She pours with skill and hands me the glass as the foam settles. I'm still getting used to her cropped hair, so blonde it's almost white. It definitely suits her; too much hair would overwhelm her small face. She's cute in a cheerleader way with light freckles clustered on each cheek like she dotted them there with a pen.

"I hope you're hungry," she says. "I made a double batch of chili."

"I'm starving. It smells great. Do you need any help?"

"Almost done, thanks." She nods towards the island dividing the kitchen from the living room. "Take a seat."

It's an order and it sounds like she's used to giving them. Pulling out a stool, I watch her work in silence and a bit of fear. She chops a head of lettuce with efficient, brutal strokes, leaving a shredded pile in her wake.

"I think I saw your cat earlier," I say, noticing two small bowls near the fridge. "The grey one?"

"The holy terror. I don't like cats and guess who ends up looking after that thing?"

"Diesel is a great name."

"I wanted Fred."

Fred?

The kitchen is open, contained only by the island and a rock wall behind the stove and sink area. With everything black outside, the floor to ceiling windows makes it feel like I'm in a spaceship. A nice spaceship.

"Your house is cool. I like all the windows."

"It's too modern for me. Garrett designed it," she says, dumping the lettuce into a salad bowl.

"Do you like living in New Mexico?"

"I used to."

She roots in the fridge for something else and I take a long pull of beer. She has all the enthusiasm of a dentist about to do a root canal and I'm happy to see Garrett reappear. He's changed from jeans into track pants and with his hair in a ponytail, the angles on his face are even more pronounced. Rylan points to his beer and he grabs it, slides behind her and kisses the top of her head. It's proper, the kind of kiss you'd give your grandmother, and she doesn't relax into it. Instead, she pulls forward, away from him, with a loaded look.

"Damien is going to stay overnight," he says, moving to lean against the countertop. "Possibly longer."

Her head whips around. "How long?"

"Not sure yet."

"Doesn't he just need to get his car fixed?"

Garrett takes a swig of beer. "Is there a problem?"

Rylan yanks on oven mitts and hoists the pot off the stove. "Grab the salad please," she says to Garrett and whisks past us.

"I can help," I offer, but Garrett shakes his head, his mouth in a tight line.

The only thing comfortable about dinner is my chair. In between cutlery clinking and lean looks, Rylan asks me about what happened and I ramble just to fill the space. When I ask what they do, Rylan glances at Garrett and he says they manage the property with some help. After that, the conversation peters out. When Rylan clears the dishes, they've barely picked at anything and I've eaten three bowls of chili and half the salad.

Garrett steers us into the living room with two more beers and I'm relieved to be out of the war zone. He stretches out on the chaise part of a leather sectional and I sit in the middle. We're both quiet, watching the flames in the gas fireplace. The noise in the kitchen finally ends and after a door slams somewhere, he sighs and scratches his thick five o'clock shadow. "She wasn't happy I went to New York by myself."

"Oh. I thought it was me."

His smile is brief. "You didn't help."

"Are you from New York?"

"Originally. Happy not to be anymore. I couldn't wait to get out of there this time."

"Family?"

"Business."

I try to imagine him – flipflops, ponytail – in a room full of New York suits and can't. "How long have you lived here?"

"Seven years."

"Why New Mexico? It's so...different."

He brings the bottle to his lips and pauses. "This place chose me."

"Is that a good thing?" I ask, after he's taken a sip.

"Yes and no."

When he doesn't elaborate, I say, "You could tell me why. It's not like I have anything else going on tonight."

His big belly laugh isn't as crazy as the one earlier, but I still like it. "What would you normally be doing on a Friday night?" he asks.

"It sounds like you're trying to change the subject."

He rolls the bottle back and forth in his hand, a smile creeping in. Once he starts, he talks nonstop for almost twenty minutes. He tells me about his father, a successful Wall Street trader, who bought the property years ago, planned to turn it into a city slickers type of cowboy getaway. Construction was almost complete when he died unexpectedly and his mother shortly after.

"I was only twenty-five when they died," he says, "working ninety hours a week at Goldman Sachs. Living in Manhattan. I knew of this place, but never came out. Cowboys, New Mexico...not my thing. But there was a lot to deal with and...I thought I could handle it." With the bottle between his legs, he leans back against the chaise and knits his hands behind his neck. "I struggled," he says, looking at the ceiling. "Needed a re-set. I decided to come out here."

"Are there guests here now?"

"It never opened."

"Why not?"

He cocks his head and I hear it too: footsteps thudding closer. Over my shoulder, whatever politeness Rylan managed earlier is long gone. Standing behind us, she crosses her arms, hip jutted out to one side.

"Should we put this to a vote," she asks, "or are you just going to do whatever you want?"

Garrett turns to look at her, and there's an entire conversation going on with their eyes. "We'll talk about it later."

"I don't mean me."

"Let me finish here please."

"You know there's going to be..."

"We're done." Garrett's cool gaze returns to the fire in no uncertain terms.

"No, we're not 'done'," she says, testily. "You need to figure this out."

"I *said* we're done."

Suddenly interested in my feet, I count silently to three before Rylan storms off. A few seconds later, another door slams. On the coffee table, chess pieces carved from stone vibrate almost imperceptibly.

"You sure it's okay I'm here?" I ask. "I mean..."

He swings his legs onto the floor and rubs his face with his hands, as if he's getting rid of any distractedness. "She'll get over it. She has to," he says. "She doesn't make the decisions." It sounds like an old-school patriarchal attitude, surprising, but then again, maybe not. I don't know him. Or her.

He shifts towards me, now all business. "Let's talk about you. Next steps. My offer still stands. You can stay here until we figure things out."

"It sounds like a good idea being here," I start, careful, "but eventually I need to get my car fixed. I need money."

"I know. I can pay you while you're here. Once your ankle's better you can do some work. I could use an extra hand."

"I thought you never opened the ranch."

"With five thousand acres, there's plenty to do."

"Ah, I'm not really a labor guy, FYI."

He eyes my dress shirt, buttoned at the wrists, all the way to my neck. "Change can be good."

"Where would I stay? In that house down there?"

"You'd have it all to yourself. We'd feed you." He clears his throat. "Of course, there would be some conditions."

Of course.

"Yeah? What are those?"

"First, we come up with a story for why you're here and stick to it. We can't risk anyone knowing your real predicament."

"You won't even tell Rylan?"

He shrugs away the implication. "The less everyone knows the better."

"Who's 'everyone'?"

"I have other people helping out here."

"Employees?"

"You could call them that."

He's very still on the couch. Weird still.

"So...uh, what's my story then?"

His answer is immediate, like he's already thought about it. "You've had some issues at home. No one is willing to bail you out.

You've agreed to chip in here to pay for your repairs. It's all true, minus a few details." He pauses. "You didn't say anything to Addy or Cassius, did you?"

"No, but what if they Google me? I'm all over the internet."

He shakes his head. "There is no internet here."

"Really?"

"Well, I have access to it," he admits.

"No phones?"

"Just my cell. For emergencies."

"You're not really selling the place," I joke, but my laugh is nervous.

"I think I am. You need anonymity, no outside world."

True, but...

"What are the other conditions?" I ask, not quite ready to say yes.

"While you're here, you need to stay away from Addy. She's not well."

"Like, contagious not well?"

"She's been suffering up here," he says, pointing to his head, "and the less..." he searches for the right word, "aggravation she has the better."

"What if she talks to me?"

"You can't avoid her entirely, and if she engages you, be polite."

This condition is a bit of a drag for me. So far Addy's been the only interesting thing about this place. His hand finally unclenches when I say, "Uhm, okay, anything else?"

"Those are my terms. You must have a question or two."

There's an extended pause and he waits for me to fill it.

"How do I know you won't turn me in?"

"Why would I offer to help if that wasn't my intention?"

"That's the right answer, but what's in it for you?" I ask, adding quickly, "no offence."

"None taken," he says with shrug. "But would you believe me if I said nothing?"

I shift my eyes to his. "Maybe."

He leans in and a clean soap smell follows. "The way I see it, we're not so different, you and I. You're in a similar place I was in almost seven years ago. You need to get your bearings. Figure out next steps. I'd like to help. You follow my conditions, I pay you to work, you fix your car. I trust you, you trust me. Deal?"

"What happens if the police show up anyway?"

It's a throw-away question and we both know it. This is one of those moments in life where I already know I've lost.

"I'm willing to take a risk if you are."

It takes serious effort to break away from his crazy eyes, but I need to just to think. Outside is the black night, a night I'm able to appreciate thanks to him. A big part of why I decide to stay is his honesty: about himself, the circumstances. But I'm not going to lie. We're not pals. We're not even acquaintances. We're strangers who've hammered out a mutual understanding. The benefits are clear and only later will I realize we never talked about consequences.

The other, more obvious reason why I agree to stay?

I have nowhere else to turn.

"Okay," I say, as we shake hands. "Deal."

NINE

WITH THE HELP of a Tylenol 3, I sleep through the night and all of the morning. After a long shower and instant oatmeal Garrett left along with some other supplies when he dropped me off last night, I head outside with a second cup of Nescafe.

I settle on the porch bench and rock, the wall of heat already familiar from yesterday. The squeak of rusted chains is the only sound until an irritating, high-pitched whine cuts the air and announces Cassius' arrival. He swerves around the corner in a battered golf cart and lurches to a stop. With a pair of crutches in hand, he takes the porch steps two at a time.

"You're finally awake," he says with a hint of accusation. "I came by an hour ago. And an hour before that." He hands the crutches to me with a stiff gesture. "These are for you. Merry Christmas from Garrett."

"Thanks." I lean them against the bench. "What time is it?"

"Two thirty. Why? You have an appointment?"

I blow on my coffee, even though it's lukewarm, and ignore his smirk.

"It's time to hustle, hombre," he says, with a snap of his fingers.

"Garrett's waiting for you in the workshop. He wants you to see your car."

"Tell me where I need to go."

"I'm driving you."

I pat the crutches. "I'm good on my own. I'll use these."

"It's too far to walk."

"I'll figure it out."

He crosses his arms over a midsize beer belly and leans against the railing. His thick shoulders indicate he was once in shape, but overall, not a body I'd flaunt shirtless. "You don't have a choice," he says.

Right then, I know Garrett has said something to him about his attitude. He's kind of pathetic in a school bully way, and no doubt thinks he's all that because of the Chinese dragon tattoo on his head. Like he suffered for his art. Moron.

"Your eye looks better," he says.

"No, it doesn't. It looks worse."

He shifts against the railing and tries again. "So you finally decided to cut loose, huh?" he says, nodding at the t-shirt.

"Maybe."

Drumming his fingers impatiently on meaty biceps, he says, "Listen. I know we didn't get off on the right foot, but I got shit going on you don't know about it. I'm cool if you're cool."

"I'm cool."

"Good," he says and pushes off the railing. "We can go whenever you're ready." When I make no effort to move, he asks, exasperated, "Do you want to see your car or not?"

"Of course," I say and take another sip of coffee.

He stalks back to the golf cart scowling something under his breath and I smile. Damien one. Cassius one. Bring it on.

To tilt the score in his favor, he drives fast up the rutted dirt road behind the guest house. The golf cart bounces wildly and I hang my leg out to avoid further damage. After a long minute, we slow to a stop and I crane my head up. "This is a workshop?"

It's a valid question. The building is the size of four city lots, wrapped in corrugated metal. It's oddly designed; two halves squished together, with the right hand side twice the height of the left.

"Yup," Cassius says, sliding off the seat mummified with duct tape. "Left side is woodworking. All the mechanical and gear is on the right. We're going right."

Four roller doors, each big enough to drive a motorhome through, dominate the right façade and three are locked to pins in the concrete walkway that spans the building. At the far end, the fourth door is raised halfway. Inside, Garrett is crouched beside an ATV, tools spread around him. He stands and waves us over when we enter.

"Morning," he says to me. "Or should I say, afternoon. How you feeling?"

"Better. The pill helped. Thanks for these, by the way." I hold up one of the crutches.

"You're welcome. How are they working out?"

"He's a pro already," Cassius answers and Garrett acknowledges his shirtless state with a cool gaze.

"How's everything down there?" he asks him.

"Lots of chit chat as you can imagine," Cassius says, and tilts his head in my direction, just barely, but I still see it. "I'd be prepared for some questions tonight."

Garrett nods, doesn't seem concerned. "Fair enough."

There's a formality to their interaction, and Cassius stands like a solider, arms tucked behind him. "If you don't need anything else, I'm going to head back. Do you want me to pick him up later?"

"His name is Damien," Garrett says, and Cassius immediately drops his head. I would too at that tone. "And no, I'll take it from here."

"Ok," Cassius mumbles and pokes one eye up at Garrett, waiting.

Garrett nods once. "We're done."

With his head still lowered, Cassius says, "I'll have everything ready for tonight."

After he leaves, the awkwardness of their exchange lingers. In the small lull that follows, Garrett's gaze flicks to me, like he's waiting for me to ask something. When I don't, he starts to collect the tools, laying them neatly in a toolbox.

"This is pretty impressive," I say, taking in the rest of the shop. It's like Home Depot on steroids. Every tool imaginable hangs neatly on the walls or on black steel shelves. In the far corner are three more ATVs, a giant snow removal blade, and a bunch of dirt bikes. "Looks like you're prepared for anything."

"We have to be out here," he says, "Around back we have a grader, a bobcat. You name it."

"You know how to use all this stuff?"

"Self taught."

"Rylan said you designed your house. Did you build it too?"

Last night I snooped around the guest house and didn't find much aside from a stack of instructional books in the living room: electrical, plumbing, woodworking, and a lot of boring ones about plants.

"I had some help with the foundation, but otherwise, yes." He eyeballs the XL t-shirt draped on my L frame, part of the care package he left with me last night. "You're doing my Alma Mater proud, but we need to get you some clothes that fit."

"You went to Princeton?"

"BA in Economics. Very useful out here." He wipes at some dirt on his arm, his cutoff t-shirt exposing muscle definition I wish I had. "How about you? Did you go to college?"

"No, but I was working towards my CPA."

"Really?" he asks, surprised.

"I know. Everyone says I don't look like an accountant."

He smiles and skin crinkles at the edges of his eyes. Under the bright lights of the shop he looks a little tired.

"You get any sleep?" I ask.

"I've had better nights," he says. "But you probably know all about that."

"About what?"

"Women."

There's a weird pause, or maybe it's just me. This isn't an area of conversation I'm familiar with.

"Oh, yeah. Tell me about it."

Another pause. Longer. Then he puts his hand on my shoulder. "You ready for the show?" He nods towards the rear corner of the shop and we head over. I can just see the tires of my Lexus peeking out from under a drop cloth.

"Jesus," I say, letting out a whistle when he whips the cover off. "They really went to town."

He tried to downplay it yesterday, but destroyed pretty much sums it up. All the windows are smashed. The hood and roof are dented. A tiny donut tire is the final insult. Garrett rubs his hand over one of the dents, inspecting it. "They must've used a baseball bat or a jack. Too bad. It's a nice ride." He steps back and crosses his arms. "What made you go with a Lexus?"

It wasn't my choice.

I might still be living in it if it wasn't for the random conversation with Eric, the ex-accountant/homeless guy I met in Santa Monica. He asked for some of my fries first; then mentioned he'd seen me around, sleeping in my car. When I didn't offer much, he was happy to do most of the talking. Before the booze took over, he had been a CPA. When I told him I liked numbers, he said companies were always hiring accountants. We ended up talking for two hours. After, he dug around in his shirt pocket for a worn-out business card: Hannah Browne, his old boss (and ex-wife I'd find out later).

His breath was stained with cheap vodka when he said, "Tell her I sent you. And that I'm sorry for everything."

Hannah hired me as a trainee with three months' probation, the youngest guy in the department, and soon realized I worked better alone. (A more positive spin to the fact no one wanted to work with me.) Not that I minded. I was a fast learner and got promoted twice in two years. With cash in my pocket, I moved into an apartment, but after living in the Lexus for five months, all the space seemed unnecessary. I should've sold the car and didn't. We went through some tough times together. It would always be a reminder, but car or no car, it's not as if I'd forget.

What made me go with a Lexus?

"I found it online."

The tightness in my voice doesn't register, or if it does, he chooses to say nothing about it. Instead, he pries open the driver-side door and the shop fills with the sound of gnashing parts not lined up properly. "I can get you a quote for the repairs," he says.

I lower myself sideways into the front seat and dig through the console, the side panels and the glove box, all of them empty. Glancing back at Garrett, I ask, "Did you take the insurance papers out?"

"No. They're gone?"

"Yeah." I finger around the ignition. "And what about the keys?"

"We couldn't find them. We towed it up with a winch."

"Were they in my jeans? Addy said she washed them."

He shakes his head. "I can ask but Cassius searched your pockets and the car before we brought you up."

The thought of Cassius digging in my pockets is bad enough. With new windows, a tire, body work and no insurance? Five grand? Six? Money I don't have access to. Even if I had my wallet, I can't leave any trace. And replacing a key isn't easy either. All my expectations plummet. I thought about driving away today, despite our deal, but without a key I'm seriously boned, and worse, totally reliant on him to get a new one.

"Maybe they chucked the keys out there thinking I wouldn't find them," I say.

"It's possible."

"Can we go look?"

"Now?"

"What if they're out there? Not having to replace the key will be a huge deal. At least I can drive the damn thing."

"No harm in trying I guess," he says with a shrug.

He doesn't seem that jazzed, although I can't deny the small sliver of hope.

"You don't mind? Is it far from here?"

"About forty-five there and back," he says and pulls the bandana off his head, shaking out his hair. "I walked over from the house. I'll have to get the truck and swing back for you."

Bumbling up and out of the car seat, he might have missed it, if he didn't come over to help me: my abrupt stillness. He follows my gaze to the jerry cans lined up on a shelf. They're bigger than the ones I chucked into a gas station dumpster three days ago, heading East on the 10, but the same fire-engine red.

"You okay?" he asks, and I know he can sense it. My struggle. Right on the surface.

"I'm good. Fine," I say.

"Lucky for you, they're empty." He smiles quickly. "Or lucky for me?"

He's trying to make this less awkward and failing. I wish he would stop staring at me. It's enough to process the rush without an audience.

"You don't have to worry," I say.

His head slants to one side. Not that I blame him. Even I don't believe myself.

"Is gasoline your weapon of choice?" he asks.

"It's not a weapon," I say, practically whisper. "That's the first thing you need to know."

There's a hazy quality to the space between us, particles of uncertainty. It's one thing to hear about someone else's urges. It's an entirely different thing to witness it.

"Got it," he says and even though he's right beside me, his voice sounds far away. "I'll be back in twenty. Meet you out front."

He walks away and I force myself to wait, longer than I need to. There are laws in the universe that are powerful, but the pull of gasoline is stronger than gravity, impossible to explain. I've tried. It's always there when I needed it, and sometimes I wish I didn't need it so bad. Now I can't live without it.

A familiar anxiety surges inside me. The rubber tips of the crutches squeak on the slick concrete floor. In front of the cans, just standing here, my head swims with anticipation.

With a shaky hand, I lift them all, one by one.

They're empty. Just like he said.

TEN

WHEN GARRETT RETURNS with the Chevy pickup, his eyes are alert. The empty jerry cans have helped me settle down, but he saw enough to make him cautious. In the truck, he hands me a baseball cap and a pair of mirrored sunglasses. "Just in case."

"You think we'll run into anyone?"

"No," he says, "but better to be safe."

I put both on and assess myself in the visor mirror. "At least I don't look like a giant walking bruise."

"Purple suits you."

"Yeah, thanks."

But I smile too. It's funny how he can diffuse situations with just a comment. I'm the opposite. Maybe he can teach me a thing or two.

"So what's going on tonight?" I ask, impressed with how he steers the truck through the dips of the road with one arm. "Cassius said you needed to prepare for some questions. About me I guess?"

"I'd like to introduce you to everyone tonight. Get it out of the way in one shot." He glances over. "It won't take long."

"How many is everyone?"

He pauses. "Thirty-six."

"What? I thought..." But I didn't think. I never asked and now can't remember why. "Do you trust them?"

"Of course. They won't say anything."

"How do you know?"

"I know."

He sounds sure, me not so much. Putting faith in other people is asking for trouble. But it's not my deal, so I don't push, and as the truck rolls past the guesthouse, my attention turns to the new surroundings. The road, lined with clumps of dusty grasses, stretches with no end in immediate sight, no people in sight. "Where do they all live?" I ask.

"At the other end of this road. It's pretty spread out. I can give you a tour when we get back."

"What kind of work do they do?"

"Some work in the garden, some up in the shop."

"Are those *my* options?"

A half smile flashes on his face. "You don't want to grow tomatoes?"

"With all the GMO stuff flying around, I don't know if I've ever eaten a real tomato, let alone grown one. "

"So you're open minded," he says and there's a subtle command behind his words, as if he's willing me to be that.

"I don't know if I'd go that far, dude."

"Dude?" The look on his face is priceless.

"You've been out here too long. You need some civilization."

"I'm civilized," he says, a little defensive.

I give his cargo pants and t-shirt a long look. "Whatevs."

Now he laughs. "Is this some kind of new language?"

"It's called the real world," I say and right now, I'm missing the real world, or at least some sign of it. It's a little *too* quiet. How he's managed to live here for seven years is beyond me.

Finally, as we approach a fork in the road, in the distance I can see a roofline and something glittering behind it. But he turns left at the fork and we disappear around the corner before I can make out what it is. The truck chatters on the next washed out section of switchbacks and he mumbles something about grading. After a particularly hairy corner, we dip down a hill and the road turns to follow a wide river.

"That's the Chama," Garrett says. "It cuts through the property for a few miles."

"Any fish in it?" I ask, craning to look out his window. The water is a gritty brown and looks deep. Long grasses and trees line the riverbank, their leaves a bright spring green.

"Trout, mostly. Brown and rainbow. You fish?"

"No. But I've always wanted to try. My family wasn't outdoorsy. Unless you count a tennis court."

"You have any brothers or sisters?"

"A sister. *Half* sister," I correct myself. "Barely."

"Not close?"

"As close as two magnets could ever be."

"Older?"

"Older, better, faster, stronger. Take your pick."

He chuckles. "What's her name?"

"Virginia. She lives in Switzerland. Works at the UN."

"She sounds determined."

"Try relentless."

"No one's perfect, right?"

I decide to let that can of worms pass and glance down nervously as we cross a shaky looking bridge spanning the river. Once we're on the other side, the road narrows to a tight single lane. Another small descent and...

WTF?

After nothing but nature, the gigantic sci-fi gate looks totally out of place. On either side of it, stretching as far as I can see is a fence, at least ten feet tall, deadly spirals of razor wire snaked along the top of it.

"This is security," he says.

No shit.

An arm pokes out and waves at us from an adjacent gatehouse. A Mexican man waddles up to the truck in jeans and a bright pink polo shirt, a beam of a smile on his face. Garrett roles down the window as he approaches.

"Buenos tardes, señor," the man says. "Another day to be thankful for."

"Hola, amigo. Como estás? Cedric, I'd like you to meet Damien. Damien, Cedric." Garrett leans back as I stretch over the console towards the open window. "He's the gentleman we brought in this morning."

"Hola," I say.

Seeing the welts and scratches on my face, Cedric makes a sympathetic sound. "I heard the bad news. It makes me nervous knowing it happened so close by. You are very lucky Señor found you." Looking back at Garrett, he says, "I have asked around but so far no luck."

"I figured. I don't think they were from around here."

"You don't need to worry," Cedric says, patting the bulge on his right hip.

"We're going back out to try and find his car keys."

"You think it's safe?" Cedric asks, concerned.

With a quick glance in my direction, Garrett says, "I think so. We'll be back in about an hour, okay?"

"No problem, Señor."

"When we come back, I'll give you a list for Gloria. We need a few things for him."

"Of course, Señor."

He waits until Garrett nods then walks back to the hut in no rush. Their interaction was the warmest so far but Garrett is clearly the boss. The gate squeals open, pulling back on its guiders.

"That's a serious fence," I say.

"So was the bill," he says, but I don't laugh and neither does he.

The bumpy terrain flattens out past the gate, and my mind, free from being jostled around, races. Garrett notices me spinning the ring on my finger.

"You alright?"

It's Fort Knox up there.

"Why do you have security?"

"Everyone needs security these days," he says, like that explains everything.

But not like that.

"With guns?"

"He's down here by himself. Safety first."

I should have recognized the small sense of dread nagging at the back of my mind, or at least given it more attention. But my thoughts are distracted when the grit of the dirt road ends, and the first shot of nerves hits. As we make our way to the scene of the crime, I look in the rearview mirror, back from where we came. There is no marker or sign for the property and maybe it's the angle, but it's like the vegetation closed up behind us.

I wouldn't be able to find this place even if I tried.

ELEVEN

AFTER FIFTEEN MINUTES, Garrett starts to slow down.

"It's coming up," he says. "Do you recognize any of this?"

"Kind of."

There is zero chance of running into those rednecks again and still, I've been sitting straighter and straighter, like rebar is growing up my spine.

"There's your pothole," he says, moving smoothly into the other lane.

Passing it, I can't help but wonder where I would be right now if I hadn't hit it. Mexico? Jail? Dead? A few seconds later, we're parked on the dirt shoulder.

"Here we are," he says. "You ready?"

"Let's do it."

Outside, Garrett points to the embankment. "I'll head up and do a sweep. You focus down here. We'll check the other side after."

"It's just two keys on a plain gold ring."

"Yeah, right," he says, with a blank look. "Would help to know what I'm looking for."

Using one of the crutches, I move dirt back and forth along the surprisingly tidy shoulder. Based on the damage to my car, there should be more debris on the ground, but it's like the area was swept clean. Garrett traverses the embankment and little plumes of dust spiral up into the hot air as he pokes at the ground with his foot.

"How far up was I?" I call out, because he seems awfully close to the road. When he points to an area barely ten yards up the slope, I almost don't believe it. Everything from last night seems to have been amplified, appearing worse in the moment than it really was. Even the pothole looked smaller when we drove past it.

After twenty minutes we scour the other side of the road. I'm close to giving up when Garrett bends down to pick something up. My stomach flutters. Then he holds up one of my sneakers with a wry grin.

"Forget it," I say, dejected, waving him back. "We're not going to find them."

But he's now looking past me, hand above his eyes. I turn around, and in the distance a vehicle approaches.

Seriously. Where were you yesterday?

Garrett jogs back to the road. His features are tense. As the truck comes closer he mutters, "What is she doing here?"

"Who is it?"

His voice turns gravelly. "Get in the truck."

"But..."

"Just go."

I've got twenty feet and make it fifteen before the Tacoma screams to a stop in front of me. A woman the size of a linebacker is wedged behind the steering wheel. She rolls down the passenger window and barks, "Not so fast sweetheart."

Garrett shakes his head imperceptibly; too late. I inch back towards him and she makes an ordeal of getting out of the truck, like we've somehow inconvenienced her. She struts over, as much as someone bowlegged can.

"Well, if it isn't Jesus Christ himself, come down off the mount," she says to Garrett.

"Eleanor. Nice to see you," he says evenly.

She pushes her sunglasses into a butch flattop. "Spare me the bullshit, Mr. Kaller. We both know you'd like me to keel over and die."

"This isn't your part of town."

She crosses her arms in a bitchy way, a state that appears natural for her. "And you'd like to keep it that way, wouldn't you? I'm surprised you've dared to come out. Figured you'd hole yourself up there forever, hiding behind the 5th."

With a tight smile he says, "If you're going to quote amendments, you should probably know what they are. You're referring to the 4th."

"You have a lot of nerve."

"No more than everyone else."

"'Everyone else,'" she snorts, "last I heard everyone else wasn't killing people. Old habits die hard. Don't they, Mr. Kaller?" She pauses for dramatic effect before turning to me. "You do know this man is a murderer, right?" After my hard swallow, her mouth curls into a sneer. "Yeah, I didn't think so. Apparently they're dropping like flies in there as of late, but no one can confirm. Or is willing to," she adds, hard eyes falling back on Garrett. "Who's this young thing anyway? A voodoo child? He didn't spring from your loins now did he? Or anyone else's for that matter?"

"Is this going to turn into a dialogue at some point or do you just need to hear yourself talk?" he asks. "If it's the latter, we're done, thank you."

The fact he can look over her head seems to piss her off even more. "The truth hurt, don't it?"

"In most cases, yes," he says, "But why don't you let me know once you've actually found it." He tilts his head towards the truck and I don't have to be asked twice. Garrett makes his way to the driver's side and Eleanor charges right after him, yelling.

"You're a charlatan. A phony. All your powers or whatever else it is you claim to have. How are your powers going to help you when you stand trial for murder?" Garrett climbs into the truck and I'd slam my door just to make a point, but he closes his like he's going for a Sunday drive. "She told me before she died," she yells, banging on his door. "She said you give them things so they don't remember. Is that why no one talks?"

The engine roars to life and a huge glob of spit lands on his window. Garrett makes a slow U-turn around her while she shouts *murderer* over and over. Only when she disappears from view do I spin back around in my seat, stunned. Garrett's face is like stone, focused on the road, right arm draped over the steering wheel, like it's holding him up. When we're halfway back to the gate, he parks and turns off the ignition.

There's a huge block of silence before he finally says, "That was Eleanor Marks."

"Who's she?"

"A nurse."

"Why did she call you a murderer?"

He stretches his neck right and left before he answers. "A woman living with us got pregnant. She had an abortion. There were complications and she died. Eleanor was on duty at the hospital."

One of them died.

"So you didn't *actually* kill her."

He looks at me for the first time since we got back in the truck. "No."

"Is abortion illegal in New Mexico?"

"No. At the same time, I don't allow children on the property," he says.

"*Allow*?"

"Those are the rules."

"Why was she talking about amendments?"

"She thinks she knows a lot of things."

"Amendments mean serious shit," I press, frustrated with his tendency to avoid direct answers. "And she said that lady knew it was you."

He watches me twist and wring my fingers. "I heard what she said."

"And...?"

"And what?"

"C'mon, dude. Don't pretend. She said people were dropping like flies. And what about the...powers. What did she mean by that?" I ask, and for a few fleeting seconds I cling to the belief that there's an explanation, a normal one, but as the silence grows, the taste in my mouth turns gross and metallic. "This is the place, right? The place that girl told me about."

He stares out the windshield. "What if it is?

It's like a trap door has opened beneath me. I close my eyes against the sensation of falling. "You told me last night we had to trust each other. What about *you* having to tell *me* the truth?"

"I haven't lied to you."

"Not saying anything is pretty much lying."

"I didn't lie," he repeats.

Deep down I know if the conversation from last night were replayed he'd be right. He chose his words carefully. For a reason.

"Eleanor said voodoo. So did the girl in the store. What's going on here? Are you some kind of weirdo cult?"

"I haven't heard that word in a while."

"Jesus," I whisper, and hot sickness pushes up my throat. "You were never going to let me leave, were you?"

"You can leave whenever you want. The door's right there," he says with a nod of his head.

"What about my car?"

"You get out now, you're on own. We never see each other again."

The sun is already low in the sky. What am I going to do? Walk in the dark? With nothing? "Are you joking?" I ask.

"What do you think?"

His voice is cavalier, uncaring, and I'm not even sure what's holding my body together right now. I feel like rubber, about to collapse. "Is there anything else you want to tell me?"

"What else do you want to know?"

"The truth!" I shout. "What's the deal here? Sacrifices? Satan shit?"

He looks insulted. "It's nothing like that."

"Then what is it?"

"I told you. This place chose me."

"That can mean a million different things and you know it."

His hands tighten on the steering wheel, like he's going to crush it.

"Well?" I prod, but he still doesn't say anything. I've never been good at gauging other people's emotions, but I do know my breaking point, and I've just reached it. "You know what? You suck."

He spins around so fast my head jerks and bangs against the window. "We're in the same boat, okay?" he yells, jabbing his finger at me. "I don't know you, you don't know me. I haven't told you everything and I doubt you've told me everything. I said I would help you and I will. Does it matter what happened before you got here or what goes on? You're not involved."

He cranks the truck again, but I shout for him to stop. Everything's swirling. I can't think straight. "If I stay here I am involved."

"Then make a decision."

His eyes are flat, challenging me, and right now, I hate him.

"Right. And what exactly am I deciding?" I ask.

"Your future," he says darkly.

I turn away in a rage. The silence becomes unbearable in the confined space.

"Are we good?" he asks.

Good? Is he an idiot? This is lose-lose of epic proportions. I grip the door handle so tight that blood drains out of my fingers.

Open it. Leave. What's stopping you?

Courts. Jail. Giving my stepdad the satisfaction.

"I said, are we good?"

The sensation of falling comes back, makes me feel even sicker.

"Yes, we're good," I yell at the window, "we're fucking amazing."

The tension hangs like napalm as he starts the truck. I refuse to look at him. When we reach the gate, Cedric heads over but the smile slips off his face when Garrett rolls down the window and puts up his hand with a grim look. He rummages in the side panel beside him, and pulls out a chipped Bic pen and a piece of crumpled paper. He places both on the console. "Write down everything you need. Clothes. Shoes. Sizes. Toiletries. I'll be with Cedric. Let me know when you're done."

He slams the door behind him and I wad up the piece of paper, chucking it at the window. I'm furious with myself for believing him. There's no reason to feel hurt - he's a stranger, someone else I can't trust – but I do. It's like a post-burn let down: that slippery half world filled with promises, of something better, and when I reach for it, there's nothing. Always nothing. A familiar pressure starts to build at the back of my neck.

"No," I mutter, rubbing my temples. "No. Go away."

But it's started and nothing, not even World War III, can stop what's about to happen.

I paw through the glovebox, the side panel. It's getting harder to breathe. *The console.*

Everything comes to a standstill when the lid opens. A thousand jet fighters roar in my ears. The Chevy is in good condition but old enough to still have a cigarette lighter. My finger trembles moving towards it. The *click*, the process starting, sends a shudder up my spine.

Working quickly, I fish the ball of paper from the floor and roll it into a tube. The lighter pops out, ready, and a hot flash rips through my groin. At the sight of the glowing red coil, my jeans swell and I fumble with the zipper. I'm hyperventilating, seeing double. When the paper catches fire, my eyelids flutter, weighted down, dragging me with them as everything dissolves into black.

TWELVE

WHEN I COME BACK from the shadows, Garrett stares at me through the driver-side window. I don't know how long he's been there. He opens the door, sniffs the air and frowns. A last smouldering piece of paper drifts in the cab like a watery flake in an upended snow globe. I'm collapsed in a heap, little spasms still shooting through me. The lighter slips out of my fingers, between my legs. Garrett's eyes flick down, sees my zipper still undone.

"I need another piece of paper," I say, my face burning as I angle away. "Please."

He yanks the keys from the ignition and pockets them, stretches his hand towards me. I drop the cigarette lighter in it, unable to look him in the eye. When he comes back from the hut with another piece of paper, his mouth is in a hard line.

"Try not to burn this one."

He waits outside, leaning against the truck. I can barely write my hand is shaking so bad. When I'm done, he takes the list to Cedric, slides back into the truck and starts it without a word. The sun moves lower in the sky and glints off the coils of razor wire as we cross back into the property. The gate creaks closed behind us and I envision myself on the other side in jeans and his Princeton t-shirt, just like now, only with the satisfaction of having called his bluff.

On the way back, everything feels tainted. The sun is too hot, the scenery bland. Even the river is a reminder it can do whatever it wants, unlike me. I sulk against the window. Instead of heading back to his place, we turn left at the fork in the road and he slows down in front of a sprawling, one level building.

"I just gave you the opportunity to leave and you didn't take it," he says, both of us lurching forward when he jams the truck into park. "Then you try and burn down my truck?"

"Opportunity?" I ask, incredulous. "Dump me on the road with nothing? Yeah, thanks. And I didn't try to burn your truck down. It was a piece of paper."

"What's next?"

"Why are you acting all surprised? I told you I light fires. I told you the *truth*. Something you might want to try."

His eyes flash before they narrow. "You can't just light things on fire."

"Yes, I can. I've been doing it for years."

"Not here you won't."

"Right," I snort. "You're just going to wave your magic wand and make it stop?"

"Don't give me attitude," he warns.

"Whatever."

We're flattened against our respective doors, the atmosphere hostile. "How do you know when you have to light a fire?" he demands. "What's the trigger?"

"You're the expert in pyromaniacs."

"I'm trying to understand you."

"You don't understand shit."

"Then make me understand."

He throws my anger right back in my face and in the crackling silence after we make the briefest eye contact.

Finally he says, "You've never told anyone."

"What's there to tell? It's not going to change anything."

"So there is more to the story."

"Shut up," I say, irritated all over again. "The story is you're a liar. Stop making this about me. You're some freaking voodoo cult bullshit and what did you expect me to say when I found out? That'd I'd just go, 'oh, ok'? I mean, what planet are you even from? Just tell me the truth and put me out of my misery. All these people I'm meeting tonight? Are they the crazy natives?"

"They're Apaches," he says, pausing. "And they're not crazy."

"And you're what?" I look over with a raised eyebrow. "Their leader?"

"I'm their guide, for lack of a better word."

"Since when do natives listen to a white guy?"

"You don't have to worry," he insists, "nothing is going to happen to you here."

"And you expect me to believe you after all this? Seriously?"

He leans his head back and stares at the roof. A full minute goes by. "Maybe this wasn't such a good idea," he says. "Maybe you go home, sort it out."

It's subtle how the air disappears after he says that, how it then all comes back in a wave and crashes around me. I'm not sure how to navigate around our obliterated comfort zones. I'm only sure of one thing.

"You want to understand me?" I ask, my voice rising. "I'm not going back. *Ever*." I cross my arms and wedge myself against the window. "I'd rather be in this weirdo place."

And somehow, just by saying it out loud, all the tension that's built up fizzles. I think he senses it too, because he sighs and his voice is softer when he says, "I apologize, Damien. I should've been up front with you. We've had some challenges lately and..." He trails off and looks uncomfortable, like he's admitted some kind of defeat. "Helping you was something positive."

"*Are* you in trouble?"

"No," he says immediately. "But with someone like Eleanor..."

"I know the type. You don't have to explain."

"Listen," he starts, and right away I know this is it, we both know I'm committed, even when he says, "Anytime you want to leave, you leave. Okay? I'll drop you off at the bus station, buy you a ticket to wherever." He offers a strained smile. "I'm not forcing you to stay in this...weirdo place."

In front of us, a rabbit bolts out from under the porch, as if the universe needed to send me a reminder: all of this is real; play your cards right.

"I'll deal but you need to tell me what's really going on here. The whole story. No short cuts."

His puzzled expression lifts when he finally clues in. "Yes. Yes. The whole story. I promise." But he doesn't say anything right away. His head drops and he rubs at the scar in the middle of his palm. "Do you mind if I give you a raincheck for now though? I've had enough excitement in the past twenty-four hours."

"Sure," I say and deep down, I'm relieved. I'm not sure how much more I can handle right now either. "As long as tonight I'm not some kind of guinea pig for whatever you do here."

"Ah..." he says. "About tonight..."

"Don't say anything about all this?"

He nods and looks almost...bashful? It dawns on me the whole Eleanor fiasco rattled him, despite how cool he acted.

"I guess we're even then," I say. "We both have something to hide."

I don't mean that as a threat, only an observation, but his smile is respectful, as if he's just seen me in a different light.

"Touché."

THIRTEEN

THE MOOD STABILIZED, Garrett slides out of the truck and motions for me to follow. "This is the common house," he explains, gesturing towards the building we parked in front of. The smooth brown walls and round wooden beams poking out the front facade look just like the guest house. "It was supposed to be the main guest headquarters of the ranch. We store most of the food here. And the beer," he adds, with a look that says he could use one, or ten.

He tucks my crutches under his arms and helps me up the stairs. Weathered deck chairs are scattered along the wide porch in a haphazard way that suggests no one ever sits in them.

"This was already built when your parents died?" I ask.

"Everything was ready to go. Staff were hired, guests booked. But it was a ghost town when I got here."

"That must've been creepy, being here by yourself. Oh, I guess Rylan was here too, right?"

"No," he says, and holds the door open for me. "She came later."

Inside, the common house is, well, common. The main entry hall is bright and bland, like a Motel 6. Beige walls are peppered with signs of use, chunks of drywall missing. A couch and coffee table by the front door look like they were rained on. Not a space I'd envision millionaires in, cowboy boots clicking on the tiled floor as they waited for their horses.

"Bathrooms are there," Garrett says, pointing left down the hall, "and the main room's at the end. It has a pool table, a fireplace. You can use it at any time. Those," he says, referencing double doors on the back wall, "go to the meeting room, but we'll see that tonight. You access it from outside, there's another door."

He's rushing, like a tour guide who's done this beat a hundred times, and I just want to slow down. I've been all over the place, mentally and physically.

"These are cool," I say, drawn to the black and white photos framed and neatly hung in the hallway. "How come all the tree leaves are white?"

"It's a special film. Infrared."

"You took these?"

"I used to play around. They're all photos of the property."

I linger on the shot of a canyon – lush and dramatic - nothing I would ever associate with this place. "Where's that?"

"It's my favorite spot. Once your ankle's better I can take you. It's a bit of a hike."

The angle is disorienting, as if it's taken from a ledge. Vertigo rushes over me. Still, I can't stop looking at it. There's a seductive quality to the light, like in a dream. It's a magical spot, I can tell.

"You can come back tomorrow and look around," he says, pressing, but polite. "The meeting's at seven and it's almost five thirty."

Our final destination definitely has the feel of finality. In the food storage room, a faint scent of bleach tickles my nose and I shiver in the sudden cold. Garrett digs out two empty cardboard boxes from a pile and dumps them in front of a grid of shelves filled with dry and canned goods. "Help yourself to whatever you want." He nods to the shiny wall of metal on our left. "Beers in the last one. Be right back. I've got to take a piss."

There's something unnerving being alone in a cold room with eight giant stainless steel fridges, and I'm half expecting a frozen body to roll out. After mustering the courage to open the first door - no dead bodies, thank god - a different kind of fear creeps in. Vegetables. The next fridge: more vegetables. Then fruit. Raw meat. In LA, I worked eighty hours a week and survived on take out. What am I going to do with a head of lettuce? On the shelves, it doesn't get much better. Lentils?

I'm digging around in one of the freezers, hoping to find a pizza, when the door opens. Instead of Garrett, Addy waves at me with a big smile. "Hiya. Long time no see."

Shit.

"Hi," I say, as she saunters over. Her breathing is pronounced, as if she's been running. Like before, she comes way too close and I take a step back. "How are you?"

"Oh, you know. Hot and bothered." She shakes her hair, a shiny black cascade. "I was in the garden and heard the truck. I didn't want you to leave without saying goodbye."

I take another step back and bang into the shelves. "I won't."

She giggles with a hand over her mouth. "Do I make you nervous?"

"No."

"I promise I won't bite," she says. "Unless you want me to."

She winks and damn, I forgot how pretty she is. Jeans and a t-shirt have never looked so good on anyone, and everything clings in the right places. The only thing I can think of to say is, "Uh, thanks for washing my clothes yesterday."

"You're welcome. It was my pleasure," she says, fingering the hem of my t-shirt. "This is better than that stuffy shirt. What do you do for work anyway?"

"I'm an accountant."

"Really?" She cocks her head. "You're *way* too cute to be an accountant."

I point to my face. "Have you seen this lately?"

She laughs, the same smoky laugh. "A sense of humor. I like that. Maybe you're not so serious."

"Kind of serious."

"So, LA huh?" she says, sliding her hands into her back pockets. "You must have a glitzy life."

"It's no so glitzy."

"You've got a fancy car."

"It's a 2013. I just keep it in good condition." I pause. "Well, I did."

"You like working with your hands?" she asks, and pushes her chest further out.

"I'm pretty creative at some things."

She grins and studies me the way I imagine Lorelei must have studied me, every Saturday in Peet's Coffee. Determined. But being around Lorelei was different. She taught middle grade and claimed misfits were her specialty. Whatever her trick was, it worked. Her ability to calm me made our movie outings less stressful. In Addy's presence it's like I'm a steak dinner and she hasn't eaten in weeks.

"What's your deal then, huh?" she asks, nudging me with her arm. "Out here on your lonesome. You're too young for a mid-life crisis. Let me guess. Bad breakup?"

"Kind of."

"You getting back together?"

"I don't think so."

Her eyes dance all over me. "You two live together?"

The gradual infiltration of Lorelei into my apartment probably doesn't qualify as the living together she's referencing, but I still say, "Yes. What about you? How long have you been with Cassius?"

"A while," she says and looks hurt that I asked. "Why?"

"Just curious."

Her smile comes back. "It's good to be curious." She glances at the crutches. "You going to be okay to drive?"

"I just twisted my ankle. It'll be fine in a few days."

"When are you leaving?" she asks.

"Not sure yet."

"In the next day or so?"

Her smile falters and maybe I read her interest wrong. "Garrett needs some help around here so I offered to chip in."

"Doing what?" she asks, skeptically.

"This and that."

Her brow darkens. "On crutches?"

"Once I'm better."

"What about your job?" she asks, her voice rising with concern. "Don't you have to go back?"

"Ah...I'm on holiday."

She turns, frowning, and in the thin streak of sunlight nipping through the windows, I can see a purple swell on her cheek, dark through the makeup. Her mouth twitches, like she's talking to herself. Eventually I look in the same direction, wondering what she's staring at.

"What are you doing here?" Garrett's booming voice is almost as chilly as the room.

Addy shakes off any distractedness and looks over her shoulder. "Morning Garrett," she says, in a pledge-allegiance-to-the-flag voice.

"It's afternoon," he says, coming up beside me. Somehow he seems taller. More imposing.

"I heard your truck. I was going to say goodbye, but sounds like he's staying," she says, crossing her arms. "Fancy that."

"I'm introducing him at the meeting tonight. Why don't you head home and get ready?"

She leans over and says to me in a loud, fake whisper, "If he *lets* you, come on over to the garden. I'll be there for a bit."

"We've got things to do," he says, roughly.

"Why don't you let him make up his own mind?" she fires back. "Or is that not allowed?"

Garrett's jaw squares. "We're done."

"Well, I guess that's my cue, isn't it?"

Unlike Cassius, she doesn't defer in his presence. If anything, she seems to be looking for a fight. But maybe she decides this isn't the time or place.

"I'll see you around Damien," she says and brushes her hand down my arm. "I know where to find you, don't I?"

Garrett's eyes drill into me like I've been caught with my hand in the cookie jar. "Uh, yeah. See you around."

"Garrett," she says coolly, a version of goodbye laced with anthrax.

She walks away, swinging her hair, like she knows we're watching. When the door closes behind her, Garrett turns to the shelves and starts to chuck cans into the box on the floor. The tension we just got rid of is back, and this time I'm not sure how to navigate out of it.

"I, uh, didn't know what I could take, so I waited," I say, moving beside him.

Another can thuds into the box.

"Take what you like," he replies curtly.

Thud.

"She just came in," I insist, hating how pathetic I sound. "I had nowhere else to go."

Thud.

Thud.

He pauses and rests both hands on the shelves. A charged silence hangs between us. His head falls between his arms with a weary sigh. "I know. Let's just get through tonight and forget it, okay?"

I nod, eager to move on. The bad blood between them is obvious. Instead of opening another Pandora's box, I respect the layered quiet, and focus on what's in front of me. Cream of broccoli? Whatever. I'm not even hungry anymore.

Garrett's box is soon loaded to the rim with only six cans in mine.

"That's it?" he asks.

"For now."

"You don't cook."

"Not really."

He holds up a package of instant oatmeal. "Breakfast?"

"I'm good with coffee."

He tosses it into my box anyway. "Lunch is made every day so you don't have to worry about that. And I know you drink beer."

"Never say no to beer."

He pulls two cases of Miller from the last fridge, crooks them under each arm. "You're welcome to have dinner with us again, although I'd understand if you said no." He focuses just past me, as if he doesn't want to see me say no.

"I'm cool with that. I've got your back." He stiffens slightly with a surprised look and I quickly add, "I mean...not that..."

"It's okay," he says, "I could use the support."

His smile is bashful again, like he's aware of what he's just copped to. I'm just glad he gave me a free pass. Not everyone appreciates my directness.

Once we're loaded up and headed back, he drives slowly and we're both quiet. It's hard to wrap my head around everything that's happened since I woke up. Eleanor. Our argument. The fire was embarrassing. Fire is always a private, personal thing for me. Just seeing it doesn't mean he understands it (Lorelei sure as hell didn't) and I'm grateful he didn't freak out too bad. To go this deep, this fast, with anyone is unheard of for me. I think it was the same for him. There's a weird kind of understanding between us now.

"I'm going to pay you back for everything on that list," I tell him, out of the blue.

He turns to me with a mystified expression. "That's the least of my concerns."

"You're not used to giving charity, I'm not used to taking it."

A smile flickers on his face. "A pyromaniac with morals."

"Bet you never figured on that."

"No, I didn't," he says. "You've actually surprised me in a lot of ways." He means that as a compliment, something else I'm not used to, and I guess my silence gives the wrong impression, because he's quick to add, "In good ways."

"I figured."

The sun has warmed the window and I lean against it, thinking about Addy. What Garrett told me about her doesn't really add up. She didn't seem crazy at all. Feisty is more like it. Maybe it's a girl thing. Lorelei was always rebelling against something.

Out of the corner of my eye, I catch his gaze. "What?"

"How old were you when you lit your first fire?"

Unlike his responses, he never asks things in a roundabout way and on any other topic I would welcome the straightforwardness. "Ten," I finally say, rolling and unrolling the hem of my t-shirt. "Why?"

"Nothing," he says. "Just curious."

His eyes drift back to the road but he's not fooling me. I'm a professional when it comes to saying 'nothing', so I know that nothing is loaded with more things than a U-Haul.

FOURTEEN

ADDY

WHAT THE HELL is going on now?

I can't blame Cutie Pie for throwing a wrench in my plan because I know it's not him behind the decision. (Bless, he's cute and all – tall and young and strapping - but he doesn't strike me as the sharpest knife in the drawer.) It's Garrett that can't be trusted. He doesn't trust me either, for good reason, and this little move of his screamed loud and clear: he's scheming as much as I am.

"Addy! Wait up."

Here's good ole JD, huffing and puffing up the road towards me.

"What are you doing exerting yourself," I say. "You don't do well in the heat."

"I know," she says, bending over, both hands on her knees to prove the point, "and thanks for always being so concerned. You're an angel that way."

"What's on your mind? Or let me guess."

She grins mischievously, busted. "I've heard all sorts of rumors and you've met him. What's he like?"

"He's just a kid from California," I shrug. "Nothing special. Why?"

"Cassius said he was mugged."

"Cassius should keep his mouth shut."

With my tone, she glances over, real quick, and I know she sees the bruise. Like everyone else, she says nothing about it.

"I heard he's young. Is he handsome?"

"Miss JD," I say, hands on my hips.

She blushes and giggles. "Oh come on, Addy. Nothing wrong with checking out the merchandise. I'm not saying I'm *buying* anything."

I don't burst her bubble. Cutie Pie wouldn't take her money in a million years even if she were buying. I've seen my fair share of unfortunate looking women (my little sister Violet #1 on the list) and JD ranks right up there. She's as wide as a Redwood with a smooshed in face like she was running and forgot about the wall in front of her. Being five-feet nothing doesn't help her cause.

"Don't tell Taza what I said," she warns, wiggling a finger at me. "I love that man, but I know he'd be at the front of the line if some new young thing showed up."

Her eyes latch onto mine and for a second I wonder if she's trying to let me know that she knows. I still carry my shank around, old habits die hard, and Taza found himself on the wrong end of it one night after a few too many beers. Old coot. His scar's healed nicely though.

"Him and Bola still at odds over the Alternate?"

She blinks a few times, like she does when her brain has to catch up with a change of topic. "A little," she admits. "I keep telling him it's up to Garrett. All he can do is be the best he can be."

"I miss Elan," I say, and I do. He was smart for an Indian, but he lost it when Nalin died and Garrett doesn't like anything out of his control.

JD looks down, scuffs the ground with her moccasin. "Yeah, me too. And the others. Feels spooky losing four so quick. Hopefully that jaguar's moved on."

It hasn't. Trust me.

"I'm still feeling a little lost," she continues. "I could really use a session."

"I wouldn't count on those starting up anytime soon."

"I know," she says wistfully, and for a few seconds we're both quiet, our shadows long with the setting sun, a warm breeze blowing east. "I should head home for dinner. See you tonight?" She smiles and touches my arm. "I might just put on some mascara." Her eyes twinkle with expectation, and she does a goofy pirouette before trundling away singing a song. It's one of those Apache ditties I've heard in another lifetime, whether I wanted to or not, back when my first cellmate was an Apache.

When I made my debut in the Christina Melton Crain Unit in Gatesville, Texas (a half-a-horse town best known for its collection of women's prisons) my choices had dried up. I had no say in cellmates or my ensemble. White overalls and a crusty Indian on the top bunk I could live with. Getting twenty-five years for trusting a man? I was *pissed*, and I wasn't going to spend the prime of my life fighting off smelly dykes while Mason, that bag of shit, walked free.

Mason Boone Carter. He was the one who tore me apart the worst, although every man I've ever loved has turned out to be junk: Donny, Earl, Mason and all the little fly-by-nighters in between. All of them junk. (Steady Steve and Cassius too, except I never loved them. Convenience never equals passion.)

Now, maybe it's my choice in men, but it seems unfair. Why love always starts out perfect and can never stay that way is a question even the Good Lord won't answer in my prayers. I've been told I'm beautiful by almost every man, and those who don't say it with words tell me with their eyes, so is it too much to ask to be loved? *Real* love.

Lasting love. The kind of love Gramma had with Gramps, bless their souls.

I swore Mason was the one when we first met and I do see a little of him in Cutie Pie: broad shoulders, dark hair. Mason had harder lines in his round face, lines from a life on the streets, though when I first saw that face I never suspected how hard he'd turn out to be. That he would turn me in to save his own ass. Fucker. The only thing good I ever got from him was learning how to build things. My trusty shank established its reputation quickly in the Crain Unit, and the dykes left me alone. I spent a lot of time alone, watching, waiting, figuring out how I was going to get out. Who would be the one to help.

Pedro was kinder than most of the guards and I knew I was the hottest thing he had ever set eyes on. He watched me eat, watched me exercise, he probably watched me shower through the peephole all the guards denied existed. In return, I gave him extra long looks, just so he knew that I knew.

He was an ugly, fat bastard with a disabled wife (I found out later), which explains why taking him down was easier than I thought. Still, it took six months of constant sucking, and listening about his train wreck of a life, to finally put me in a position other than on my knees.

Of course, I lied; told him on the outside we could continue our ways, if he would only help. I've always been a good little actress and he really believed we had a kinship. On a bitter cold Sunday morning, when staff was short and the only other guards were snoozing off their thanksgiving turkey dinner, Pedro turned the other cheek and I got out.

I'll never forget that morning. 2 am. Frozen to the bone. The sky as black as my past. The relief of finding the bag of civilian clothes and five twenties, where Pedro promised they would be. When the headlights of the blue Nissan peaked over the hill, I started to cry.

Little did I know, out of the frying pan into the fire.

The driver of the Nissan was an electrician, recently laid off and in need of money (hence the convict pickup). He was supposed to drop me off somewhere near Brady, a safe house Pedro had set up, but that never happened. You can learn a lot about someone after spending eight hours in a car with them. If you're both desperate, sometimes the connection is much more powerful. He was freaking out because his cancer had come back and he had been given a year to live.

Our fate was set.

I needed a new life.

He just needed to live.

In exchange for new ID, the safety of his El Paso apartment and some of my *services*, I told him what I heard from one of the inmates, a half-breed native who said part of her tribe had defected to live with a white man who was believed to have powers. Powers only the Good Lord should have. Powers that could change the cancer in his body. I told him this group, this man, was somewhere in New Mexico, way north. He went over the edge with hope.

For the next two weeks, he was a man possessed. He tracked down whatever information he could and finally, with a scrap of a tangible lead, we left El Paso the same way we arrived: at ten in the morning, with nothing but uncertainty in front of us. It took another week of false starts and dead ends before we pulled up in front of a security gate that put the Crain Unit to shame. A dirty Mexican manning the property told us off. Said we were wasting our time. This man wasn't a doctor taking patients. His people lived under his rule, his laws, and didn't have an open door policy.

Cassius refused to leave.

We never laid eyes on Garrett for the first week. The Mexican, Cedric, was the only person we communicated with, if you could call it that. In fairness, he took pity and brought us some food and water while we camped out and almost gave up.

Finally, on day eight, when we were half starved, filthy and out of hope, he came.

I had only half listened to the inmate when she blabbered on about this guy, this Black Magic man, over dinner. In jail, you take every story you hear with a grain of salt. Those bitches could spin tales better than Dr. Seuss, and the way she went on about this guy, you'd think she was a Jew and he was the first coming of Christ. No one could be that special.

But that fucking half breed was right.

Some people you meet and right away you know they're different. Physically, there was no question of his authority. Garrett was a Greek god come to life, in stature and looks. But it was his mind, I swear I could feel it: a force so tough, so inscrutable. He dominated me even in silence.

He didn't say a word for the longest time, just stood at the fence watching us like animals in the zoo. Cassius poked me, hoping I would start things off, but I was stunned into muteness. I've never fallen in love on the spot. Cassius started with his sob story and it was the only time I ever saw him cry. It was a pathetic sight, on his knees in the dirt. He promised things he didn't even have to give and never had I expected his expertise in electricity would be the ticket in.

Turned out, there was a bunch of electrical work needing tending to, serious work, and the bunch of useless natives living there didn't know their ass from a hole in the ground. After eight days, five hours and thirteen minutes, our journey came to an end. But as we drove the Nissan through the gate, I felt it, like Gramps' arthritis used to tell him a storm was coming. Trouble. More trouble than I've ever been in, and I've been in lots.

We had dinner with Garrett and Rylan that night, and after she went to bed the three of us stayed up talking. He was very clear about our arrangement and the expectations. If he helped Cassius, we were here to stay. There was no more outside world. Those conditions required discussion, but Cassius was having none of it. He committed us on the spot.

After all I had done to help, he batted away my protests like I had dropped an ice cream cone and could get another one, instead of my entire life changing on a dime. I told him I needed a say in all of this and he disagreed. A more violent discussion later on got me nothing but a split lip and an ultimatum: if I dared to leave or double cross him, he'd have my ass thrown back in jail before I could say boo. Modern romance. Ain't it grand?

Now, if I could have made inroads with Garrett, I could've turned a blind eye, accepted this place, but he's always, always, been cautious with me.

At first, I thought he liked me and was just being careful around his bitch girlfriend. Then, after the second session, I realized he wasn't able to control me the way he did the others. His special concoctions didn't work, my mind stayed shut, and he didn't like it. He needed control.

You see, Garrett does have powers. Real powers. The only reason Cassius is still on this earth, his cancer gone, is because of those powers. But the devil comes in many disguises, always tricking, and I know Garrett is the devil. Only the Good Lord has the real power to give life, to fix life, to take life. Anyone else laying claim to those powers has made a deal with darkness, and when power comes to you corrupted, eventually it will corrupt you. That's what scares me. Something's not right with Garrett anymore.

And if Cutie Pie is staying, the numbers aren't adding up. I have to figure out why.

After the long walk, our cabin finally comes into view and my stomach grumbles, not from lack of lunch. Cassius is outside, sitting on the porch steps, a stupid puppy-dog look on his fat face. He reaches for me as I pass, like he always does after the fact. I know well enough this will last for a nanosecond, and his good will isn't a metric to be relied on for anything.

Men, I've learned, can't be trusted.

FIFTEEN

DAMIEN

DINNER IS LESS tense tonight and I chalk it up to the wine. I'm not used to heavy reds, and after two glasses, I'm nicely buzzed. Despite no wine, Rylan is friendlier. She asks about movies I've seen, but that line of conversation dies when it becomes clear she knows nothing about horror movies. Garrett is focused and says little, continues to be quiet as we drive to the meeting, all of us piled in the truck.

The wine was supposed to kill my nerves, but when the common house comes into view, so much for that. Golf carts and old pick-ups are jammed around it, like it's Friday night at the bar and I'm the entertainment.

"Full house," Rylan mutters.

"But where is everyone?" I ask.

Garrett wedges the Chevy into a spot behind the common house.

"Inside. They know to be early."

Parked, he leads us towards an enclosed gangway connecting the common house to a square-ish structure that resembles a bomb shelter. A small flight of steps leads to the only visible door. Inside the windowless gangway we turn right, passing through another door into a coat room lined with benches. Above them, dusty jean jackets and hoodies hang on wooden pegs.

Garrett shakes out his arms like he's getting ready for a performance. Beyond him is a third door, leading into the meeting room. Voices talk quietly inside. "Sit in the front row, on the right," he instructs.

Rylan stretches out her arm. I'm first in.

In my mind I was ready for this.

Living it is a whole other story.

The muted conversation dies as soon as I step inside and the silence is deafening. Thirty-two Native American heads swivel in my direction. I don't even realize I've stopped moving until Rylan nudges me in the back. "Up front."

Walking up the aisle, a wave of hushed whispers breaks out. By the time I get to the front row, my legs are shaking. Rylan sits next to me. The noise quiets down as Garrett makes his way up front. Despite the t-shirt and jeans, his command of the room isn't even a question.

"Good evening," he says, and waits for a ripple of 'good evenings' to float back. "Thank you all for coming. I know visitors are not part of our community, but unusual circumstances demand unusual responses. When I first came here, I had my own challenges. An unprecedented situation followed and you welcomed me, we welcomed each other, and together we got through a difficult transition." He tucks his hands behind his back, scans all the faces. "Two nights ago we had another unprecedented situation. Cassius and I found this young man, Damien," he says, acknowledging me, "beaten and left for dead on the side of the road." A couple female voices gasp. "If we hadn't brought him here, he might not be with us tonight.

"He's had his own challenges so for now, I'd like us all to make a temporary adjustment. Damien will stay with us for a short period of time..." The wave of questions - "What?" "How long?" – only dies down when Garrett raises his hand. "To keep things harmonious Damien will be staying in the guest house."

"Does that mean it will be available when he leaves?" a woman calls out.

"No," Garrett says in a tired way, like he's had to answer this question before.

The same woman whispers to someone behind me, "Why does he get to use it?"

"Give it a rest and be thankful for what you have," a man mutters in reply.

"Are there any questions?" Garrett asks.

"How do you know you can trust him?" one man asks, and by the way he poses the question, I can tell Garrett doesn't intimidate him.

"I trust my instincts," Garrett says.

"After last time, we agreed to vote on these things."

"I understand, Bola," Garrett says patiently. "This was a matter of life and death. There was no time to vote."

A couple of murmurs float through the room. I summon the courage to peek over my shoulder. Bola's features are strong - sloped forehead, thick lips - and he stares at me, unblinking, like I've offended him.

"I don't trust him," Bola says.

"You don't trust him or you don't trust me?"

Utter silence.

"I've made my decision," Garrett continues.

"What if your decision is wrong?" Bola presses.

Chairs squeak as bodies shift. Rylan frowns, her hands clasped tight in her lap. Thin strips of windows near the vaulted roofline are the only natural light in the suddenly claustrophobic space.

Garrett's gaze doesn't waver from Bola's direction. "Your opinion is always welcome, however, the final decision rests with me." He paces, hands still tucked behind his back. "Our status quo isn't threatened by Damien. He's here temporarily, and while he is here, I expect all of us to be respectful of him as he will be of us."

The finality in his voice is clear, but the equilibrium in the room remains precarious. What Garrett says next will push it past the tipping point.

"The second piece of tonight's agenda is also unexpected," he continues. "I've decided on an Alternate."

A surprised wave of chatter breaks out and Rylan's head snaps to attention.

"As a reminder, the Alternate is the stand-in whenever I'm not here or am incapacitated. If there are decisions or choices to make, the Alternate will look to our guidelines first, and if a decision can't be determined from those, the Alternate has discretion to make a decision that best represents the consensus of the group." His eyes drift behind me, to Bola. "I've made my decision and again my decision is final." The anticipation in the room ratchets exponentially for every second he says nothing. Then, with zero fanfare, "Cassius Odette."

Under her breath, Rylan mutters, "Are you fucking kidding me?"

Garrett starts to clap, and it takes several seconds for the rest of the stunned room to join in. Behind me, in the back row, Addy and Cassius sit by themselves and Garrett waves a constipated-looking Cassius to the front. They shake hands awkwardly.

"Cassius will be briefed on the full responsibilities and, as with Damien, I expect full respect towards my decision," Garrett says to the crowd.

Cassius leans towards Garrett, whispering, and Garrett nods distractedly, motioning me to join him up front. "Before leaving," he calls out to the crowd, "please come up and meet Damien."

I join Garrett at the front of the room and he tilts his head towards mine. "Almost done."

Cassius shuffles back to Addy and their discussion looks intense. Rylan marches past Garrett and me without saying a word. On display, I force a smile as the natives line up to file past us like a wedding procession. They shake my hand and introduce themselves, eyes black as oil, before moving on to Garrett. In front of him, they bow and he rests his hand on each head for several seconds, muttering words I can't understand.

A squat woman in line keeps craning to look at me, impatient at the slow procession. When it's her turn, she shakes my hand vigorously. "Hi," she says, gushing. "I'm JD, short for Jack Daniel's. Jack almost killed me, before I..."

"Save your gut spilling," the man beside her interrupts. His long braid falls over his shoulder, ending at his belly button. Most of his teeth are a yellowy brown. "Shake his hand and move on."

"It's such a pleasure to meet you, Damien," she says, giving the man a dirty look. "Nice to have some *young* blood around for a change. If there's anything I can do, or it you just want to..."

"Taza," the man says gruffly, elbowing her out of the way to shake my hand. "Never mind the wife. Even sober she's a handful."

JD pouts, but moves on to Garrett. "I think it's wonderful what you did. And never mind Bola," she says, lowering her voice because he's a few feet away. "You did the right thing. Saving his life. You're a good man. We all know that. And by the way..."

"Thank you, JD," Garrett interrupts and Taza snickers as JD blushes.

Bola is the last guy to come up and he doesn't shake my hand. He stands tall in front of Garrett, the respect and tension between them equal.

"Remember your honor," he says. "You were chosen. For *us*."

Garrett nods. "Always."

Bola remains longer than anyone else under Garrett's touch and while Bola looks calm, Garrett's features are strained, eyes closed, and the hard consonant sounds flowing out of him sound alien. When they're done, Bola pushes up the thin, gold wire glasses that have slipped down his nose and finally addresses me.

"Name's Bola. Like e-bola. And just as deadly."

"I'm Dam..."

"I know your name," he interrupts.

"Bola," Garrett warns.

I force myself to hold his gaze even though his presence is overwhelming.

"Don't fuck with us," is all he says, before he turns and walks away.

Those are the only words he'll say to me for the next three weeks.

When we're alone, Garrett runs his hands through his hair with a long exhale. "Well, that's over with. You okay?"

"Aside from the fact it was borderline revolt?"

He laughs. "They'll get used to you, including Bola."

Right. Like getting used to a rash.

"I don't have to work with him, do I?"

"Absolutely not." The cloud hanging over his head since dinner is gone and he smiles. "You up for a beer?"

"Best idea ever."

In the coat room, Cassius and Rylan are huddled in conversation and spring back from each other when we enter. Cassius radiates nervous energy.

"Where's Addy?" Garrett asks him.

"She left," he says. "Uh, can we talk?" His eyes shift to me. "Alone."

Rylan's pulls on her jean jacket and is about to leave when Garrett orders, "Give Damien a lift and come back for me. Twenty minutes."

She gives him a look slightly warmer than ice then shoves the side door open, the frame banging against the wall outside.

"Raincheck on the beer," Garrett says and I can tell he's pissed. "I'll find you in the morning, okay?"

"Yeah, sure. No problem."

Outside, the air has lost the afternoon heat and the Chevy is the only vehicle left. Rylan guns the engine with impatience as I fumble inside with the crutches. Dust kicks up as she reverses, and she drives fast, bangs through potholes. The truck drifts to a stop after she does a half donut in front of the guest house.

"You'd definitely fit in in LA," I say, thankful the Dakar Rally is over. "Thanks for the lift."

She hasn't said a word since I got in the truck and now her eyes, and body language, soften. "Hey," she says, "I'm sorry. He just caught me, all of us, a little off guard with you. I know you're not the enemy."

I'm not sure she believes that, and I have nothing to add.

After an awkward silence, she asks, "Can I ask you what he's told you about us?"

"Not much."

"He's told you something."

"Only that he's the guide of...all of you."

"And?"

"I mean..." I start, "he did mention...the powers."

There. I said it.

Her head tips back and she looks down her nose at me, like I'm some sort of interesting new species. "Really."

"I don't believe in that stuff though," I add, hastily. "So, it's like, whatever."

There's another gap of silence and she flicks her thumb absently against her index finger. "You never heard of him before? Honestly."

"No."

"And you really don't have anyone to help you back home?" she continues, skeptically.

Tired from the day, the wine and her questions, my reply is fierier than intended. "My mom's a vegetable. My dad's an asshole. End of story okay?"

"Oh my god," she says, covering her mouth with her hand. "I'm sorry. I had no idea. He never told me."

"He probably didn't want to make you upset."

She laughs bitterly. “Wouldn’t it be nice if he was that considerate?”

If that were a question, its clear what the answer would be. But she’s in a place beyond answers. Whatever her distress is, its acute, her long-distance runner’s body all sinew and tightness. She stares out the window for so long it’s like she’s forgotten I’m here. I figure its fair game to remind her.

“Is that Alternate thing a big deal?” I ask.

With an emotion-roughened voice she says, “I don’t even know what he’s thinking these days. No one does.” She swipes at her eyes and turns away from me.

“You ok?” I ask.

“Yeah. I’m fine. I better head back.”

I’ve slipped out the door, about to close it when she asks, “Are you going to have dinner with us every night?”

“Do you mind?” I’m not sure if it’s a trick question.

“No,” she says and smiles, the first time I’ve seen her smile. “But if you are, you can tell me what you like and I’ll make it.”

“Thanks. I’m not picky. I’ll eat anything.”

“I’m really sorry about your mom,” she says, the smile fading. “That’s awful.”

We say good night, but it’s too early and I’m too wired for sleep. I’m still on the porch swing, nursing a beer when the truck roars past later. At the top of the hill, both doors open, then slam shut. If there was conversation going on, I probably don’t want to hear it. Something tells me my comfort level here is going to be like a glacier: for every two steps forward, there’ll be one giant step back.

I finish the beer, head inside and, just before sleep takes me away, convince myself that after today things can only improve.

Wishful thinking.

If I had known what was coming down the pipe tomorrow, today would have been a piece of cake in comparison.

SIXTEEN

RYLAN: "Are you trying to make things worse?"

Garrett: "Define worse."

"Jesus, you're an asshole."

"You've been telling me that for years."

"I finally got used to you being cruel. Now you're just indifferent."

"I never asked..."

"Don't you dare throw that in my face."

"You knew the deal."

"'Deal'," she says sarcastically. "Like father, like son. Everything's always a deal." A pause. "So what's the *deal* with this kid then? I mean, really?"

"I already told you."

"I know what you *told* me. The same shit you told all of us with Cassius and Addy. That's been a real charmer decision hasn't it?"

"You accuse me of being cruel when I saved his life."

"Don't give me that excuse."

"I've made my decision."

"Right. God has spoken." Another pause. Longer. Then, a different tone. "He's a good looking kid."

"Is that supposed to be a threat?"

"Fuck you."

"Sleeping in the spare room won't facilitate that."

"*Facilitate.* Good God. Can you stop being a pretentious jerk for one second? Ever wonder why I'm not sleeping with you? You're a moody shit."

"Is that what you tell yourself? Would it be better if I pretended to be happy?"

"You wouldn't know happy if it bit you on the ass."

Rylan stomps down the stairs into the entrance hall and doesn't break her stride even when she sees me. "How long have you been here?"

"Uh, just now. The door was open and ..."

She waves her hand *whatever* and yanks on her sneakers. Garrett appears on the steps shirtless, in shorts and bare feet, a surprised look on his face.

"Um..." I mumble. "I didn't know when you were coming down."

"It's okay," he says, distracted.

"I'll just wait for you down there."

"Why don't you come with me?" Rylan asks, and when I look at Garrett, she says firmly, "You can do what you want."

"Where are you taking him?" Garrett asks.

"I think someone in the garden could use some eye candy," she replies with a smirk. She yanks on my shirt. "Let's go."

She waltzes out the door and Garrett says, "Give me an hour, okay? I'll come pick you up."

I hobble out to the Honda Pilot idling in the driveway and knock on the passenger window. When it rolls down I tell Rylan, "It might be better to keep a low profile while I'm here. You know, keep to myself."

She shakes her head. "Get in."

Making conversation just to fill the space has never been my strong suit and the space between us is as big as the Pacific. Luckily, Rylan seems pre-occupied with whatever their argument was about, so I focus out the window and try to pinpoint why Garrett looked different this morning.

"So now you know," she says out of the blue. "We're not fucking."

Woah. TMI. TMI.

"I don't think I should get involved."

"You're involved now."

"I meant I'm not very good with relationship stuff."

"You've never had a girlfriend?"

"We broke up."

"Did you cheat on her?"

"No," I say. "I'd never do that."

She looks at me, unconvinced. "Never, huh?"

I won't go so far as to say that she relaxes, but by the time we pass the common house and turn onto a narrow lane, her hands are no longer clutching the steering wheel in a death grip. We park in front a shingled cabin, straight out of Yellowstone Park.

"End of the line," she says. "Welcome to the garden."

She's not joking.

A massive garden plot occupies the frontage and three industrial-size greenhouses dominate the embankment behind the cabin. One of the women from last night, Feather (I remember because she has a feather in her hair), pokes her head out of a cabin window and waves as we climb out of the SUV.

"This is a surprise. You working with us today, Damien?"

"I guess," I say, with a questioning glance at Rylan. "For a bit."

"Garrett's going to pick him up in an hour," Rylan explains, looking like a model in aviators, cargo pants and a jean jacket. "Can you leave him with JD?"

Feather laughs. "Really? She's going to be tickled pink. I'm not so sure about him." Rylan laughs too, like it's a secret joke. "We have to pack up lunch. Why don't you wander down to the garden and say hello to JD?"

"Can I check out the greenhouses first?" I ask.

"Maybe later," Feather says and behind her sweet smile authority screams loud and clear. "I'll bring out some tacos once we have everything ready, ok?"

"Sure. I'll meet you in the garden."

Feather disappears from the window and once Rylan's in the cabin, I hurry up the embankment, glancing once over my shoulder. It's always easier to ask for forgiveness instead of permission. Besides, greenhouses are ten times more interesting than a freaking garden and I've never been in one.

As soon as I'm through the door, an invisible veil of moisture greets me, the air fresh with the smell of plants. Growing stuff is serious business by the looks of it. Elevated rows of seedlings run the entire length of the space, lines of lush green against the dark soil. With a stuttering hiss, the irrigation system kicks in, just as a blur of long legs and black hair disappears out the back door.

Addy.

"Hey," I call out, but she doesn't hear me. By the time I reach the back exit, she's slipping inside a smaller greenhouse - a residential-sized one - tucked at the end of a worn path. I follow her as quickly as I can. She'll know more about what went down last night and I want to ask her before Feather re-appears.

But once I've caught up and peer through the glass door, I'm confused, because at first I don't see her. Tiered shelves are crammed with exotic looking plants, planters are clustered on the floor and she's wedged between two shrubs, clipping foliage from one of them with garden shears, muttering to herself. The bright sunshine streaming in highlights several bruises on her back - some purple, some faded yellow. When I knock on the door, she shrieks and spins around so fast she topples onto the tray of seedlings beside her. "Good Lord," she says, eyes wide. "You gave me a fright."

"Sorry. I didn't mean to scare you. I can help you clean up."

"No, no no, no, no" she says, holding up her hand. "And don't be sorry. I was in my own little world, that's all." She shovels seedlings and cuttings into the tray, making more of a mess.

"You can finish what you're doing. I can wait."

"I'm done in here," she says, standing to herd me out the door. "Let's go."

Her pace is brisk until we're back at the embankment. With a smile that feels forced she asks, "What are you doing here anyway? I mean, not that I mind."

"Killing time. Garrett's picking me up in an hour."

"I'm surprised he let you out of his sight."

She's wearing short shorts and a tiny bikini top. Two bullets stick straight out from the small triangles of fabric. She notices me notice and pokes me with her elbow, grinning. "I knew you were nothing but trouble," she says. "Lucky for me I like trouble."

"How are you?" I ask, focusing on her face.

"Awww. Look at you, all embarrassed. Don't worry," she says, swatting my arm. "You're only a man. I'm good by the way, and thanks for asking. You're so polite. I like a man with manners." She sways back and forth in a playful way. "I'm just glad grumpy old Bola didn't scare you off last night."

"Yeah, what was up with him anyway?" I ask, relieved she's brought it up.

"He's very protective of Garrett."

"Really? It felt like he was challenging him."

"Someone has to."

"Addy! Get some clothes on," Feather yells from the doorway of the cabin. She starts marching towards us, her long cardigan flapping behind her. "You were wearing your shirt this morning. Did it suddenly disappear?"

"It's hot," Addy says with a pout. "Besides, there's no harm in him looking."

"Is that what you're going to tell Cassius when he finds out you've been parading around half naked?"

"Are you going to tell him?"

Feather ignores her glare. "Come and help us get lunch packed up."

"I'll be there in a minute."

"I'm in charge here, in case you forgot."

"How can I forget when you remind me every day?"

"And what are you doing up here?" she asks me. "I told you to go to the garden."

"Uh, I've never been in a greenhouse," I say, lamely.

She's about to say something when a loud clanking sound catches her attention. She takes a couple steps forward and squints in the direction of the small greenhouse. Her eyes narrow on Addy. "Were you in there?"

"In where?" Addy asks, innocently.

"You know where." Feather scans the tray of debris in Addy's hands. "You know we're not allowed in there."

"I wasn't in there," Addy insists.

"Then why is the door open?"

"And now I'm supposed to know everything? The other day you said I knew nothing."

Feather crosses her arms with a grim look. "You're always pushing the envelope aren't you, missy? Why do you need to make things more difficult?" To me, her tone crisp, "You make your way to the garden and help JD like you were supposed to. Never mind this one."

"Can I say goodbye in peace, please?"Addy asks impatiently.

"I'm going to tell Garrett what I saw."

"You didn't see anything."

"I saw enough," Feather says and ends the discussion with a withering, "Lunch. Two minutes."

When she's out of earshot, Addy mutters, "It's like I can't even change my mind without everyone watching. Damn Indians."

"Isn't it Native American?" I deadpan.

She spits out a laugh, and the sun hits her cheek, the bruise from yesterday more noticeable.

"What?" she asks at my stare.

"I saw the bruises on your back earlier. Those are serious."

"I fell."

"That's a nasty fall."

Something stirs in her face. "What are you doing tonight?"

"I don't know. What is there to do?"

"Why don't I swing by your place? Nine?"

Her hand grazes my arm and I'm suddenly unsteady, like the ground has shifted. "Uh, I don't think that's a good idea."

"Shhh," she says, and on tippy toes places a finger on my lips. "No one has to know. Besides," she continues, "You seem a little uptight. I can help you relax."

"Addy!" Feather yells.

"I'm coming," she yells back. Then, muttering to herself, "Jeez Louise, that woman drives me nuts."

"She sounds tough."

"If she has a good side, I've never seen it." She leans in and lowers her voice. "Thanks for not saying anything about the greenhouse. I appreciate it."

"What's so special in there anyway?"

"It's all of Garrett's 'magic' plants."

"Magic?"

"Now, Addy!" Feather shouts, gesturing at her to head down.

"We need to talk," Addy says. "See you tonight, okay?"

She jogs down to the cabin, the tray of seedlings bouncing off her hip.

I'd be lying if I said my thoughts weren't bouncing along with them.

SEVENTEEN

"DAMIEN!" JD gallops over and wraps me in a sweaty bear hug before I'm even through the garden gate. "I'm so glad you're here."

"Yeah, me too," I say, pulling away.

"Are you on garden duty?"

"He's not on any duty," Feather scolds, kicking the gate closed. She sets two plates loaded with tacos on a picnic table half sunk into the soft dirt. "Garrett will be here after lunch to pick him up. Try not to scare him away before then please." To me, she says, "I hope you like carne asada. It's my special recipe."

"Like hell it is," JD blurts out. "Garrett found it on the internet."

Feather ignores her and puts a hand on my shoulder. "If you need anything else, more food, just holler, okay?"

"She made herself the boss without asking," JD grumbles after she leaves. "Typical Feather. She probably already told you, because she likes to talk too, even though she pretends not to, but no one works with me because, apparently, I talk too much, but I say phooey on them because I like working by myself just fine, and the less interruptions I have the better. *Anyway*," she says, taking a breath, "much obliged and glad to have some company. Especially someone as nice as *you*."

Her smile is full of crooked teeth, but it's the two beads of sweat sliding off her chin I can't look away from. They drop onto intricate scrollwork blooming out of her deep cleavage and she pulls her ratty t-shirt lower before I can stop her.

"The right one says 'forgive', the left 'faith'," she says, proud to display her tats and tits. "I had to forgive a whole lot even to be here today, and faith is the only thing that keeps me alive. My baby daddy doesn't deserve any forgiveness, but he's all my son has right now."

"That's some serious ink."

"Thank you," she beams, finally letting go of her shirt. "I figured you, being from LA and all, would appreciate it."

We dig into lunch (delicious, internet recipe or not) and JD gives me one of her tacos, says Taza wants her to lose ten pounds. She talks nonstop, tells me who does the most (Cassius), the least (Feather), who she considers a friend (Addy), who she doesn't (Tanis, Bola's wife). On overload, I zone out when she launches into another baby-daddy monologue.

"Anyone home?" she asks, waving her hand in front of me.

"I'm here. I'm listening."

She gives me a long look.

"Honest, I was listening."

"I could make you feel worse and ask you what I just said but I get the hint; enough about me." She crosses her arms, the skin underneath jiggling like the Jell-O cubes I used to spoon into Mom's mouth every Sunday. "Tell me about you."

"There's not much to tell. I'm an accountant."

"Oh come on," she scoffs, "a nice looking young man like you. Los Angeles. You must have a hundred stories."

"I worked a lot."

"You didn't even photocopy body parts at the office?"

When I finally stop laughing, her disappointed face is gone, replaced with a mischievous grin. "It's nice to see you smile. You looked like a deer in the headlights last night," she says, and clucks sympathetically. "Mind you, Bola took it all too far, as usual. But, it's the circumstances. Everything's been a little different lately."

"Why's that?"

"Well," she says, leaning forward conspiratorially, "Tanis, she's Bola's wife, she told me Bola wasn't even sure anymore about Garrett, and he's the one who brought him to us."

"Brought him?" I ask, confused. "I thought he moved here from New York."

"He did come out here on his own, but Bola was the one who found him. He was out riding one day and found Garrett, lying in the dirt. Poor thing. You see, Bola knew. He knew right away. His granddad had the power, seen it with his own eyes. Garrett had no clue why he was chosen and..."

"Chosen?" The word sounds even more ludicrous when I say it.

"Garrett didn't know at first what it all meant," she said, waving my question away, "and the Tribal Council didn't like him one bit. They didn't trust a white man. Said he was stealing what was ours. They were just scared because he was too powerful, more than they'd ever seen. They said if we joined Garrett we would be banned from the reservation forever, stripped of our status. Of course, they didn't have the power to do that, just blowing hot air as Elders do. But Bola, he stood up to them and asked those who believed to come. Not everyone did."

The whole situation here is starting to make a bit of sense. Finally. "That sounds like a serious decision. Being stripped of status."

"It was, but it was the right decision. The *only* decision," she insists. "Of course, there were some bumps along the way, there always are. Sometimes you have to compromise."

"Is that why your son is still back on the reservation?" I ask, and immediately wish I didn't. Her smile is more than a little broken.

"My baby-daddy sided with the Council. Wouldn't let me take

him. It was the toughest decision I ever had to make." She stops and brings her hand to her mouth, eyes watering.

"Sorry. We can talk about something else."

She pats her chest, composing herself. "I miss my little Sammy more than anything in this world. Anyway," she continues, "Taza always had a crush on me, and since we all had to pair up to come over here..."

"Had to?"

"It's the natural way of things. Two, not one. You being single here wouldn't work out in the long run. It causes trouble, if you know what I mean. Anyway, things have been running okay here. There was a little blip when Cassius and Addy arrived earlier this year, kind of like you, out of the blue, and..."

"They only got here this year?"

"You sure do interrupt a lot," she says.

"Sorry. It's so much information. I'm trying to keep it all straight."

"I thought he told you all this?"

"He did. A little."

"Well," she says, and leans back. "You should have told me. I don't want to be the one telling you things he should be."

If I could get a word in edgewise...

"Why did they come here then?" I press, and she holds out for about five seconds.

"Well, alright. Just don't be blabbing to him that I told you all of this, okay?" She leans forward again. "Now, I don't know if we ever got the real story about those two, but all I can say is there's a reason for most things. There's a reason why Bola found Garrett. There's a reason why Addy and Cassius found us. There's a reason why he found you."

"What reason?"

"Why do you think you're here?"

"A flat tire."

"Don't be smart, even if you are," she says, wagging a finger at me. "What I mean is, we're all running from something. Some things we know about it. Some things we don't. Even you. Thing is, he finds it all. Makes it better."

"How?"

"The sessions." She pauses with a suspect look. "He told you about those, right?"

"A little."

"You'll have to ask him about those yourself," she says, warily. "He's been taking a break from them and we're all feeling it, but it's his decision and we respect it." Her eyes drift over my shoulder. "And now, with this jaguar running around..."

"Jaguar? Like the cat?"

"Uh, huh. New Mexico has jaguars. They're rare, usually south, but we have 'em. This one's killed three of our own in the past few weeks. You be careful walking around at night by yourself."

"A jaguar has killed people here." It's too outlandish I don't even bother posing it as a question.

"None of us has seen it, of course, only the aftermath. But having one around has put us all on edge. The jaguar is a very powerful spirit animal. It represents death and rebirth."

"What's a spirit animal?"

"Animals are a big part of our universe. They protect us and give us wisdom. Help us deal with issues. But if a jaguar shows up in the outside world, it means disruption. It forces us to look inside and see what's no longer needed. They can make things better, but its havoc gettin' there." She pauses and puts her hand on mine. "I think that's why Bola's a bit nervous about you showing up. Especially with everything else going on. But don't worry about him. You keep good thoughts in your head and you'll be okay."

I don't need anything else in my head right now. It's about to explode. I don't even know what to ask next, and I'm spared when Garrett's truck rumbles up the path behind us.

"Oh darn it," JD says. "Time flies when you're having fun." She helps me up, and hands me the crutches. "Will you come back tomorrow?"

"I don't know what's happening yet. I have to ask Garrett."

"Tell him you want to work with me, okay? Don't let him put you on maintenance," she warns. "That's the worst of the lot."

At the gate, she wolf-whistles and Garrett looks over with a wave. She pats my heart, eyes crinkled against the sun. "You're my ch'onii, okay? That means friend in Apache."

"Ch'onii," I say, the word unfamiliar on my tongue. "Okay. Thanks. I'll see you later, okay?"

Back at the truck, Garrett asks if I'm up for a tour. I say sure, distracted; my brain revs in overdrive. Native Americans are deeply spiritual. The connection between the people and their beliefs is practically unbreakable. For part of a tribe to move away permanently from a reservation is serious shit. And now a killer jaguar? Part of me doesn't really want to know more, but my curiosity is out of control.

When we're settled inside, Garrett hands me a paper bag. "I brought you some lunch."

"Thanks," I say, putting it on the console. "I already had some tacos."

I crack my knuckles. Then tuck my hands tight between my legs. Move them under my legs, back between my legs. He watches the whole procedure until it's over. "Anything on your mind?" he asks.

"Yeah," I say. "I'm cashing in my raincheck."

EIGHTEEN

"YOU HAD some quality time with JD I take it?" he asks.

"You could call it that."

"Fair enough," he says, like he was expecting this. "I was going to show you the cabins, but we can start somewhere else."

He reverses the truck with one hand, looking over his shoulder, at which point I finally clue in to what's different about him. He's clean-shaven and looks ten years younger.

"Where are we going?" I ask.

"You wanted the whole story, right? Or have you changed your mind?"

The way he asks it...

"No. I haven't changed it."

He swings the truck straight and a rectangular metal box slides off the dash and tumbles between my feet. Inside, bullets as big as my index finger are wedged tight.

"What's that for?" I ask, like a moron.

He nods to the backseat. "You ever shot a rifle?"

I've never seen a gun in person and the long, silver barrel is daunting.

"No way. Guns make me nervous."

"It's not loaded," he says, like that should make me feel better.

"Does everyone here have guns?"

"I have a couple rifles for hunting."

"What do you hunt?"

"Deer, elk."

"Jaguars?"

Garrett frowns.

"Is it even safe here?" I ask. "JD said three of your people have been killed by it?"

"It is true, unfortunately," he says, like he's admitting he prefers peas to carrots, instead of a killer cat slaying people. "As far as safety goes, jaguars are nocturnal, so the attacks have happened mostly at night. You shouldn't wander around by yourself." He glances at my crutches. "The others can run but you can't."

How he manages to take my anxiety and turn it into a joke is impressive, but kind of annoying.

"Have you seen it?"

"Only tracks."

"Does Eleanor know about *those* people?"

He shakes his head. "We buried them on the property."

"We're not going there I hope."

He doesn't reply. We lapse into a silence that continues past his house and the workshop. After that, the road gets rougher and he drops the truck into four-wheel drive. He navigates expertly up a steep slope before the hill flattens out and we skirt along a ridge, way up. At a lookout area he pulls over. The sky, light blue with a hot noon sun, goes on forever.

"At the bottom, there in the corner, you can see the fence," he says, pointing at a thin silver line deep in the valley. "That's the property line."

I roll down my window and squint. "Your fence goes around five thousand acres?"

"Almost all of it."

"It's kind of overkill, don't you think?"

"When we first started, it was a little tense," he admits. "I don't know what JD told you, but knowing her it was probably everything."

"She said they all defected to be with you."

"The Jicarilla Elders weren't happy about it and made a lot of noise to anyone who would listen. For a while, we had reporters and TV crews showing up at all hours. Rylan and I were sleeping in the guest house and some guy actually walked in at 2 a.m." He shakes his head at the memory. "The next day, I started on the fence and building the new house. Cedric was the contractor. He's been with me ever since."

"It's funny you call it the guest house when you don't have guests."

"You're a guest."

"True," I say. "But at the meeting someone brought it up, about not being able to use it. How come no one lives there?"

"I decided it was better to have separation." He pauses and scratches his chest. "Not everyone's happy with that."

"And Rylan doesn't mind if I stay there?"

His face clouds, and he puts the truck back in gear. "It's not her decision."

From the heavy silence up the next ascent, it was the wrong thing to ask, but he can't expect me *not* to notice. Its obvious things aren't going well between them and I'm no expert in relationships. Maybe she doesn't like having a stranger sleeping in her old bed. But as before, the awkwardness between us disappears as quickly as it appeared and the conversation steers back into neutral territory. He points out different things as we drive – mostly plants – until we arrive at a clearing surrounded by a half ring of trees. In the center, thick rectangles of stone are arranged in a circle.

"What's that?"

"It's a kiva." He parks and kills the engine. "They're used for ceremonies and rituals."

"What do you use it for?"

"Contacting spirits."

"For real?"

"For real." He cracks his door. "Let's go."

Closer to it, it becomes apparent the stones aren't just lying on the ground. Crumbled mortar affixes them to another layer below. Two ends of a ladder jut out from the opening. I circle around it, cautious.

"Is it okay to walk on it?" I ask.

"Go ahead."

Peering down into opening, I can't see anything. A cold, earthy smell fills my nostrils, crawls down my throat.

"It's creepy," I say, edging back. Like that weird hum from the other day, this feels like bad juju. "You go in there?"

"Not lately," he says, his eyes scanning the area. I wonder if he's just picked up on the same sensation I have, like we're being watched. He nods towards two boulders shaded by trees. "Let's sit over there." Once we're seated, he asks, "Do you know anything about shamans?"

"No. Nothing."

"They're members of indigenous tribes around the world, including the Jicarillas. Each shaman operates within the guidelines of the tribe and has varying functions but mostly focuses on the well-being of the members."

"Like a medicine man."

"Kind of. What I do, we call them sessions. They're used for healing. Internal things like trauma or emotional issues. I contact the spirits and ask them for help, channel bad energy into good."

"That sounds heavy," I say.

And so not real.

"It can be. It's a complex experience and not always smooth. It's accessing levels I don't have full control over. There's an exchange of energy and I can steer and shape it, but there's always a risk."

"What happens when you can't control it?"

"So far, nothing bad," he says, but his voice trails off, like he's not sure. "I have to be careful though. The sessions take a toll, physically. I'm taking a break right now."

"Oh," I say, like any of this is actually making sense. "Does not knowing what's going to happen freak you out?"

"It did at first," he admits. "Then I realized what I could do." He knits his hands behind his head and leans back on the rock. "Everyone thinks money is power, but anyone can earn money. This is real power."

"Do the sessions have to happen in there?"

"It's what they wanted," and when he says *they,* his brow furrows. "I told you I came out here by myself, after my parents died. I wasn't in a good place. Drinking, doing drugs. One night I was high and started to hike, ended up here."

"On foot? We must've gone four miles."

"Not quite," he laughs. "But it was February, snow on the ground, freezing cold. I wasn't prepared at all and passed out. When I woke up it was dark and snowing. The next thing I remember is the earth moving beneath me. It started to shake and the ground split open, like a sinkhole, and I fell in."

"Holy shit. I've seen videos of those. They're crazy."

"Yeah, and this hole was deep. I could barely see the sky. Tried to climb out and couldn't. I have no idea how long I was in there. I thought I was dead, or going to die. And right then, honestly, I didn't care. I wanted to die. Then they came."

"The spirits?"

"Yes. They appeared out of nowhere. One of them spoke, not out loud, but I could hear every word, like I was telepathic. It was a language I didn't understand. Apache, I realized later. They said I would live, if I honored their gift, their people. I had no idea what they meant." He holds out his left arm and turns it, the jagged white scar bright in the sun. "They cut me open and said they'd let me bleed to death unless I embraced it."

There's a great dead space in my gut. He's talking like this is all real, but drugs make people do weird shit: like cutting themselves.

"And then all these animals showed up. This energy surged into me. It was ancient, more powerful than an earthquake. After, I could understand them, even the animals. I was connected to planes, different levels of consciousness. A whole universe I wanted to understand. Like being deconstructed is the only way I can describe it. A rebirth." He's rocking back and forth now, like there's a rhythm only he can hear. "So I said yes. When I woke up, Bola was beside me, asking who I was, how I got the scar. The cut had healed on its own somehow."

"How did Bola find you?"

"He was riding through the property from the reservation. The Jicarilla Nation has a small southern annex. We're close to it. Bola lived near the southern tip with his wife, Tanis. I stayed with them until I got my strength back. I didn't really understand what had happened, but Bola did. His grandfather was a very powerful shaman and had a scar almost exactly like mine. Bola knew right away when he saw mine. He tried to explain to the Elders the significance, wanted them to embrace me, but they said forget it.

"Bola already wanted off the reservation, didn't like the oil and gas deals, how the Tribe was being run. We made a deal, sorted out how it would work. And here we are." He sits up and blinks, like he's just come out of trance. "So, the long answer to your question is that's where it all happened. The pit I fell into is in there."

I've heard my share of ghost stories and conspiracy theories and believed none them. This is different. The kiva, that hole in the ground, has taken on mythical proportions. "Wow. I mean it's almost unbelievable."

"*Do* you believe it?" he asks, as if sensing my ambivalence.

"It's not like you're lying," I say, glancing at his scar. "But you have to admit, it's pretty out there."

Like way out there.

"That's why I didn't say anything at first."

He chews on a fingernail, spitting out whatever he tore off.

"So you really are a guide in some way. You help everyone with their problems."

"More or less," he says.

"It sounds like a lot of responsibility."

"It is. That's why I'm taking a break."

"Does having this power mean you have to stay here forever?"

Shifting on the rock, he says, "Forever's a long time."

"I know. It's so isolated here. I'd be way too lonely."

He looks down at his lap. "Won't Colombia be lonely? You won't know anyone."

"Yeah, I guess you're right." He's reminded me of what's still to come, and I don't really want to think about it. I force a smile. "Maybe this is good training, huh?"

"Speaking of training," he says, "if you want to be a fisherman, I can teach you how to fish before you go."

"Really? You'd do that?"

"Of course." He looks pleased until I start to laugh and his voice is the tiniest bit defensive when he asks, "What?"

"I don't know. You're like this dark wizard, channeling the underworld, and then, 'Oh by the why, I can teach you how to fish.' It's pretty rad."

"Rad, huh? That's a first."

We both chuckle, and he leans back onto his elbows. I'm finding that I like talking with Garrett. It's easy, especially considering that most people have the depth of a puddle; I could spend hours and never touch the bottom with him.

"What does that mean?" I ask, noticing the faded words on his t-shirt: Man is condemned to be free.

"It's Sartre. He was a French philosopher. It means that as humans we're free to do whatever we want, choose what we want. We're totally responsible for our lives. But despite that freedom we get paralyzed with choices. Second guess ourselves."

I think about that for a bit. "So being condemned means we struggle with freedom?"

"That's right. Even being totally free, whatever your version of that is, you still have to make choices, and you still have to be able to live with them."

Choices, decisions: a hundred different ones that brought me here.

"Do you ever second guess all this?"

"I have," he says, and there's something in his voice that tells me not to push, so neither of us rushes to fill the gap in the conversation. Then, out of nowhere, an ice-cold wind rips past us, over the clearing. It gusts in forceful waves and loose dust whirls around the kiva entrance. For a second it sounds like someone's screaming.

"Where did that come from?" I ask, looking around nervously. The day is still scorching hot.

But Garrett's gone completely still. He scans the trees, alert. This time, I'm certain he feels it. The premonition from earlier, of being watched.

"What?" I ask. "What's going on?"

He pushes up from the rock. "Let's get out of here."

I don't need to be asked twice and when we drive away, I'm surprised how relieved I am to get away from the kiva.

You couldn't pay me to get in that thing.

NINETEEN

THAT NIGHT, it takes a long time to fall asleep. I can't stop thinking about Garrett's story. Every bone in my body tells me to reject it – it's fantasy, Dungeons and Dragons stuff – and I can't. My dreams are filled with talking animals and snow storms. I toss and turn and wake up drenched in sweat. Garrett picks me up at ten and I'm still sluggish after three cups of coffee.

After my second yawn he asks, "Rough night?"

"Not as rough as yours."

He matches my sly smile. "Hey, I was rusty. I'm open to a rematch."

After dinner yesterday, I challenged Garrett to some chess and kicked his butt four games in a row. He took the defeat in stride and even asked where he went wrong. I knew every time. We stayed up late talking about probabilities and statistics and Fibonacci numbers. He's freaking smart.

He also gave me an overview of how things work here. In the morning, he trades; manages his own inheritance and the monies each of the natives brought with them. They pool resources for food. Garrett covers major expenditures like the fence or electrical upgrades they did a few months ago. From their investments, each person can buy what they want for themselves, clothes or personal items.

The deal we made is this: he's agreed to pay me twenty dollars an hour, in cash, and at that rate it should take me at least six weeks, including recovery, to earn the five grand to fix my car. A couple days ago, the thought of six weeks here would've killed me. I'm still not one hundred percent dialed in, but I like Garrett even if he is the grandmaster of native spirits.

Instead of the garden, this morning we drive to the shop. I get the feeling Garrett doesn't want me to spend more time with JD, and he'll hear no complaints from my end. Working with Cassius is the only downside, and he shuts down the table saw when we arrive. He's covered head to toe in sawdust, and with safety goggles on he looks like an extra from a Mad Max movie.

"Well, look who's decided to man up and play with the big boys," he says, flipping the goggles up. "Or did the garden wenches can your ass already?"

"He's here to help you since no one else wants to," Garrett says, sternly. "What's he going to start on?"

"Something easy," Cassius replies, and flicks a dark look in my direction. "Sanding boards. I can adjust the work bench over there if he needs to sit."

Garrett assesses the area with an approving nod. "Good. Make sure he knows how to use the tools properly. I'll be back around two to pick him up."

Cassius frowns so I pipe up, "I can stay longer. No problem."

"No. I have some other stuff I want to show you." To Cassius, "We're good?"

Cassius nods crisply, and when Garrett leaves he gives me a suspicious once over. "He seems pretty stoked to have you around."

"He said you could use some help."

"I don't need help."

"What about the boards?"

"You ever used a sander?" he asks doubtfully.

"No."

From next door, an engine fires up, and Cassius stalks over, slamming the door between the shops closed. "Fucking rednecks," he mutters. "Over here," he says irritably, waving me over to the work bench. Cedar planks are lined up against the wall, ten deep, multiple rows. He shows me how to refill the hand sander - sixty grit paper first, one hundred for the final pass – and instructs me on a test board.

"These are just going to be picnic tables so we don't need them smooth as a titty" he says. "Once you're done, wipe them down with a damp cloth and stack them on the horses over there. Job number two will be staining. Got it?"

"Got it."

"These aren't Armani or whatever you wear back in LA, but put them on," he says, handing me a pair of goggles. "And remember to empty the dust container every once in a while." He fishes around in his coverall pocket for a pair of earplugs wrapped in plastic. "Wear these. The saw is pretty loud. If you need anything, wave."

Faced with the ocean of planks, it's the kind of work I've always feared – physical labor, repetitive – and I'm surprised it's so satisfying. The feel of the wood as it gets smooth with each pass, the tangy smell of the cedar, the sander vibrating in my palm. I get into a zone and complete fifty boards before Cassius comes over and says it's time for lunch.

"Not bad," he says, rubbing his hand over a couple of finished boards. "Didn't think you had it in you."

Outside, the native guys unload boxes from the back of Rylan's SUV. Two of them carry jerry cans, and from their flexed arms I can tell the cans are full.

"Should we help?" I ask.

"Nah," Cassius says, lowering onto one of the picnic tables outside the shop. "I do ten times the work they do every day."

Rylan comes over, a bankers box leaning against one hip.

"There better be ham and cheese," Cassius grumbles without a hello.

"We're out of ham until tomorrow," she says and dumps the box on the table. "There's plain cheese."

"Great," he says, and digs in the box like a dog burying bone. "If I was a fucking mouse."

"How about don't kill the messenger?"

"I asked for Coke, too," he says, holding up a juice box with disdain. "I'm not an eight-year-old."

"You want to be on lunch duty?" she fires back, and shoves the box towards me. "There's tuna, egg salad and cheese."

"Chicken of the sea, farts or mouse food," Cassius continues like a petulant kid, as if Rylan's somehow to blame for the selection.

Ignoring him, she says to me, "I hear you're a pretty good chess player."

"I'm okay," I say, fishing out two sandwiches, a juice and some cookies.

"It's all he could talk about this morning."

Both hands are on her hips like she's accusing me of something. She has tiny hands. Tiny wrists.

"Really? He lost every game."

Cassius laughs, brays like a donkey, and Rylan, fed up, whisks the box away with a sour look. When she's with the Natives, he asks, "So did he let you beat him or did you actually beat him?"

"I beat him fair and square."

He smirks. "Good for you."

Shoulders hunched, he devours his sandwiches like a lion with fresh kill. He's solid, in all the opposite ways from Garrett: short, wide, no angles. Earlier I noticed curls of orange hair crawling up the three thick ridges that make up the back of his neck. If he were a wrestler, he'd be the Flying Orangutan. All he needs is a cape.

"What are you looking at?" he asks.

"Nothing."

He licks his fingers with a stubby tongue. "How much longer you here for anyway?"

"Not sure exactly. A couple weeks."

"Your job doesn't care you're gone?"

"I took an extended leave."

"Addy said you're an accountant. How'd you get into that?"

Addy. Shit. I totally forgot. She was going to come over last night. I wonder if she did.

"Numbers are reliable."

"Oh," he says and burps. "I figured you were an actor. All that precious hair." He pulls out a pack of cigarettes from his overalls and jams the last one in the side of his mouth. "Thank Christ I don't have to worry about that shit anymore," he says, and flicks a lighter. "You want one?" he asks, my eyes glued to the flame.

"I don't smoke."

"Could've fooled me," he says and inhales deep, the cigarette crackling. "It looks like you were about to blow a load."

I re-arrange myself on the bench uncomfortably. The lighter is on the table, beside the cigarette box.

"Speaking of blowing loads," he says. "You banging anyone back in LA? I hear the chicks are all pretty eager. You know, trying to make it in Hollywood."

"Nah. Flying solo right now."

"Playing the field?"

"Not really."

He squints at me. "But you're thinking about it, right?"

"Isn't everyone?"

Rylan heads back to the SUV without saying goodbye, and Cassius watches her leave with a moody expression.

"You know anything about wine?" he asks.

"A little."

"What's a Sigh-ra? Any good?"

"You mean Syrah?"

"Whatever, Mr. Bigshot. Is it any good?"

"Yeah, they're nice. It's red."

He flicks his ash in my direction. "Thanks, fuck wad. I know it's red. Garrett gave me a bottle."

What does Addy see in this buffoon?

After a long drag, he asks, "Speaking of Garrett, how's everything going up there anyway? I hear you've been having dinner with them."

"It's good."

"What do you guys talk about?"

"I dunno. Regular stuff."

"They ever mention any of us?"

"No."

He scratches at another tattoo on his forearm, some celtic knot thingy. "Ever?"

"Why are you asking?"

"Just wondering what's up," he says, trying his best to sound casual. "Garrett's been a bit distant lately."

"I'm probably the wrong person to ask."

"I think you're the right person," he says, switching from defence to attack with surprising dexterity.

"What does that mean?"

"I can tell he's taken a shine to you. Seems odd, given how he's been." He places his cigarette on the edge of the table and unwraps some cookies. "You know, he insisted we bring you here. I told him you were better off in a hospital."

"And...?"

"What do you think?"

"About what?"

"Why he didn't bring you to a hospital."

"I was unconscious. I never asked why."

He gives me a flat look. "You end up at some strange place and never ask a single question?"

"Like I said..."

"I heard you," he interrupts. "I also heard what Garrett told us about you. Believing it is another thing."

"You don't trust him?"

"I never said that," he says, looking away. He finishes both cookies, then picks up the cigarette and puffs on it a couple times to get it going. "He saved my life. He tell you about that?"

"No," I say, surprised. "How?"

"I had cancer. Five months to live." He snaps his fingers. "Gone."

I roll my eyes. "Right. No one's cured cancer."

"I was last-legging it. Had two tests after. Both clean."

"C'mon, you think I'm that retarded? It's impossible."

"Ask him," he says, indignant. "It's a fucking Christmas miracle."

"Dude, if he cured cancer, I mean, there'd be people lining up for miles. He'd be famous."

"That's the last thing he wants. You see the security this place has? It's fortified to the tits. No one gets in. Or out," he adds, cryptically. "That's the way he wants it. How it works here."

"What do you mean 'how it works'?"

He flicks his ash, assessing me. "Maybe you should be asking him for more details since you're so buddy buddy."

"If he saved your life why don't you trust him?"

His face flushes. "You think I'm not grateful for everything he's done?"

"I never said that."

"You..." He stops, searching for the word.

"Implied it?"

He drops the butt on the ground, crushes it with his boot heel. "Smart ass."

The natives break out in raucous laughter, two of them looking over their shoulders in our direction. Cassius glares at them until they turn away.

"I hear you and Addy talked yesterday," he says.

"Uh," I stammer. "Yeah, but not for long."

"Jesus, the look on your face," he laughs. "No offence amigo, she'd never do a punk like you. She likes 'em macho." He flexes his bicep, but his smile fades into what might be the first serious expression I've seen on his face. "What I want to know is does she seem alright to you?"

"I guess," I say, "I don't really know her."

"Duh. That's why I wanted your opinion. First impression."

"She seems...nice. Normal."

"Normal huh?" he asks, pulling on his bottom lip. "Do me a favor, would ya? Let me know if she starts talking," he spins his finger in circles beside his head, "crazy talk."

"What constitutes crazy?"

"Good question, amigo. When it comes to chicks the sky's the fucking limit right?"

What an idiot. "I'm serious."

He cocks his head as if he's caught off guard, that he actually has to think. "Well, you'll probably be gone before you have the chance to notice anything, but, she's wobbling between the lines, if you know what I mean. Just take whatever she says with a grain of salt."

"If she's sick, shouldn't she get some help?"

"You try telling her that and let me know how it goes," he says. "She's a little sensitive about the whole matter. Denial is a wonderful thing."

"Are you asking me to spy for you?"

"It's not spying if it happens in front of you," he replies, annoyed. "All I'm asking is for you to tell me. It's not a big deal."

Annoyed right back, I start to get up. "Forget it."

"Hey, hey, hey. Calm down," he says, motioning for me to sit back down. "I'm just making sure you're on my side, that's all."

"I'm not on any side."

"You might want to re-think that."

"Why?"

He lowers his voice and leans towards me. "Just so you know, bringing in strangers doesn't really jive with the overall plan here. I'd watch your back."

"Weren't you two strangers?"

His face turns an ugly shade of red. "You fucking lippy punk," he says. "You think you know everything, well you don't." He stands up so violently, the table lurches with the sudden release of weight. "Stay away from me. Stay away from Addy. And here I was about to tell you you're doing alright. Asshole."

He flips me the finger and stalks back to the shop. Minutes later, the saw fires up.

I untangle my legs from under the picnic table with a heavy sigh. If this is how it's going down, the next few weeks will be slow and painful. But I'm not caving. If he's going to dish it, I'll dish back. The situation isn't ruinous by any means, I've dealt with worse, but a few more confrontation-free minutes won't hurt.

Deciding on a cat nap, I'm about to lie down when the sun pops out from behind a cloud. Something shiny flickers in the dirt. When I realize what it is, butterflies start to churn in my stomach. Keeping a nervous eye on the shop, I maneuver myself off the bench. Cassius was so mad he didn't notice the cigarette box tumble to the ground when he got up.

Or the lighter.

Brushing the dirt off, it slides effortlessly into my pocket like a needle into skin. Just knowing it's there gets me through the next hour, until Garrett swings back to pick me up.

TWENTY

"DAMIEN. OPEN UP. PLEASE."

The doorknob spins again. She's crying. Always crying.

"Damien. Please."

I squish my body into a tight ball. The shower stall is splattered with blood.

Outside, another voice cuts in. "Leave him alone and get back to bed."

"Franklin...." she pleads.

"I said, get to bed."

"You've been drinking. It's always..."

"This has nothing to do with my drinking."

"He's my son."

"Gwen," he warns. "Move. Away. From. The. Door."

"No," she says. "Not this time."

He laughs, an awful sound. "You're giving me an ultimatum?"

The stretch of silence goes on too long for him. Even I've learned this.

"Answer me!" he yells. Then, "You fucking bitch."

I can feel the slap through the door; hear the futility of her strug-

gles. A loud crunch reverberates the glass wall of the shower. Mom screams. I thought I knew all her screams.

"Damien! Help me. Call the police."

He tells her to shut up, and their sounds move away, down the hall. He's freaking out, screaming bitch, slut, cunt and there's a shriek that's different from the screams then thumping sounds I used to make when I slid down the carpeted steps of our old house.

For a long time I don't hear anything.

When he knocks on the door, his voice is calm. He tells me to open up. He knocks again, waits; knocks a third time. Goes away. Shortly after, a siren wails outside and he comes back.

"You stay in there now if that's your choice. If you make a sound, you know what's going to happen. I swear to God."

No way I'm going to stay. Not this time.

When there's voices downstairs, I slip out and dash to my bedroom. I pull on four t-shirts, a sweatshirt, a hoodie. Stuff what I can, as fast as I can, into my backpack. My bedroom window opens soundlessly and the thick scent of night jasmine pours in. In the driveway, ambulance lights flash blue and red. A grim faced attendant unpacks a gurney. Three. Two. One. I jump and land wrong, limping away in the shadows.

At school, three days later, I'm called to the principal's office. When I come around the corner, he's there, laughing with the secretaries. He turns and smiles his fake smile, on his fake plastic surgery face. He's wearing a black three-piece suit with a bright red tie, his undertaker look. Coming to bury me.

We sit in his Bentley, parked in the handicap spot. The car smells like new leather but all of them do. I keep one hand on the door handle, just in case. When his phone beeps and flashes he pretends to ignore it, although his eyes shift down every time. The gloomy silence is like the purple leaves from the jacaranda tree beside us, slowly falling, smothering us.

"She's going to be okay," he finally says. "But the police want to talk to you even though I told them you weren't there." He takes a deep drag of his cigarette and starts to tap the steering wheel with his gold pinky ring, slow, steady, three seconds between each tap. I know that ring. The diamond sticks out. It left cut marks on her face and mine. "Just so we're on the same page, I haven't told them about the fires. I wouldn't want you to get blamed for that warehouse."

He pauses. Doesn't ask how I've been, where I've been. He doesn't even look at me. Right now, he's doing what self-made millionaires do: cutting a deal. Negotiating.

"We both know it was you," he continues. "Now that you're sixteen, you can get tried as an adult. Arson means jail. We don't want to go there, do we?" His gaze drifts to a group of jean-jacketed boys walking past. He lights a second cigarette with the butt of the first one, flicks the butt out the small gap in the window. He hasn't smoked in years. "We're good then?"

The sickness of finding out he's lied, that she's never going to be okay, is days away, and it will never trump the sickness I feel in his presence.

"I said, are we good?"

"Sure," I say, opening the door, dizzy from smoke, the sun warm for January. "We're great. We're fucking amazing."

A week from now, after the police interview me, there will be keys to a Lexus on the kitchen counter, his business card beside them.

Like I don't know who he is.

The trunk of the Lexus is tiny and maybe he's right after all. Maybe my life doesn't mean anything if it can all fit in a trunk.

TWENTY-ONE

"DAMIEN. OPEN UP. PLEASE."

I jolt up on the couch. Garrett's woodworking book slides off my chest and lands on the floor with a clunk.

"Damien. Please. Help."

Stuck in the half-world between sleep and waking, I stagger up on one crutch. "Hold on," I call out, limping towards the foyer. "I'm coming."

I've barely opened the front door and Addy rushes past me, streams of crimson running down her face. At the sight of so much blood, fear coils up my spine. "Jesus. What happened?"

"Lock the door," she begs, her eyes wild, filled with terror. "Please."

I close the door and flip the deadbolt, queasy. It looks like she's been stabbed. "Calm down," I say, fighting to keep my own voice neutral. "It's okay."

Cowering against the wall she whispers, "Sorry. I didn't know where else to go."

Her sudden arrival, her trauma, is like a shot in the arm. I'm fully alert and not in a good way. ""Don't be sorry." I reach for her hand. "C'mon, let's get you cleaned up."

She lets me steer her through the bedroom, into the bathroom. Shoulders stooped, she curls up tight on the toilet seat. Her body twitches with the occasional sob. Using wads of toilet paper, I daub at the cut on her scalp. The deep gash extends close to the hairline. Soon, my hands are slick with blood, balls of red toilet paper piled in the sink. "I don't know, Addy. You might need stitches."

A drop of blood splatters on the white tile floor and she flinches. "You think so?"

"Can you grab the Band-Aids? There's a box under the sink. I'll need a few."

When I'm done, four Band-Aids, almost breached with blood already, lie like railroad ties on her head. She pats them gingerly and looks up at me. "Thank you." There's a long stretch of silence and her eyes skip around. "I like your bathroom," she says with a weak smile. "It's big."

I lean against the counter and cross my arms. "This wasn't you falling."

"I know," she admits.

"How long has this been going on for?"

She fidgets with her hands, nails short, a little ratty. "A while."

"And no one here helps?"

"They don't care about me."

"Have you talked to Garrett?"

"Garrett?" she asks, a frown creasing her forehead. "He's the last person who would help."

"Have you asked? Maybe he can talk to Cassius."

"And say what? Stop beating on Addy?" She shakes her head at the suggestion. "Like that's going to happen."

"If it's so bad, why do you stay with him?"

"We made a deal with Garrett," she finally says.

"What kind of deal?"

"The kind you can't break."

There's something behind her look I can't figure out and there's no time to, because she stands gruffly and says, "Forget I said anything, okay? You can't help."

"Hey, wait," I say, as she brushes past me. "Wait!"

I follow her into the bedroom and she spins around. "What?"

"How can I help you if you don't tell me anything?"

"You want to help?"

"Girls shouldn't be treated like that."

"You've never hit a girl?"

"Never."

"Even when you were mad?"

"Especially then."

She scans my face, must decide I'm telling the truth. "So you'll help me?"

"If I can, yes. But you need to tell me what's going on."

I thumb towards the bed and we both sit on the edge. She's restless, edgy, legs firing up and down like pistons. "You need to take me with you when you leave."

"Okay," I say, slowly, "but I still need to get my car fixed."

"How long is that going to take?"

"A few weeks. Garrett's paying me to help out here, and once I have the money I can do the repairs."

"You know he has more money than God, right? He could fix your car right now and not make you wait."

"I can't ask him to pay for it."

"Why not?" When I don't reply, she asks, "How much money do you need?"

"Five grand."

"So we drive back to LA, earn some money to pay him back and it's done."

I clear my throat. "It's not that easy."

After a sticky silence, she asks, "You going to be up front with me or play games?"

"I'm not playing any games."

"Right," she says, unconvinced. "Let me tell you what I see. You say you're broke but you drive a fancy car and live in LA."

"Just because I live in..."

"Hush," she interrupts, holding up her hand. "And you could sell your car to pay back Garrett if you really needed to. He also has the money to fix your car."

"Yeah, but..."

"I'm not stupid, Damien," she interrupts again. "Do the goddamned math."

"I don't know why he's not fixing my car," I say, throwing up my hands. "I'm in no position to demand anything."

"Why's that?" she asks, eyes narrowing.

"Uh, because."

It's the lamest answer and we both know it.

"Oh, I get it." She leans forward with a crafty smile. "You're in trouble, aren't you? I mean, real trouble."

"No, I'm not."

"Sweet Lord," she says, voice filled with wonder. "What did you do?"

"Nothing," I insist. "Listen, don't put words in my mouth. I'll help you but...it's going to have to wait." Suddenly everything is moving way too fast. "And what about this deal you made? You said you couldn't break it."

She smiles. Laughs. "Silly," she says. "I can break it with *you*."

"I don't want you to get into trouble."

"The longer we stay here, the more trouble we'll be in," she says. "Both of us. *You're* in danger if you stay."

"Danger?"

The whole room has just got hotter.

"Garrett's turned," she whispers.

"What does that mean?"

"It means something's gone wrong. He turns. Changes. I saw. I wasn't supposed to see." The urgency in her voice grows. "There isn't a jaguar here. It's *him*. He's going to kill me. Maybe you."

"What?" I laugh, nervous.

"I'm the only one who's seen it happen."

She has a fevered look in her in her eyes. *She's wobbling between the lines.*

"Maybe it was just the dark," I say, uncomfortable with her intensity. "Maybe you..."

"I know what I saw," she insists. "We need to get out of here."

Her hand slips onto my leg and I freeze. She's way too close again. Her chest moves in and out with rapid breaths and I can see the curve of her breasts, the dark hollow in between them. She follows my eyes and cocks her head inquisitively. The air tightens. Her hand drifts higher along my thigh. She smells like candy, sugar, but she's the one licking her lips. It feels like slow motion, but her kiss comes fast, warm and soft. I make a little sound right into her mouth before she jams her tongue in. I pull back, wiping my mouth.

"Oh my," she says, breathlessly. "You taste real nice."

Her hand is still on my leg, dangerously close to *there*. I inch over so it slides off, my heart thundering. "I don't think we should do that again."

"You didn't like it?"

"I liked it."

She leans forward so she can see can my face. "How long has it been since you've slept with a woman?"

"Not long. Not that long."

"Are you a virgin?"

My cheeks flush. "No."

"Nothing wrong with being one."

"I'm not. One."

Her eyes drift down to my nipples, hard under my t-shirt even though it's boiling hot. "Uh, huh," she says. "I bet you could use a woman's touch in your life. How about I'll help you if you'll help me?" She draws a little circle on my thigh with her finger. "You need some help, right?"

"Possibly," I say, my hands, toes, ass, everything clenched tight.

"Don't be scared. I won't hurt you." She moves hair off my forehead. "You've got a dreamer's face, you know? Sensitive."

Behind closed lips, my teeth grind.

"You knew someone else in my situation, right?" she asks.

"Yeah. One."

"Did you help her?"

"No."

"Is that why you'll help me?" She grabs my hand and her thumb moves across it like a windshield wiper.

"I guess, yes."

"We'll help each other then? You and me?"

I swallow hard. "Okay."

Her mouth pushes onto mine again and a wave of helplessness sinks in, my thoughts falling into a place where I can't stop them.

I push her away and stand up. "Sorry...I...I.."

"It's alright," she says, sounding flustered. "You okay though? You're sweating like mad."

"I'm fine." I angle away from her, hips hunched. "I think I got too much sun today."

She stands, smoothing the front of her skirt. "I should go anyway, it's late," she says. "Thank you. For everything."

"Where will you go?" I ask, muddled thoughts swept away with fresh concern. "You can't go back to him."

"You're sweet for caring. You're *very* sweet. I'd like to stay here," she says, scanning the room with a sad expression, "but it will only make things worse. We'll talk more though, okay?"

At the front door, I'm uncertain. Sending her back to Cassius is like a one-way trip into the dragon's den. But she can't stay here. "I can walk you home, if you want."

"With crutches? It's almost a half mile. No, I'll be fine. Our truck is back at the common house. I didn't want anyone to hear me come over." She opens the door and slips onto the porch. Her skirt ruffles in the breeze and in the distance a coyote howls.

"Are you sure? What about the jaguar? Garrett said all the attacks happened at night."

She glances at the house on the hill. "Don't tell anyone what I told you. About Garrett turning."

"I won't, but..."

"It's important," she stresses.

"I won't. I promise."

"Okay. I trust you," she says, and blows me a kiss. "Good night."

Once she's gone, I lock the door. Her cotton candy smell swirls like a whirlpool. A familiar sensation rips through me: disorientation, my body wanting one thing, my mind needing another. In ten minutes, I've torn through every drawer, every corner in every room of the house and come up empty. My head throbs, like someone is jamming ice picks into my temples. My heart beats dangerously out of control. There's nothing to light on fire. I'll have to improvise. Cassius's lighter is tucked away safe in the bedside drawer and I need it, like a junkie going through withdrawal.

TWENTY-TWO

ADDY

EVERYONE HAS A WEAKNESS. You just have to find it.

Poor Cutie Pie. He isn't fooling me. Girlfriend, my ass. That boy has had one stuck in the chamber since time eternal. He darn near came in his pants right then and there tonight. I tend to have that effect on men anyway, but this kid...it's going to take some serious patience to stop him from crossing the finish line before me.

But I'm one step closer, and patience is something I've learned in spades.

On the way home, I rip off the bandages he placed so carefully on my wound. I should win a goddamn Oscar for my performance back there. It took a couple tries before I could smash that rock against my head and it hurt something awful; even worse the second time. But I needed it to look legitimate. I knew Cutie Pie was a softie, that I could bend his will with a little sob story. And while I had my suspicions all along, now I know for certain Cutie Pie is scared. Running from *something*. And if there's anyone who knows what it's like be on the run, it's me.

Ever since Gramma died, life has been a marathon to Shitsville.

Me and Gramma were always close, almost as close as me and Daddy. When the debacle of my fourteenth year broke me, broke my faith, she was there. She tried to give me good advice. If only I'd listened.

Gramma didn't like Mason from the moment she laid her one good eye on him. As soon as he was in the bathroom (stealing one of her figurines I found out later) she told me to kick his ass to the curb. But I wailed away, like girls do. I was *in love*. He was *the one*. She tried to convince me otherwise, said his type only led to misery and unwanted children. I'm only glad she never lived to witness her premonition come true. Her funeral was small - Mason and me, my sisters and a few fossils from Gramma's ragtag circle of friends. Mason didn't want to come. He refused to buy special clothes - "No one there knows me so who gives a shit?" he argued – and would only get his stupid ass to the service in a black t-shirt and shorts.

I hadn't seen my sisters in years and nothing had changed. Veronica was squeezed into some abomination of a dress. If you squinted and didn't mind her potato shape, she was passable. Violet? Well, she got the short end of the stick in every department, especially looks, and by short, I mean even a plastic surgeon would throw up his hands in defeat if she walked into his office. She was still buying clothes in the children's section, by the looks of it.

I ignored their charged glances and sat up in the front pew with the fossils. My sisters wouldn't even have been there if it weren't for Gramma naming me executor of her will, something those two snags never saw coming. And when the service was over, right as rain, Veronica sidled over. She would've rather ended the day without talking to me, but now she had to.

"Well, look who showed up."

"Veronica, nice to see you."

Pleasantries aside, she cut to the chase. "We're going to challenge, contest, whatever it is we have to do. You sneaked around behind our backs. That money is ours too."

"Fight all you want. It'll probably cost you more in legal bills than the money you'd eventually get."

"You self-centered bitch," she spit out.

"Look who's talking. I was the only one who gave a shit about Gramma. You two never even visited her after Mother died."

"I have children," she said in that way that only mothers do, like her shit didn't stink because she gave birth to two ugly brats.

"Sucks to be you."

"We're paying for the funeral costs," she reminded me, "up front."

"I'll cut you a check."

Her face pinched, like the material on her too tight dress. "You have some nerve. We haven't heard a peep outta you in years. You left us to fend for ourselves and now you're here reaping all the rewards."

"Rewards?" I asked, laughing. "Is that how you look at it? Gramma is dead. I'd trade all the money and then some to have her back."

But relationships were transactions to Veronica. She kept methodical records of who did what and when, who was to be rewarded or penalized. I was forever in debt, no penalty too severe, and didn't care. That's one of the reasons I left in the first place.

"We need the money," she said, trying another tack. "Steve lost his job and we can't afford insurance right now."

"What about all the money you sucked out of mother after I left? I know you were spending her checks. I never saw a dime after you sold the house."

"I tried to find you," she said, two red spots burning on her cheeks, "but you're always hiding."

"Right," I said, and started to look around for Mason. "Why don't we just call it even? Send me an invoice for the funeral."

She glanced back at Steady Steve, her husband, and waved for him to join us.

"Vera," he said, coming in with a shit-eating grin. "Nice to see you again."

I didn't correct him on my name. I was Isis at that point. "How long you in town for?"

"Just came for the funeral," I said. "We leave tonight."

"Where you living these days? Last Ronnie told me it was somewhere in Texas?"

"Still in Texas."

"That your boyfriend?" he asked, gesturing at Mason lounging in one of the pews, bored, sunglasses on.

"Yup."

Veronica squinted, too vain to wear her glasses, and gave Steady Steve a *what did we expect* look.

"Well, it sure is nice seeing you again," he gushed. "I don't know if Ronnie told you, but we're in a bit of a pickle financially and we were surprised to find out Ronnie and Violet were cut out of the will."

"Were they ever in it?" I asked, and watched in silent glee as Veronica's nostrils flared.

"Now Vera," he said, in that placating tone I had come to hate. "It's true you had the closest relationship with your Gramma but this isn't right. The only reason why there's a funeral today is on account of our good will. We tapped into our line of credit to pay for all this."

Time hasn't been kind to Steady Steve. His pear-shaped body has bloated into watermelon roundness and strong cologne, something drugstore brand, probably on sale, surrounds him at all times like a separate atmosphere. Even a boatload of the stuff could never do much to cover up his bad breath. I'm certain part of his attraction to me was that I liked it doggy style, but sweet baby Jesus, it was the only position I could do it in with him and not gag.

"I already told Veronica I would cut you a check for the funeral costs. As for the rest of it, all of you, including Violet and mother, already did everything possible to drain Gramma out of every dime while she was alive. How any of the policy premiums got paid is a true mystery." I made sure to give Veronica a heavy glance. "I got diddly squat from the house sale and it ain't my problem you're on the dole."

My diatribe stunned them into momentary silence until Veronica said, "You always were a conniver. And a slut," she added for good measure.

"You might want to treat me a little better if you expect a check."

"Don't you even think of asking for our help down the road," she hissed before elbowing Steady Steve. "Make sure you give her our address."

She stormed off to commiserate with Violet while Steady Steve dug around in his suit for a business card. He was so fat he couldn't even do up the suit jacket.

"You were selling tractors?" I asked, looking at the card. "What happened to your bank job?"

"I got laid off. Times were tough and I had mouths to feed," he said, looking at my tits. "Just make the check out to me and send it to that address, okay? I know our financial concerns aren't yours, but we sure would appreciate the funds sooner than later."

"Why am I sending a check to a business you no longer work for?"

He turned flamingo pink, and right away I knew there was some shady business going on. There always had been with him. "I know you two aren't getting along," he said, changing the subject, "but Ronnie and the kids are going to stay with Violet tonight. Why don't you stop by for dinner?"

I fought the urge to laugh hysterically, imagining the tableau: Mason at the dinner table, while Steady Steve plotted ways for he and I to resume our shagging ways. The only reason I gritted my way through months of disgust with him was because I needed the money, something he had zero of now.

"Thanks for the offer, but we have to head out." I gave Mason a wave, and he came over, rubbing his nose. A drift of white powder lingered in one nostril, his skin peeling like the Verizon logo on his t-shirt.

"Can we go?" he asked, hopefully.

"Mason, this is Steve, my sister's husband. Steve, Mason."

The look on Steady Steve's face was pure torture. He had loved fucking me, hadn't minded paying handsomely for it. After meeting Mason though, I had called it off. Thank god. Two abortions were enough, and they have messed me up permanently. Something I've come to regret.

Mason took his sunglasses off and squinted at Veronica and Violet, huddling near the back wall. "Man, are your sisters ever ugly." He glanced quickly at Steady Steve, realizing what he just said, and laughed, stoned out of his head. "Uh, sorry dude."

I grabbed his arm and we ran outside, collapsing into giddy laughter.

I never sent the money, even though I planned to. I'm sure after watching the news they probably figured out why. Mason made me cash the whole check right away because he had a plan. He knew a guy who could double it, with one deal, and since thirty thousand was the most money I ever laid eyes on, the thought of doubling it was too good to be true.

It was.

In the end Mason was just like every other man: a liar. There never was a guy, or a deal. There was another girl and when I woke up in that motel room, my head way too fuzzy from just booze, I knew Mason and my money were both gone for good.

In hindsight, I should've taken out my anger in more conventional ways. The motel manager truly was an innocent. He thought someone was dying in room 105. I never heard him come in, only saw his horrified reflection in the bathroom mirror...what was left of it. We tussled something fierce. I didn't mean for the cut to be so deep he would bleed to death. The jury didn't see it that way. They saw a pathetic junkie. They said put her away. And they did.

In jail, I promised myself never to get trapped with another shit of a man, and guess what? A shit of a man picked me up on the side of the road the day I got out, and now my days consist of sleeping, eating, and working with a bunch of dumbass Indians. If I dare complain, Cassius tells me how he feels about it without saying a word. He's wrong to do that, wrong in so many ways, and I will do anything to get away from him for good.

The good news is Cutie Pie's desperate, but in a whole different way. The thing is, I have to be careful. Tonight, in the middle of my performance, I admit, he caught me off guard. Those brown eyes, full of concern. That sexy, wide mouth. I couldn't resist and damn, he felt good. But I can't let my desires get in the way of the plan. Cutie Pie's integral to my escape, but disposable once we clear that fucking gate.

And speaking of fucking....he *does* have those beautiful long fingers. Oh my. The places they could go.

Maybe I won't dispose of him *right* away.

Like I said, everyone has a weakness.

Including me.

TWENTY-THREE

DAMIEN

"YOU'RE ALREADY DONE?" Cassius asks, lifting up his goggles in disbelief.

I've been on a role this morning and the remaining boards are sanded and stacked. "I can start staining, if you want."

He almost looks impressed. "Take a breather for now. You can start up again after lunch."

It was tough on my ego to walk back into the shop after our argument yesterday, and I don't know if Cassius or I was more surprised to see me come back. I had won the argument, but Cassius' smug look stung; he knew I had nowhere else to go. Yet he's been surprisingly civil since Garrett dropped me off this morning. Cassius is a hothead, but he's also too stupid to remember to hold a grudge.

After washing up, I head outside. It's cooler today with the breeze, but still warm. The picnic table groans as I lie down (Cassius calls them 'old whores,' the reason they're being replaced) and as soon as I'm horizontal, I drift off, waking up when something wiggles my foot.

"Sleeping on the job already?"

Addy leans against the table, smiling. Long, tanned legs stretch out of tight shorts. Her cropped tank top says Keep Austin Weird.

"Hey," I say, sitting up awkwardly.

"You were smiling before I woke you up," she says. "What were you dreaming about?"

"Nothing. Or I if I was, I don't remember."

"I had a *very* interesting dream last night. You were in it. We had a good time." She grins and sits down beside me. "A *great* time."

Her two pigtails make her look even cuter, like a farm girl. Whatever manic edge bubbled under her surface last night is gone.

"JD usually brings lunch to the shop, but," she flashes a brilliant smile, "I'm bored down there."

With the sun behind her, I put my hand over my eyes and squint. "How's your head anyway?"

"How do you know she hurt her head?" a voice asks from behind.

We both spin around and Addy flashes a *don't say anything* look in my direction. "He didn't..." she starts.

"Shut up," Cassius says and points a finger at me. "You wanna tell me what the fuck is going on?"

"Nothing," I say.

"Nothing. Really."

With both hands he grabs the front of my t-shirt and yanks me up and off the bench.

"Dude," I say, pushing him away. "What's your problem?"

"Stop it," Addy says. "He didn't do anything."

"Then how did he know about your head?" he asks her. "You said you wiped out in the common house."

"I did..." she stammers, "but I was worried and..."

"Relax, man," I tell him. "She came to the house. I helped her clean up."

"I bet you helped her."

"Yeah? Well, I bet she didn't wipe out at all."

The natives have gathered around their tables and start to chant *fight, fight, fight*.

"Is there a question in that?" he demands. "Because you better think long and hard before going down the path you're about to go down, asshole. You think you know what's going on? She's banging into shit all the time. Clumsy like a mule."

"Right. Is that what you tell yourself?"

His eyes bulge and he moves fast, faster than I would have imagined he could. In a second, he's dropped me, twisting and driving my right arm up behind my back. "Why don't we come to an understanding here and now," he hisses in my ear. "What goes on with Addy and me is none of your business, so drop the knight in shining armour bullshit. Capiche?"

He says it ca-pee-chee, like the idiot he is.

"What are you going to do? Break my arm?"

"Don't tempt me," he says, and cranks it another notch.

"Leave him alone," Addy shouts, pulling futilely on his coveralls.

He whirls around and shoves her so hard she has no chance to break her fall. She slams onto the ground, flat on her back, dust kicking up. The natives, now unsure where this is going, huddle together in silence.

"I told you to stay away from him," he snarls as Addy blinks and gasps, hands around her throat, the wind knocked out of her.

Enough is enough.

I lunge at Cassius head first, and he latches onto me, laughing, because I'm no match for his bulk. He spins me around like I'm a toy, holding onto my t-shirt until it rips off, almost taking my head with it. While I'm staggering around, he jabs his foot behind my knee and I crash in the dirt. Before I can get back up, his foot stomps onto my chest.

"Just say the word, pussy," he growls. "Fucking hairless freak."

I clasp onto his ankle, trying to keep the weight off me as he pushes harder, his eyes glittering with hate.

"Cassius!"

Garrett comes running up the hill towards us. Cassius jerks his foot off me and mutters, "Well, aren't you lucky."

"What the hell is going on?" Garrett demands, helping a dazed Addy up first, me next.

"Why don't you ask boy wonder?" Cassius grumbles.

Garrett's eyes land on me, questioning.

"It wasn't his fault," Addy cuts in, her breath halting, still coming back. "He was only trying to help."

"Bullshit," Cassius says. "You go crying to him I beat on you and then you come home telling me you fell down. Which one is it?"

"I want to hear your side of the story," Garrett says to me.

"What a surprise," Cassius mumbles under his breath.

"She showed up last night, bleeding bad, said Cassius hit her and..."

"That's fucking impossible," Cassius interrupts. "She came home with that cut. I never touched her."

"Let him finish," Garrett says.

"That's it," I say. "I cleaned up the cut, put on some bandages..."

Cassius whirls towards Addy. "You never came home with any bandages on. Tell them the truth, dammit. Tell them what you told me."

Addy glances at Garrett and pauses, her brow furrowing, like she's remembering something. Garrett's looking at me, and suddenly aware of my pale skin, I pick my t-shirt off the ground, shake it out and slip it back on.

"Helloooo?" Cassius says.

Her heads snaps around and she glares at him with defiance. "It was you."

"Sure it was, you loony bitch. Then why did you go crying to him, huh? A sympathy fuck? Maybe he'll listen to all your crazy talk?"

"I know what I saw," she says, her voice suddenly small.

Garrett jumps in with, "What did you see?"

Unconsciously, we've formed a circle around Addy. She stands like a statue in the middle, head lowered.

"Exactly. You gonna tell them or should I?" Cassius taunts. "Little buttercup's suffering these days. Aren't you? Seeing things. Hearing things. Just like your mother. Cuckoo for cocoa puffs."

"Shut up," she says, miserably.

Cassius waves his hand with disgust. "Get out of here. I'm going back to work."

"No," Garrett says, and we all freeze at his tone. He points at Cassius, eyes flashing. "You don't work in the shop anymore. You're on maintenance as of tomorrow." To Addy, "You don't come on this side of the property for anything. No lunch, no nothing. You don't talk to Damien, you don't even look at him. Do you understand? Both of you."

From the looks on their faces, this is serious.

"Fine," Cassius snips, anger rippling off him. "Just remember I told you it was a mistake bringing him here."

"Let's not talk about mistakes," Garrett fires back.

The hard look between them is a definite showdown and if it came down to brute strength, I'd call it a draw, but there's another dynamic here too, something only they understand.

"Get in the truck," Cassius growls at Addy.

She looks at me expectantly, like I need to do something and I shrug - *what can I do?* When they're both in the Nissan, Cassius guns the engine and spins away in a kick of dust.

Garrett caught my gesture to Addy and I'm prepared for the worst as he walks over. Instead, he tousles debris out of my hair. "You okay?"

"Yeah. I'm fine."

"Hold on," he says and walks over to the natives. The conversation is hushed, and based on the replay, they're confirming what happened before Garrett showed up. A couple of them look over at me with sympathetic glances. Garrett returns with a handful of sandwiches, cookies and two pops. We eat in silence, doing our best to look anywhere except at each other. Finally he asks, "So, was she cut?"

"Yeah. It was pretty bad. Deep, on her head."

"You definitely think he did it?"

"You don't?"

He leans forward on his elbows and I force myself to keep looking at him. "What else happened last night?"

"Nothing."

"You sure?"

"Yeah."

"You remember what I said about her?"

"I know, but she just showed up. What was I supposed to do?"

"She seems to show up unexpectedly a lot around you," he says, rolling a saran wrap ball back and forth in front of him.

"You see how he treats her," I push back. "She sure as hell didn't fall. Don't you even care?"

He shrugs. "I don't agree with it."

"Well, you should say something. He'll listen to you. He should anyway."

"He should?" he asks, cocking his head. When I look away, he asks again, more forceful, "He should?"

"He said you cured him of cancer."

I say it like I don't believe it and he takes his time before he replies.

"I did."

Considering the magnitude, it's the most casual confession. "But that's impossible."

"What do you want me to say to that?"

"If it's true, you could save lives. Thousands of them."

He nods, as if he's thought about this. "I could, but I told you, the sessions impact me physically. I can't do them all the time."

"So you cured him in one of those...sessions?"

"Yes." He unwraps some cookies and offers me one, takes the other. "But I shouldn't have done it."

"Then why did you?"

"I made a mistake."

"How is curing cancer a mistake?"

"What I do isn't for exploitation. That's not what it's for."

I get it...in a way. He'd become a freak show if the world knew what he could do. But it seems unfair that Cassius of all people gets to benefit.

"How did Cassius and Addy end up here anyway? They're not Apaches."

He takes a bite of cookie and with his hand in front of his mouth, "No, they're not."

I lean back, hands wrapping behind my neck. Here we go again. "You know you're the king of the non-answer, right?"

"Then you're the prince of questions," he says and pops the rest of the cookie in his mouth. His weirdo eyes are suddenly bright and full of humour.

"You think you're pretty funny, huh?"

"Maybe," he says and raises his eyebrows a couple of times in a joke-y way.

I shake my head and laugh. "Sometimes you're a real doofus."

"A doofus that's saved you not once, but twice," he reminds me.

"I never needing saving back in LA."

The birds that were rustling and chirping while we ate suddenly go still, like Garrett. "You want to go back?" he asks.

"No. Of course not."

But he doesn't look convinced. "If you have any other questions, now's the time to ask them."

Even if I didn't have another question, he's staring at me so intently I'd make one up. "Okay," I say. "Why did Cassius say it was a mistake to bring me here?"

"He says a lot of things, in case you hadn't noticed."

"True, but why didn't you take me to a hospital?"

"You were unconscious, it was late. The hospital is two hours away. You needed immediate attention."

"But what if I had died?"

His features cloud. "I was trying to avoid that." He takes a deep breath and places both hands on the table. Looks me right in the eye. "If I need to tell you again, here it is. I'm committed to helping you. That's not changing. But I need friction at a minimum to make this work. You keep to this side of the property they'll stick to theirs. Okay?"

On one hand, I'm relieved; the less interaction I have with Addy and Cassius the better...for now. Cassius – once a douchebag, always a douchebag. I never need to see him again. Addy is the dilemma. Once I leave here, it's a solo mission, and while no woman deserves to be abused, her tagging along would only mean trouble for her. There's no easy solution and whatever deal she made with Garrett weighs on my mind. He's not the type of guy I want to piss off.

"By the way, everything's still clear," he says. "I looked this morning."

That's his code for telling me I'm safe. For now.

"Thanks for checking. I'm still hoping for world disaster so they forget all about me."

"Me too."

I crack a smile. "So you liked it when I tried to burn your truck down?"

"Maybe not that." His eyes are soft on mine, the tiniest smile. "How are you doing without a phone or TV?"

"So far, so good. I was never Mr. Social Media."

"I can set up Netflix on your TV if you'd like."

"You know what?" I say, after thinking about the suggestion. "I'm cool. I'm going to have to get used to living like this anyway, right? Colombia. Middle of nowhere."

"Right," he says, and shifts on the bench, away from me. It's like a veil has draped over him, closing him off. Every time I think I'm beginning to get him, this happens, and it's driving me crazy because I *want* to figure him out.

"Or would you rather us watch TV and avoid your nightly beat downs?" I ask, referring to our post-dinner chess games.

He laughs that crazy freaking laugh, and just like that, he's back. "I'll win. Eventually."

From deep in the shop, an engine rumbles to life. It's a reminder that without Cassius around I might be stuck in the garden for the next few weeks.

"Is it okay if I keep working up here on my own?" I ask.

"You enjoying it?"

"I've never worked with wood before. It's cool."

Garrett pops the top off a Coke and takes a long swig. "Says the 'I'm not a labor guy.'"

"'Change is good,' right?"

He nods and smiles. "I could help you learn some of the tools."

"Awesome. I started to read your woodworking book last night. I have some ideas if you want to hear them."

Garrett's smile broadens. "You plan on building your own house?"

"If you play your cards right, maybe I'll hire you to help me."

He laughs and pushes up from the table. The rest of the afternoon zips by. We stain the remaining boards, I tell him about the new porch swing I'd like to build and he practically has to drag me out of there for dinner.

There's a lot of different lives I used to dream about; ones I wish I had. Being an accountant hiding out with the only person on the planet who's cured cancer wasn't one of them.

Go figure.

TWENTY-FOUR

I READ SOMEWHERE it takes thirty days to create a new habit. For a quick learner like me who craves routine, two weeks is enough. Especially when I like what I'm doing. Working in the shop isn't even work.

Since the *incident*, Garrett's been with me every day, and that's the best part. I already knew from playing chess we'd work well together. He's patient and makes sure I understand why things are done one way, and not the other. He listens even when I challenge him and doesn't press on my mistakes. The new swing is coming along and it's cool, building something from scratch. With Cassius gone, things are peaceful. Garrett's been different too, more relaxed, and its not just me who notices.

JD brings us lunch most days, and yesterday, after Garrett got up from the picnic table, she said, "It's like he's a changed man. He used to always be paranoid about having kids, younger people, around. I swear it's you that's having this effect."

"Why doesn't he like kids?"

"I don't what all his issues are, some sort of unhappiness, but having someone younger around allows you to see beyond yourself. I think he's needed that." She covers her mouth with one hand, eyes glistening. "Life is a cycle, and if you deny it, you're denying the creator, your very reason for being."

"You okay?" I ask.

"Yeah," she says, letting the tears fall. "I just miss my boy."

I put my arm around her, awkwardly. "Maybe he'll change his mind."

"If he does, I'll have you to thank," she says and nestles into my shoulder. "I really was worried for a bit, but don't tell anyone, okay?"

We finish lunch as we usually do: her filling me in on the gossip. Cassius isn't happy on maintenance and the crew doesn't like him either. Feather is still bossy. When I ask about Addy, she says, "She's been zippered up lately. Won't tell me anything about what's going on in her mind. I think she has a thing for you, so it's probably best you two are kept apart. She has to sort out her lot with Cassius."

The truth is, I've thought less about Addy because I haven't had the time. The past two weeks have gone like this: I'm in the shop at eight, and Garrett joins me at ten, after trading. Around two, we cut out and he takes me to different places on the property. The first time we fly-fished I almost lost my balance in the excitement of catching a trout. (Garrett helped me get the hook out so I could release it.) Another time, he set up targets in a big quarry and let me try the rifle, stood behind me to help steady my aim. I kept the stock wedged tight in my shoulder, nervous about the kick. Garrett said the muzzle brake on the end of the rifle would help lessen the blow and it did, but I was a wreck right up until I pulled the trigger. Turns out, I'm not a bad shot. But I couldn't kill anything to save my life. Except for spiders.

Yesterday, we hit golf balls with rusted irons into a ravine. Garrett moves with the easy grace of an athlete in everything he does, and his shots were spot on, even landing balls right beside certain shrubs. My shots sprayed everywhere. I got more and more frustrated while he said nothing. After whiffing on another ball he finally asked if I wanted some pointers, and helped guide me through the motions, directing me to relax and focus. My next shot went way high, and the sound - a perfect thwack – was kind of addictive.

We talk about a lot of things - New York, LA, stuff we've done - and we both like quiet stretches too. Aside from trading and the Sunday meetings, he's spending all his free time with me. I was worried it might make things worse with Rylan but lately, when we play chess after a perfectly civil dinner, she simply takes off. Overall the mood feels okay. Maybe it's good they spend some time apart.

Garrett's been paying me, like he said he would. So far I have two grand. Cedric got a quote for all the repairs, including a new key - $5,100.00 - close to where I thought it would be. In another three weeks I'll have enough cash to leave. I should be thrilled, ecstatic, except last night, when Garrett and I walked back to the guest house, the night was warm, the air sort of sweet, and we were in the middle of laughing about something stupid, and it felt good, *I* felt good, and it was like a knife twisted in my stomach, because I couldn't remember the last time I had felt good. Then it dawned on me that I hadn't thought about fire at all in the past two weeks, not even once, and fire was the only thing that used to make me feel good.

I stopped and Garrett turned around, asked if I was okay, and I said yes, even though I wasn't. I couldn't tell him what I was thinking - that the days were moving too fast. My time here was always going to be finite; what did I expect? But later in bed, my mind raced. I tried to visualize myself in Colombia, back in LA, anywhere but here, and couldn't.

After lunch today, Garrett finally takes me to his favorite spot. It's a cliff far up the property, a fifteen minute drive on the ATV. The hike up is a little sketchy like he said, but my leg is better now and the view is totally worth it. Carved into the cliff is a deep, natural ledge, big enough for four or five people to sit on. Below us, the burnt red ground falls away into an untamed canyon that sprawls into the horizon.

"This is incredible," I say.

"I never knew about this place for the first few months. It took me a while to explore the whole property. Now I come up here to think."

"I get now why you've stayed here so long. It's really cool."

"I'm glad you had the chance to experience it," he says. "At least you'll have the memory of being here."

A wave of unsteadiness hits, the same feeling of vertigo when I saw the photograph of this canyon in the common house.

"You okay?" Garrett asks when I lean back. His arm drops like a guard in front of me. "Don't look down if you feel sick."

"No, I'm good," I lie.

He's dangling his legs over the edge, and once the dizziness ends I let mine drop too, force myself not to look down. My stomach is already in knots. Last night I practiced what I wanted to ask, said it over and over, until the words stopped having meaning.

So, ask.

"I was thinking, if you, uh, needed my help, I could, you know, work more. Stay longer."

Instead of the reaction I was hoping for he looks over, confused. "What about Colombia?"

"It's still there. I can go whenever."

"I thought you missed the ocean."

"I do. I mean, I did."

His eyes flick back to the canyon. "You don't miss other things?"

"Like what?"

"Friends."

"I never had a lot of friends."

"Girlfriends?"

"I only had one. Sort of."

"Sort of?"

Heat flushes on my cheeks and I'm glad he's not looking over. "I'm not very good with girls."

After a beat he asks, "Did you love her?"

"I liked her."

"And she knew?"

"About what?" I ask, my hands clutching the ledge so tight, fine particles crumble and float like mist beneath me.

He gives me a funny look. "The fires."

"Oh. Yeah. Eventually. That's why it didn't work out."

"Do you wish it had?" he asks, staring straight ahead.

A hawk dips and weaves until it coasts on an invisible airstream, its wings twitching side-to-side for balance, before it plunges down into the canyon. It flies away, dinner squirming in its talons.

"No."

Garrett swings his legs back and forth, and in the long silence I can hear my heart beating way too fast.

"What about you?" I finally ask. "Do you ever, uh, miss things?"

"I do."

"Like, stuff in New York?"

He shakes his head and I panic, just a little. Things aren't going as I imagined. "Do you usually come here by yourself?"

"Rylan doesn't do heights."

My eyes clench shut. "Does she like New Mexico?"

His legs stop swinging. My eyes re-open. Our heads move in slow motion to face each other. "Do you?" he asks.

"Yeah," I say, "I do."

After another beat, he says, "You haven't burnt anything since that day in my truck."

"I know."

He leans back and his legs splay out. His knee touches mine. "Maybe this is a good place for you."

"I think so."

He glances over with an inquisitive look. In this light, his blonde hair glows like a halo. A weird lump forms in my throat.

"If you really want to, you can stay," he says.

"You mean it?"

"If that's what you want."

I'm about to burst with relief. Whatever weight was pressing down on me, lifts. He starts to swing his legs again, his knee still on mine.

"What's up with those shoelaces anyway?" I ask.

He sticks his feet up in the air, admiring them. "I got them in New York. What do you think?"

"They're bright."

"You don't like them."

"Maybe if I liked orange."

He chuckles. "It was these or neon green." After a pause, he kicks my foot. "I like them."

I kick his foot back. He kicks mine again and then we're both laughing. He's got a goofy smile on his face and looks content to be on a rock ledge, acting dumb with me. It's one of those moments I never want to end, and when it does, we both look out at the horizon. The sunset is a couple hours away, but the early evening sky already blazes with pink, blue, banana yellow.

"You know the photo you took of this place? The one in the common house?" I ask.

"You remember it."

"There's so much color here and you chose black and white. Why?"

"Good question." He scratches his chin and chuckles at a private thought. "What do you think?" he asks, swiveling towards me. "Should we start a new collection? All color?"

The smallest thrill rockets inside me when he says 'we'. He puts up his hand and I high five it.

"Color's better."

Rylan's not home when we get back. A pot of crusted spaghetti and sauce is cold on the stove. Eating quickly, we take advantage of the remaining sunlight and play chess on the deck until it gets dark. He's almost won his first game when I sniper him out of the blue.

It's our tradition for him to walk me back to the guest house when we're finished and tonight, a hint of smoke lingers in the air. Paper thin leaves of the nearby trees rustle in the breeze.

The new porch swing isn't quite finished, so we rock on the old one, knocking back beers. A shooting star blazes in front of us, the first one he's seen. We watch for another and he's loose and animated, gesturing and smiling. We swap work stories and I tell him about my old boss, Hannah, how during the last performance review, she said I 'excelled' at my job and she expected me to mentor. I told her I was good at my job because I didn't waste time telling other people how to do theirs. When I detail our argument, how she finally stood down (probably to get me out of her office) Garrett laughs so hard that he spits up beer.

"God," he says, wiping his mouth. "Performance reviews. Another reason to be here."

After, there's a lull in the conversation. Stars speckle all around us. On the hill, his house is dark and he seems pre-occupied looking at it. He finishes his beer and stands. "I should let you go," he says. "But I'm glad you're going to stay. It's good to have you here."

I stand too. "I'll work extra hard. Whatever you want."

He stuffs his hands into the pockets of his cargo pants. "That's not what I meant."

A flutter ripples in my stomach. We're so close I can see his t-shirt move up and down with his breathing. He tilts his head, like he's waiting for me to say something.

Say something. Anything.

"I really like it here."

"I like it here too," he says, smiling.

The seconds pile up. His eyes glow as if he's lit from within.

"Goodnight," he says.

"'night."

In the pause that follows, something passes between us. It's there and then it's gone, like him. He disappears into the night without looking back. When the lights come on in his house, its like I'm watching a movie: a world going on right in front of me that I want to be a part of and don't know how. Regret wads in my throat and I can't swallow past it. It's like I'm drowning, fighting for breath.

Inside, it only gets worse. The house is claustrophobic. I pace, sit, try to read, pace again. I think about the cliff. The way he looked at me on the porch. How words I wanted to say dissolved in my mouth. In bed, I toss fitfully, the pressure building. Finally I give up and yank the bedside table drawer so hard it almost comes off its hinges. Cassius' lighter stares back at me. I'm trying hard not to go there, so hard, but it's too late. I reach for it and a dark shimmer spreads over my skin, like I hoped it wouldn't.

"Fuck you," I whisper.

I'm very still, hardly breathing. Everything goes quiet, real quiet. My thumb drifts over the tumbler before I spin it hard. The gas erupts into flame and the desire, the need for consummation swells. My other hand reaches under the covers and it's almost painful, the release not far away. I've been here before, more times than I can count, but it's too intense, nothing I'm used to. My teeth clench and grind. Tears burn in my eyes. The flame cooks the flesh of my thumb but I grip the lighter tight, its existence the only thing that matters right now.

The beams on the ceiling start to crash together. It's like my blood has started to boil, cooking me from the inside out. The pressure finally bursts and when it's over, I'm panting, dizzy, and wait for it.

Nothing.

C'mon.

Nothing.

COME ON.

Where is it?

I fight the panic, what it means. The fact I don't know what it means.

We had a deal. Fire used to manage my ups and downs better than any pill. It satisfied me in ways relationships can't. It made things better, the only thing that could. But tonight there's no reward, no relief.

In the silence, there's nothing.

TWENTY-FIVE

IT'S HOT TODAY, no wind. The shop is sweltering so we ditch it before lunch to swim in the river. The cool water runs slow, and after a second dip, we sit on thin towels drying in the sun.

I was nervous this morning but Garrett came in the way he always does, around 10 am, after trading, with a thermos of coffee the way I like it: black with sugar. I was unfocused and quieter than usual, but he didn't seem to notice.

Now, he's lying beside me in shorts, eyes closed. Glancing at his scar, I try to untangle my thoughts: the sessions, Cassius and the cancer, Garrett's whole experience here. It's a part of him I don't know anything about, and I'm not sure I want to. I force myself to speak.

"Do you think you'll start with the sessions again?"

He squints one eye open. "Eventually. Why?"

"I was thinking I should try one."

"They're serious," he says, blocking the sun with a hand to his forehead.

"I know."

"They're meant for healing."

"I know."

He props himself up on his elbows. "It involves drugs. Psychedelics. We need to be in altered states to channel the energy."

I wrap my arms tight around my knees. "How does it all work?"

"It's an organic process. The main thing is we can't go in unprepared. There can be a lot of fury in the energy. If it doesn't know what to latch onto, it can be dangerous."

His body is tanned and strong. I can't imagine anything being dangerous if he's close by.

"But you can control it, right?"

"Yes and no."

"But mostly yes?"

He sits up now, his eyes careful, searching mine. "It can change things. Permanently."

"Change is good, right?" I say, my laugh weak.

He picks up a stick and starts to dig deep lines in the dirt beside him.

"How long does it last?" I ask.

"It depends," he says, not looking up. "Usually a couple hours but every session is different."

"Will you be scared to try again?"

The stick pounds harder into the ground, his strokes almost violent. "Will you be scared?"

"A little," I admit.

The digging stops and he stares at the hole. Then he chucks the stick and it arcs high before splashing into the river. "Me too."

In the silence after, I busy myself and scavenge rocks into a pile. He watches the pyramid grow.

"We can't tell anyone."

I glance up at him. "I don't want to get you in trouble."

"I won't be in trouble," he says, but it sounds like he's trying to convince himself. "I just don't know how much strength I have right now. This will be a test."

"Will you be okay?"

For a long time he doesn't say anything. Then, "Yes."

"Will I be okay?"

"I'll make sure you're okay."

"Can you stop it once we start?"

"No. Once we're in, we're in. We have to let it run its course."

It sounds...I don't know what it sounds like. I've never done drugs. I've never done anything like this. The whole thought of getting into the kiva makes my skin crawl. All I know is this morning I chucked the lighter in the garbage and never want to touch it again.

I can feel his gaze and turn towards him. "What?"

"Nothing," he says, but he's not quick enough to avert his eyes from where they were.

"You were looking at me."

"You're right beside me."

His stomach is ripped, flat against the band of his shorts. Light hair covers his chest, a thin darker strip under his belly button.

"Now you're looking at me," he says.

I look away. "No I'm not."

He lies back on the towel, eyes closed. I sneak another look. Compare his toes to mine. His are straight and compact, the angle from big to little toe a perfect line. Mine are different shapes. Different lengths. But I like noticing his toes. Seeing little differences between us. The ways we're the same.

"I don't want to light fires again," I tell him. "Ever."

"Okay."

"I've been lighting them for a long time."

He turns to face me. "I know."

His hand reaches over to cross the distance between us. In the sunlight, the scar jags down his arm and glows bright white. With my thumb, I graze the hard tissue near his bicep. The ridge of the scar is thick and smooth. His face is lined with tension, breathing shallow, as my thumb slides down the length of it. In his palm, I lay my hand flat against the angry knot and press down. When our fingers intertwine, the sun is hotter on my skin, the water of the river rushing and loud.

He grips my hand tight and we sit like that for a long time, with nothing but the sweet melody of tree leaves rippling in the breeze.

When the afternoon sun starts to slip in the sky, we do one last swim. I tread water in silence. My head is just above the surface, watching Garrett. He floats on his back, eyes closed, arms and legs spread like a starfish, the water around him tiny diamonds sparkling in the sun.

And this is how I'll always remember him: at peace, both of us at peace, on a hot, sunny afternoon when I finally felt like I belonged in this world.

PART TWO

TWENTY-SIX

IT'S STILL LIGHT, but the first star twinkles in the sky. Loose dirt crunches under my feet. I've been pacing for twenty minutes. I scan the perimeter of the clearing like I'm committing it to memory, as if it's the last time I'll see it.

Garrett's head pops out of the kiva. "You ready?" he asks.

"Sure," I say, the taste in my mouth all stress.

I can still change my mind.

Should I? Can I? What am I doing?

"C'mon," he says.

I rub my hands together and try to settle the nerves. Here we go.

The wood of the ladder is smooth under my hands, and step by step I sink out of light into darkness, from warm to cool. Inside the kiva, the air is heavy and smells old. It's bigger than I imagined. A large SUV would fit in here with room to spare. The wood-lined ceiling clears Garrett's head by five feet.

He brings the ladder inside and closes the latch. The only light now is from several candles on the dirt floor. Beside them are sticks, what look like drums and other things I can't make out. Stripping off his jeans, shorts underneath, Garrett addresses my layers. "You might be too warm. It's better not to be distracted once we start."

I take off my hoodie and tie it around my waist, my fingers thick and slow.

It's three days after our conversation at the river. Last night, and at lunch today, Garrett went over everything again, but being in here is a whole different level. He pulls a small baggie out of his shorts and hands me several shrivelled buds of peyote.

"Are you going to take anything?" I ask.

"I already did," he says, and only now do I notice his pupils: black saucers, thin rings of white popping around them.

The peyote is bitter, so bad I try to swallow it whole and end up choking. Garrett pats me on the back and opens his other hand to reveal a glass vial.

"Wash it down with this," he says.

"What is it?"

"It will help with the transition."

I undo the cap and sniff. It's vaguely floral, sweet. "But what is it?"

"Just drink it," he says, eyes firm. He's not used to being questioned. Not in here.

It goes down easy, taking the peyote taste with it. Heat expands instantly inside me.

"Remember to focus. Anything else will disrupt the energy," he says, taking the vial away. "When it's over I'll let you know."

Focus is the big deal. That's how it works. He relaxes me first, lets the drugs kick in. To help move us to the other levels, he uses sounds and chants. Then it's all about me. Once I'm focused he calls up the spirits. That's where it gets interesting. According to Garrett, he can't tell anyone what to expect. It's the personal part of the journey. This is where I'm a little worried.

Two nights ago, after chess, we talked about what I wanted to heal. I got flustered and he gently prodded, "It's your stepfather, right?"

"Yeah."

"Ok," he said, his eyes watchful when I didn't elaborate. "You need to think about what started it, a specific incident. You don't need to tell me now. Once we're there, think of the images, the sounds, the smells. That's how it will manifest. From there, I can find it and shape it, start to change it."

"Is it going to be scary?" I asked.

"Maybe a little."

"But you'll be there the whole time, right?"

"Of course."

He gave me a cigarette with the filter ripped off. The tobacco was my offering and I needed to bury it and send a message to the spirits so they would help. I've done so, but feel a little weird about it. What I asked for isn't exactly what I told Garrett.

Now, he helps me sit down on one of the cushions scattered on the floor. Crouched beside me, he presses a book of matches into my palm, and wraps my fingers around them. "Put them in your pocket."

It takes me forever to even find my pocket. Whatever I just drank has blitzed through me. Even seated I still wobble. Saliva starts to build in my mouth. Garrett draws patterns in the dirt with a stick and talks quietly to himself. Then I can hear drum beats. They get louder, a symphony moving towards a crescendo and I'm carried with it, up, no resistance, warm, everything's warm.

"You ready?" he asks.

He drifts out of focus. The walls of the kiva have started to throb. My body feels good. Relaxed. What was I so worried about?

"Let 'er rip."

"Remember," he says, "don't fight it. Close your eyes."

I do.

I will wish I never had.

I'm floating. My eyelids are too heavy to open and patterns pulse and swirl behind them. I'm supposed to focus but a hundred different thoughts stream through me, each one an entire universe of colors and sounds. At one point I 'm laughing and can't stop. I call out to Garrett, but he doesn't respond. The only evidence of him is the slight shifting of air around me. The drums.

I'm aware of every bone and muscle, how they're connected. I've never felt looser or freer or more relaxed. I could get used to this, I'm thinking, when the temperature drops so viciously, all my muscles seize up at once. A dull hum, low and savage, fills the air.

I've heard it before. Once.

My eyes snap open. A lone candle flickers in the corner.

"Garrett?"

I look around, then down at my crossed legs, confused.

How did they get crossed?

I try to move them and can't.

How do I uncross them?

In the now arctic cold I shiver, no longer relaxed. Above me, the latch is still closed. The ladder is where it was, against the wall. Why is it so cold?

"Garrett," I call out, louder.

But he's gone. The kiva is empty.

It's your mind playing tricks, I tell myself. Just get up, walk around, find Garrett. I yank on my legs, try to pry them apart, but they're glued together. Frustrated, I yank harder, lose my balance and tip over, face plastered on the cold earth. "Shit."

The hum gets louder and it's like a magnet is sucking me against the dirt. The candle in the corner goes out with a gust of wind. Then the voices start: tortured, awful screams, the sounds of death. The wind whirls, tornado-like, whipping my hair, dirt everywhere. The noise is deafening. Curled up like a fetus, heart rate in stroke territory, I clasp my hands over my ears.

"Garrett!"

Where the hell is he? He never told me about this part.

The screams abruptly stop and there's a second, maybe two, of silence before the pressure plunges and my stomach rises and falls like I'm on a roller coaster.

Behind me, the air shifts.

A dank, rotten smell, worse than any dumpster, slithers into my nose.

Then something moves. Something big.

Whatever it is paces back and forth, the floor shuddering with its weight.

It's beside me. Oh god, it's beside me.

I squeeze one eye open. Somehow, even without light, I can see muscles pulsing under thick fur.

Bile lurches in my throat.

This can't be real. This can't be real. This can't be real.

It edges closer. I can smell its reeking breath.

Warm piss shoots down my leg.

"I'm done Garrett," I shout. "Please. Make it stop."

A prehistoric sound slices through the darkness, like a demonic call to arms. The floor starts to vibrate. I scuttle backwards, hands damp from crawling through my own piss. My bowels loosen and I tense up. No way I'm crapping myself on top of it all.

"Garrett!"

The earth splinters open with a horrendous crack. My fingers claw into the disappearing dirt but I slide lower and lower. Beneath me, my legs bicycle uselessly in ice cold empty space.

Snow starts to fall, sticky flakes landing on my eyelashes. My entire upper body is clamped in the last of the dirt. There's another rumble and I sink lower, into that abyss. My fingers cramp as I hold on for dear life.

Don't let me fall in there. Please.

I blink up to see the mouth of the thing open. Sharp teeth glisten. It looms closer and closer, its mouth stretched wide, a pink slimy wormhole of a throat pulsing.

Dear God. No. NO.

It swallows me alive as the ground, the kiva and what's left of my mind, collapses.

The air is cool, very still.

Instinctively, I know the space around me is endless.

I'm alone, although every bone in my body tells me I'm not really alone.

In the soft dirt, I wiggle my arms and legs, amazed to be uninjured. I'm certain I fell a great distance, yet not certain of anything. Far above me, dots shimmer like pixels on a screen. It takes a minute before I realize they're stars...in the sky.

I'm at the bottom of a pit.

The pit.

Jesus. This is real. This is happening.

Move, I tell myself. Just move. Find a way out.

On my hands and knees, I force myself to crawl. It might be forward or backward, the right or the wrong way, I can't tell. This is the most fucked up shit I've ever experienced. And where the hell is Garrett?

"Garrett?" I try again.

I'm not sure why I bother, only that hearing something is better than hearing nothing. Shoulders tense, I keep crawling, half expecting some other creepy thing to materialize. Every time my right leg moves forward something nudges against my hip. I sit up and feel around in my pocket. The matches. They were generic, from a gas station or diner, a pink *Thank you!* on the top flap.

A shiver runs up my spine.

Or was it blue?

In the cold silence I can hear his voice clear as day: Remember to focus, he said. Manifest it. I'll shape it. Change it.

Except Garrett's gone AWOL. How is he going to change anything?

Fingering the matchbook, everything starts to unhinge. My mind spins backwards, falling into a place I've tried to forget.

A wall of flames rushes out of the ground in front of me, a heavy *whoosh,* like a gas grill being lit. In seconds, the blaze circles me and I'm in the middle of a ring of fire. I'm not scared of fire, not after all these years, but this is different, familiar in a way I don't like. The flames whip and spin, create a tall matchstick raging in the dark. A heavy scent of smoke, the smell of burning cypress, spikes the air.

"No," I whisper. "Not that."

But sometimes the world is that cruel.

Images are rushing past my eyes: a pool, a shed, a sloped roofline with windows.

It's hot. So hot.

In my mouth, the bitter taste of gin.

From the giant flame, a phantom figure takes form, like a soul leaving a body. Once free, it hovers and spins like a funnel cloud. Thin wisps of smoke ravel around it like strands of DNA. The darkened circle near the top of it cracks open. Gleaming daggers spill out like a scroll, a deadly silvery smile. It's unnatural voice hisses,

"How am I going to explain a goddamned burnt tree?"

Focus on something else.

But it's too late. Even before I pull the matches from my pocket and they tumble into the dirt, I know. The *Thank you!* is gone. Blue letters twinkle in the light of the fire. *La Nazione.*

It's like a knife going deep and twisting.

Andrew.

The creature darts forward. "What happens to little bastards?"

Run. Run!

But I can't run. I can't even move. The dirt has become tacky, like quicksand.

"Get away from me," I yell.

Weird insect arms pop out from the phantom at ninety-degree angles, the bottom parts flapping, like broken chicken wings. Its long nails are shiny. Manicured nails. "What happens to little bastards?" it screams.

Smoke starts to billow, so thick I can hardly see. The creature disappears behind it. I can't tell where it is. Then a bright, hot pain rips through me and the back of my calf splits open like an exploding hot dog.

"Fuck you," I cry and reach for the wound, hot blood spurting through my fingers.

The creature's head bobs inches away, daggered teeth dripping red. It lunges again, one of its daggers slicing down the front of my right thigh. With cryptic awe, the pain still a second away, I can see tendons, warm muscles pulsing.

This is the first time I think about dying.

"Garrett!" I scream. "Help me. Please."

The creature's skeleton fingers clamp onto the back of my skull and push me head first into the dirt. It lashes my back over, over, wet strips of skin flapping, the pain excruciating until shock takes over and starts to dull it.

This is it, I think. This is how it ends. Fucking face down in the dirt.

The ground starts to rumble again and a cannonball sound explodes. My eardrums pop. A flash follows, so bright, even the dense soil beneath my face fills with light. The creature's hand lifts off the back of the head. I can hear it dart away. Using the last ounce of my energy, I roll onto my side.

In the brilliant light, the creature hangs a few yards away. It makes shrill, nervous sounds, its focus beyond me. Blood mixed with dirt oozes on my split thigh like subterranean ketchup and I'm paralyzed, mesmerized by the horror of it. If there was a moment where I could believe this was all still a dream, or maybe just the drugs, it's come and gone.

But the real horror is yet to come. I can smell it before I see it: a heavy, rotting scent.

If I live to be a hundred I'll never forget that smell.

Each lumbering step it takes vibrates my teeth. It's behind me and then walks right over top of me, damp hair from its swaying belly grazing my skin. With a deep-throated snarl, it circles the creature, once, twice, three times, slow and methodical. It reminds me of Roman times, in the coliseum, what the tight anticipation of the crowd must have been like just before the tigers were released on helpless humans. The creature must sense it, too. It hisses and lashes out with its arms.

"Kill it," I mumble. "Just kill him."

The jaguar pounces.

It traps the creature in its jaw and starts to whip it back and forth. A strange sound like radio fuzz pours out of its mangled body. Wind and snow start to blast again in thick gusts. My eyelids sag as I drift in and out of consciousness.

With a final, vicious snap of its head, the jaguar swallows the creature alive. Just before I pass out, it stares right at me, right through me, with its blue and green eyes.

TWENTY-SEVEN

AM I DEAD?

My eyes flutter open. In the muddy light I can just make out the wooden ceiling, the kiva. A small, relieved sound sputters out of my mouth. I'm alive. I'm back. It's over. Or did it even happen? *What* happened? I struggle to remember...anything.

Rolling onto my side, my arms and legs are heavy, like I weigh twice as much as before. After a quick inventory of my limbs, I'm shocked. Everything is in one piece. There are no wounds, no blood. Was it all a dream?

A candle flickers on the far side of the kiva. In the shadows, he's hunched against the wall, head hung.

"Garrett?" I whisper.

He doesn't move.

"Garrett."

He lifts his head and my heart skips a beat. His eyes are dull, face slack. A small triangle of tongue hangs out of his mouth.

I push myself up to seated. "Are you okay?"

"No," he says, his voice deep, two octaves lower.

I crawl over but the closer I get, my skin starts to crackle from heat. He's a million degrees. Trembling. "Can you get up?"

He shakes his head. "I need to rest."

"C'mon," I say encouragingly, though mostly for me. If I stay another minute in here I'm going to go insane. "You're boiling hot. Let's get outside."

A wave of nausea rips through me as I stand, forcing me to hunch over, hands on my knees, waiting for the sickness to pass. With the tiniest movement of my head, trailers stream off my peripheral vision like cobwebs. The ladder still leans against the wall and I stagger towards it, my legs unsteady.

"Don't," he warns.

"I need to get out of here Garrett. Seriously." Except my muscles refuse to cooperate. I struggle with the weight of the ladder and weave around with it like a drunk. "Can you help me?" I ask, frustrated. "Grab one end?"

He pushes up, grabs the ladder out of my hands like it's a piece of Lego and chucks it back onto the floor. "I said don't."

There's nothing but black where his eyes should be, the shadows making his cheekbones sharper. A weird fairy glow surrounds him.

"You can't order me around. Not after that."

He moves closer, his steps slow and purposeful. "I can do whatever I want in here."

"Really? Is that how it goes down? You just do whatever you want?"

"I just saved your life," he says, a dangerous edge in his voice. "A thank you would be in order."

Is he joking?

My insides boil with indignation. "Fuck you."

Out of the dim, two fists grab my shirt and lift me off the ground. "What did you say?"

My toes are pointed, spinning like a ballerina on the dirt. I claw uselessly at his hands. "Stop it. You're hurting me."

"Who's Andrew?" he demands.

"What?"

How does he know about Andrew?

His fists clench tighter, the shirt cutting into my neck. "Who's Andrew?" Our faces are inches apart

"Someone...I used to know."

"Did you think this was all a joke?" he yells right into my face. His breath is toxic, ammonia-like. "We barely made it out of there because of you. You were supposed to tell me the truth."

Truth? I don't even know what's real or not right now. All I know is whatever happened in that buried world was bad, for both of us.

"You were supposed to help me. You call *that* help?"

A faint vibration rumbles in the air between us. His eyes are glossy, back from the dead, and there's something about those green and blue lanterns that spark my crippled memory. "Jesus..." I whisper. "Addy was right. It is you."

His roar becomes its own thing – a sound so encompassing, I don't know how we fit in the small space with it – and he flings me to the ground. Sprawled in the dirt, he hulks over me, sweaty and crazed, a demented action figure come to life.

The thought is far away, but close enough to be real: he could kill me right now. That, combined with the horror of the fire creature, the need to get out of here, mobilizes me. I'm on feet swinging before I even know what I'm doing. Then my hand is limp at my side, knuckles ringing from the contact. He touches his jaw with disbelief.

After that, everything speeds up.

He tackles me and we land hard, my shoulder crunching under his weight. It's a mess of arms and legs, both of us rolling in the dirt. My punches do nothing to stop him. His arms wrap around me like an anaconda and with a final surge, he flattens on top of me.

"Get off me," I yell, jackknifing my leg up. He pushes against me, harder, and my ribcage flexes to the breaking point. "You're crazy, you know? This whole place is fucking crazy."

We're both out of breath, lungs heaving. "Don't fight me, Damien," he says. "You'll never win."

His face is pressed against mine, left cheek on my right. The heat of his body is like a sauna. Suddenly it's too much effort to try, to fight; just *lying* here is exhausting. "It's all about winning for you, isn't it?" I say. "You don't care about anyone but yourself." My body slackens with defeat. "You don't care about me. You never did."

His heart pounds faster, right on top of mine. Then he slowly pushes up, hands on either side of my shoulders. Strands of his hair drift onto my cheek. "That's not true," he whispers.

When I remember this moment later, it will be murky, but right now, I'm hyper focused like I'm carrying a tray of full champagne glasses through a crowd.

"Yeah? Then prove it."

Our lower bodies are still fused and I shift my hips, the dirt gritty underneath me. He slips into the space I've created. The cords on his neck tighten. I know he can feel me. His mouth twitches like he's trying to form words. Then I'm pulling him towards me, plastering our mouths together. His lips part against mine, shocked breath warm in my mouth. The very thought of being this close to him, maybe closer, pushes me someplace I've never been. It's like skimming the edge of a black hole, waiting, wanting to be sucked in deeper.

I wait for it, but it never comes.

His hand pushes violently against my chest. For a horrible second, his panicked eyes lock with mine. He scrambles to his feet. I can hear him pant; hear him move further away. Dread balloons in my stomach.

No. Its not supposed to be like this.

I want the earth to open up again and swallow me, never bring me back. The entire pathetic scene only gets worse as tears burn a trail down the side of my face.

"I'm sorry," I whisper.

An eternity seems to pass before he says, "Let's go."

It's dusk when we climb outside. A three quarter moon hangs in the sky. We barely say anything to each other. Garrett loads up the ATV and I silently will him to move quicker. All I want is to get back, have a shower and sleep. Something fundamental has shifted and trying to organize my thoughts now is hopeless. They tumble around like socks in a dryer. All I know is nothing's changed, but everything's changed. Permanently, like he said.

A breeze slips in with the impending night and I jam my hands deep into my jeans. In the ring of trees just past the clearing, there's a slip of shadow in the falling light. It slowly makes its way towards us, lean and black. Sensing my gaze, it stops, sniffs the air. The hair on the back of my neck bristles to attention.

"Garrett," I whisper.

He follows my line of sight and stills.

"Garrett," I say, louder.

"I see it," he hisses back.

I've never been this close to a wild animal. I can hear the jaguar's deep, rumbly breathing. It flicks its tail, watching, waiting. I glance over at the ATV, at the rifle leaning against it.

"Are you going to shoot it? It's the one, right?"

"Shhh," he says, putting up his hand. His eyes are locked on the cat. It starts to pad closer.

"Garrett," I say, inching backwards. "Shoot it."

"No," he whispers. "It's them."

At the edges of the clearing, trees start to rustle. Like inkblots, animals start to take shape: wolves, deer, bears. In the waning light I blink, certain my eyes are playing tricks, the drugs still messing with me. But they're real. Eyes glassy and black.

Tight knots of unease pulse in my temples. "Give me the gun Garrett."

The air starts to hum in a way that isn't natural. Garrett steps forward to face the jaguar, the circle of animals. Their silent faces bob like ghosts. The jaguar snarls at him.

It's a test.

I don't want to stick around to see who wins.

I lunge for the gun.

Garrett whips around and yells, "No!"

He rips the gun out of my hand and I storm towards the jaguar, shouting, waving my arms. It backs up, teeth bared, eyes flashing red. The other animals scatter, disappearing into the dark hills.

"Get away from it," Garrett shouts.

Metal on metal cracks.

The air splinters like an atomic bomb has gone off.

TWENTY-EIGHT

"WHO'S THERE?"

Surrounded by black, my heart thuds out of control.

"Hey," Garrett whispers. "Sorry. It's just me. I dropped the clock."

I shimmy up against the headboard, struggling to get my bearings in the dark. The crash of the clock ripped me out of a catatonic state. On the night stand, the digital numbers now glow red and steady: 8:02.

"I just changed it," he says, sounding oddly apologetic. "It was stuck on twelve."

"Is it still today?" I ask, confused. I don't remember coming back here. I'm dimly aware of being moved, the moon bright, Garrett crouched beside me. The blast of the rifle still rings in my ears. He didn't shoot the jaguar. I saw it run away. I think.

"No," he says. "You slept a whole day. How are you feeling?"

It's strange. My memory is jumbled yet my head feels clear and light like it's been scrubbed with bleach.

"I don't know," I finally answer.

"I brought you some dinner. Even if you're not hungry, you should try and eat something. I'll wait in the kitchen."

After he leaves, little snippets from the kiva drift back. Things I don't understand. Things I don't want to understand. Trepidation swamps me. He's the last person I want to see right now. I force myself out of bed and in the bathroom mirror, I look gaunt despite my tan. Two days ago I stood in front of the same mirror with a whole different set of expectations, all of them vaporized. Nothing he can say will change what's happened but he owes me an explanation. Big time.

Garrett is filling up a glass of water when I come into the kitchen. I hunker into a chair closest to the wall. A plate covered in tinfoil sits on the table.

"No alcohol tonight or tomorrow," he says, putting the water in front of me. "Your system needs to flush out."

"I know. You told me before."

He pulls a chair out, spins it around and straddles it. His hair is combed, pulled into a ponytail. The only thing about him that isn't disheveled. His stillness makes me want to scream. Finally,

"That wasn't what I was expecting."

"Is that supposed to make me feel better?" I ask.

"It was intense for me, too."

Twisting further to face the wall, I grumble, "Then you shouldn't have done it. You should've said no."

"I knew what I was getting into."

"I don't think you did."

"I knew it was a risk," he corrects. "I told you that. But I was willing to take it for you."

"Yeah, well, so much for that working out."

He shifts in the chair and clears his throat. "Listen..."

"I don't want to talk about it, okay?" I say, swivelling to face him. "We survived, right? Hallelujah."

"Survival wasn't the goal."

"Goal?" I snort. "Yes, let's talk about goals. How about *not* dying? Not being eaten alive by some...whatever that thing was."

"I told you..."

"You've done these a hundred times and nothing like this has ever happened?" I interrupt. "You must have known."

"Every session is different."

I roll my eyes. "Another Garrett non-answer."

"Don't pretend you had nothing to do with this."

Unbelievable, I think. He's actually pushing back.

"That jaguar, in there, was you, right?"

He leans back, hesitates. "Yes."

"Is that why you stopped the sessions?"

"Partly."

"Did you kill those people?" I ask, and glare at him. "Don't fucking lie to me."

"No. You saw the jaguar after, outside. The real one."

"Why didn't you kill it then?"

"I couldn't," he says. Then, quieter, "It was *them*."

"The spirits?"

"I'm not supposed to hurt them. But they're not supposed to stay in the physical world after."

"So why did they?"

"Something happened." He pauses. "After Cassius."

"The cancer?"

"It was so far along. It took so much energy getting it out of him." A look of uncertainty flashes on his face. "Then it got trapped before I was done and...I couldn't get rid of it."

"And it transferred to you?"

"Not directly, not the disease. But something was corrupted in the process."

"I don't get it. These, them, the spirits, whatever you want to call them, they're pissed?" This entire conversation is ridiculous. I can't even believe I'm having it.

"I made a mistake," he repeats, and a slow realization sinks into me.

"Did you do this to try and get rid of that, instead of helping me?"

"No," he insists. "I wanted to help you. There was just too much confusion. With you, with me."

Sick to my stomach, I can barely ask, "I could have died, right?"

"I would never have let that happen," he says, reaching for my arm.

I pull away disgusted, revolted. "Jesus Christ."

"Please. You don't understand."

"No. I DO understand. That's the problem. This is all about you. You didn't kill that thing because you didn't want to. You kill it, you lose your powers."

"No, that's not..."

"Yes, it is," I say and slam my fist on the table. "You told me that day at the kiva how great it was to be able to have something no one else has. You wanted to get rid of whatever got stuck and go back to how it was before."

"Damien, I'm sorry."

"No. No. It's too late for sorry."

"We can try again," he pleads and I look at him like he's insane.

"No. It's time for me to leave."

His hands turn white as they grip the spindles of the chair back. "You mean that?"

"Yes, I mean it."

"When?"

"Tomorrow."

"What about your car?"

"Keep it."

"Then how?"

"Dump me at the bus station like you promised. I'll figure it out from there. On my own."

His eyes, wild and confused, bounce from me to the floor to the ceiling and back to me. "How do we fix this?"

"We don't."

"But we..."

"Shut up! Shut up, okay?" I shout, drained, exhausted, wanting this conversation over. "There is no *we*. I don't need your fucking help. I. Don't. Belong. Here."

"I think...I think we both just need some time to recuperate," he says, his voice wavering.

I can see him on top of me, pushing against my chest, getting away; the humility of it. "No. I'm leaving tomorrow. End of story."

"You don't have to go. Please."

"Sure," I say, laughing at his desperate tone. "It's just me, you and your girlfriend, right? One big happy family." I point at the kitchen entrance. "Get out. Leave me alone."

His lips mash together and the Garrett I thought I knew – strong, invincible – is a little boy, broken, eyes glittering. He stands and rests his hands on top of the chair, head lowered. He's only inches away, although the space between us feels vast. We don't look at each other; we don't dare. Then his footsteps move out of the kitchen, down the hall and the sounds of him pulling on his shoes, the door closing behind him are layers peeling off, my world shrinking, collapsing.

When he's gone, the realization of what's happened hits me. The decision I just made. My eyes dart around the kitchen, as if it holds some sort of solution. The worst kind of unanswerable panic crawls on my skin. I never noticed it before, but he changed the clock on the stove too. It's 8:27.

The stench of warm, cooked meat fills my nostrils, makes me ill. He brought me dinner she cooked and now he's back up there, with her, when he should be here with me, and they'll sleep in separate rooms and live separate lives and it hurts so bad because wasn't it always going to end this way and I was just too stupid to see it?

I stand abruptly, the chair clattering to the floor. It's like I'm being filled with air and I want to be the Incredible Hulk and explode, shred everything, and my scream sounds like I've been murdered, because that's what it feels like inside, and the plate obliterates against the wall, ceramic shards, mashed potatoes and beef flying, peas scattering across the tiles like green marbles.

Then I'm outside, and the ground is white and clear from the moon. I run and don't stop, until lights pop in the distance. Taking the common house stairs two at a time, I slip and stumble on the tiles inside, skidding left down the hall. Light peeks out from under the doors and I crash into the room. She's inside, waiting, and maybe I always knew she would be.

She looks up from her book with that mysterious smile.

"Well," Addy says. "Look what the cat dragged in."

TWENTY-NINE

"SWEET LORD, WHAT HAPPENED TO YOU?" Addy asks, her hand on my forehead. "You're burning up something fierce. What's going on?"

What's going on in *here*? It's like the movie set of an Old West saloon. Curve-backed couches; uneven wooden planks on the floor. A bar running against the far wall has western saddles for seats.

"Not my style either," Addy says, watching me scan the room. "I guess it's what millionaires expect at a ranch. Here, c'mon." She puts her arm around me and guides me onto the couch. "You look like you've seen a ghost." From a leather bag beside her, she digs out a water bottle filled with purple liquid. "This'll help you settle down," she says, unscrewing the cap.

I sniff it, the burn of alcohol like wasabi in my nose. "Vodka?"

"And grape juice."

I take a swig and cough.

"But mostly vodka," she says, laughing. "You can finish it."

Blood still rushes through me from my run and I'm parched. Without thinking, I drain the bottle and the booze hits the back of my brain like a semi.

She curls her legs up underneath her and watches me shudder in calculated silence. Finally, "I've missed you. I waited every night for you to come here."

"I couldn't," I say. "You know that."

"You could've," she says with a hurt tone. "It's been two weeks. I was getting worried. I came looking for you last night. Where were you?"

"At Garrett's."

Twirling hair around her finger, she says, "Hmmm....that's odd. Rylan came here looking for him, and she didn't seem happy. What time did you get home?"

"I don't remember."

Which is the truth.

"You two *have* been spending a lot of time together."

I pick at the label of the water bottle. "So?"

"Come on, Damien," she says. "This isn't LA where you can hide. You don't think I've heard. JD downloads everyone's business. All your...activities."

"So we do stuff, big deal. It's nothing like that," I add.

"Like what?"

"Like what you're saying."

"What am I saying?"

"You know what you're saying."

"You mean that no one ever spends that much time with him?" Her grin is cocky and annoying. "Alone?"

My face reddens and not just from her accusation. I'm burning up inside. The coffee table starts to weave in and out of focus.

"We did a session," I blurt out. "*That's* where we were."

Her mouth freezes in a shocked 'o' of surprise. "Really?"

"Yes, so stop saying what you're saying because you're wrong."

Face scrunched, eyes fixated on mine, she says, "None of us have done a session in weeks. Why did he do one for you?"

"I asked."

"What was the reason?"

"Nothing."

"There's always a reason."

It's getting harder to keep myself upright. There's a swell in my head like a tumor gone rogue.

"Damien."

"What?"

"Did you see Garrett turn?"

"No," I say, agitated.

She stares at me for an uncomfortably long time. "You've just come in here all out of sorts and now you tell me you just did a session and nothing happened? Bullshit," she says, her voice hard. "What did you see?"

"I don't know what you're talking about."

"You know damn well what I'm talking about. I can see it in your face."

"Whatever," I say, and try to stand up, operative word being *try*. It's like my bones are dissolving.

"You're a fool on top of it all," she laughs, watching me flop back onto the couch. "You're not supposed to drink after. It's all those drugs he gives you." She moves closer, too close. "Now tell me. He became the jaguar, right?"

"No," I say. "No. But we saw the real one."

Her eyes sharpen. "What real one?"

"The jaguar. The black one. It was outside the kiva."

"Are you shitting me?"

"I told Garrett to shoot it but he wouldn't."

"Are you sure?" she asks, looking utterly confused.

"A hunnred percent," I say, my tongue thick. "But it doesn't matter. I'm done. I'm leaving tomorrow."

"What? Wait," she says, grabbing my arm. "You're *leaving* leaving tomorrow?"

"What elsh does leaving mean?"

"But you said you'd take me with you."

"I cannn't. I'm sorry," I say, and pull out of her grip. It was a mistake to come here, I realize. I stagger to my feet, only to crash spectacularly into the coffee table. "Owww. Shhhit."

"No, no, no, no, no," she says, pulling me back onto the couch. "You're never going to make it on your own. I can help you. I've got connections, outside."

"I donna need any help."

"Yes you do. You need a plan."

Her face has turned into two shiny plates. I blink and it's the still same. "Why shuddda I trust you?"

"You've been trusting the wrong person so far."

"What about Ca, Cashsius?"

She gives me a hostile stare. "What about him?"

"I donnna know…I jussst…" my voice trails off.

"Now listen real good, okay?" she says, her voice laced with anger. "You know what he does to me. You know it's not right, and you, what's more, know how to treat a lady. Men who know how to treat a lady should be rewarded. Why don't you let me reward you?" Her hand slips between my legs. "I told you, you needed to relax. You're not thinking straight. I can see."

Her lips touch mine and my head starts to pulse. "No…" I say, pushing her away. "We canna do that."

"Damien," she presses. "I can help."

The room blurs as I stand up. My legs are Jell-o and panic sets in. I rush towards the door, dimly aware of Addy calling to me, asking if I'm all right. In the hallway, I collapse against the wall, everything spinning.

"Slow down," she says, coming up behind me. "There's no way you're making it back in this state."

Just get outside. Fresh air. Just…

I inch down the wall. My hands are slick with sweat. It's slow going yet somehow I make it halfway down the hall when the wall, the door to the men's room actually, gives way. In slow motion, I tumble backwards onto my ass and the door swings shut behind me. It pushes open seconds later.

"Why are you being so stubborn?" Addy asks. "You're a mess."

Spittle bubbles at the side of my mouth. I start to spasm on the floor.

"Oh my. It's his plants. I warned you. If you're going to be sick let's get you to the toilet." She wraps her arms under my armpits and starts to pull. "Can you push? It's not far."

Despite my legs tingling like they've fallen asleep, I manage to kick and push. Together we make it into the closest stall. I drape around the toilet, the cool porcelain a relief against my burning face. After a minute, the nausea settles and she helps me onto the toilet seat.

"Better?" she asks, brushing hair off my forehead.

"For now."

"I know you've been fighting it, fighting us," she says quietly. "We both know fighting's no good."

"Yes. No. No good," I mumble.

"Its time we help each other right?"

"Yeah. Uh, huh." Drowsiness takes over and my heads bobs and weaves. She sits down on my lap, straddling me. "Wha...hey..."

"Shhh," she says, wrapping her arms tight around me. "Relax." Her head burrows into my neck. Soft lips move along my skin, munching like a caterpillar.

"No. Ishh....is not a good idea."

"I think it's a great idea," she mumbles, her lips moving from my neck onto my cheek. Her hand finds mine, and she slips it under her shirt, onto her bra.

"We shouldna," I say, but sag into her warmth anyway, no fight left.

"That's right," she laughs, as my fingers explore her soft flesh. "I knew you'd find something you liked."

She starts to undo the button on my jeans and yanks on the zipper with frustration. "C'mon. You have to help. On the count of three. Up." On three, I rise, barely, but it's enough for her to jerk my jeans and underwear to my knees. When I sit back down, the toilet seat is a cold dose a reality.

"Wait. Way...Way."

"Oh it's too late to back out now Cutie Pie," she says, and I want to ask *who's Cutie Pie?* but only a moan garbles out as her fingers wrap around me. Her breath catches. "Fuck me you're packing heat. Goddamn."

It's like I'm in a cocoon: warm but trapped. Her hand starts to slide up and down and the surge inside me is almost violent. "Jesus," I gasp, my hands gripping into her.

"Don't you take his name in vain, even when I'm pleasuring you," she whispers. "That's the only rule." She rocks back and forth, grinding on top of me. "I've been waiting for this. Too long. And so have you. This is why we'll make a good team." Her hand is flying. It's sweet torture. "Every night it'll be like this. Just imagine that."

I wish she would stop talking. I'm thinking of a hundred bad thoughts just to make it last. Her breath - short, hard bursts - are warm and moist through my t-shirt. "That's why we leave together, right?"

"No, I cannnnt..."

Her hand and its warmth disappears. It's like I've been flung into a cold shower. "No," I say and grab feebly for her hand. "Donna stop."

"You can't have it both ways," she grits out, in between pants. "If you want me to finish you off real nice, you've got to take me with you."

"Ok. Ok. I will. I will."

"Promise?"

Her fingers run up and down me, teasing. The whole moment tilts. I don't know how I got here or what's happening, there's only burning inside. "I promish. I promish. I promish. Please." She slides off my lap and my voice becomes frenzied, not even part of me. "What? Whereare...?"

"Shhh," she says, swatting my hands away. "No grabbing." She pushes my legs wide and sinks between them. "Be a good boy now. I've got to focus."

My head collapses backwards, arms falling limp. I'm free falling, aware of nothing and everything, as every circuit in me overloads and the bathroom stall shatters into a million pieces of agonizing bliss.

"You okay?" she asks from behind the wall.

My head is buried in my hands, elbows on bare thighs. "Juss gimme me some space."

Water starts to run and a paper towel dispenser cranks. She hands me a wad of wet paper towel and closes the door. I wipe, toss the mess into the toilet. With clumsy fingers, I pull on my underwear and pants. On the count of three, I try to stand, turning around just in time as my stomach empties. I'm still on the floor when the stall door opens and she's there with more paper towel.

"That's not the reaction I'm used to," she says, laughing as she pats me on the head. "Poor baby."

The intensity of what happened has faded, and all I do is feel sicker. I just want her to leave but she crouches down, her blue eyes hard when they find mine.

"I have to go now but it was a pleasure doing business with you. You've got a beautiful mouth and I loved kissing it, but you'll forgive me if I don't give you a good night kiss, right?" She stands back up and surveys me with arms crossed. "Men. So predictable. You never listen. I warned you about the sessions. Hopefully you realize I'm on your side now. That I'm the *only* side." She nudges me with the toe of her sneaker. "It's time for you to get to bed, sunshine. Rest up. Our big day is around the corner. And not to worry..." she grins, "we'll have plenty of opportunities to fix your quick draw issues. Ta, ta."

It's only after she's gone, and it's just me on the toilet, button on my jeans undone, the tang of puke in the air, that the funk comes back. It doesn't just trickle in either; it lands with a crushing thud.

And tomorrow...tomorrow she thinks we're going to be together, like she wants, and we'll drive back to LA and it will be movies and glamour and she'll forget this place because she doesn't want to remember, only I can't forget, and she has no idea in those spiraling seconds, when she believed it all had to do with her, every image in my mind was of Garrett.

THIRTY

ADDY

I NEVER WANTED to be a killer. I certainly don't condone it. The Good Lord may forgive my transgressions, but I'll never forgive myself. Not a day goes by when I don't think of that motel manager lying on the floor, his faded Levi's stained from soiling himself, a little brown hand in a claw, reaching for me as he died. It was horrible, all that blood.

Life is meant to be sacred and I'm tired of all the killing. Tired of all the evil Garrett's spreading. Never mind that he tried to keep Cutie Pie and me apart, tried to control the situation like he always does. Doing a session with that little lamb is darn right cruel. Cutie Pie's got more issues than a bird's got feathers, but still...he's *weak*. He's not session material. Sessions are your worst nightmares come to life. No wonder he was so out of sorts tonight.

Well, not *so* out of it I couldn't seal the deal.

I'm still a little hot from our encounter, and what's going on with me and that boy anyway? He's not even my type. A woman's gotta leave them wanting more so why am I suffering? There's just a sweetness to him I can't shake. He's so damn...*malleable.* He wants to be loved so bad. Seeing him in such a tizzy tonight made my heart break. Maybe it was good, having two weeks apart. Absence makes the heart grow fonder and all.

Deep down I always knew Cutie Pie would be back.

JD blathers on about Garrett taking him under his wing and how it's all so magical and special, but I know well enough no one can spend all that time with Garrett and not fall under his tricking spell. And look what has happened.

It makes me a little ill, especially when I think back to when I first got here; how Garrett's presence was a giant drain I swirled helplessly towards. I wanted him so bad, it hurt. Even the handful of times I mainlined, never have I experienced a feeling as intoxicating as being around him. I swear he is looking right at me, into my soul, every time he talks and paces, with that quiet control of his.

Always in damn control.

He says we became less in control with more choice, and if there was ever someone less in control due to more choices, it's me. But he wants us to have less choice, so he can control *us*. The sessions are how he does it. His devil work. Brainwashing. With secret potions concocted from his plants. He uncovers your deepest fears and uses them against you. And after, when you are weak and unsure, he summons you to the decompression chamber. The red-walled room. Empty, like him. He sits close to intimidate. Keeps talking and reminding about what happened, even though your mind can't process squat. Even Cassius said he couldn't remember anything after the session. No one can, except me. Psychedelics never affected me. Something about the way my brain's wired. And I never drank those vials. I pretended, I wasn't that stupid. After the first session, he suspected, but we never got around to a second one. After he cured Cassius, he said he was taking a break from the sessions.

Shortly after, the jaguar attacks started.

First it was Sosa. After we buried Carson, Garrett told us to stay inside at night or walk in twos. Trouble is that after a year of waking up at 3 a.m. in Christina Melton, I'm still an early riser. With nothing to do in the cabin, I often head to the common house to read or shoot some pool until breakfast. I was on my way there that morning when it happened. At the edge of the garden, Elan was staggering, drunk as all get out. He liked the hard stuff and it liked him. His wife, Nalin, had kept him on the straight as much as she could, but now she was gone, dead from the botched abortion, and Elan had spiraled out of control.

I had had my fill of managing drunks and didn't feel like getting involved. I stopped and hid behind a fence post. Waited to let him pass.

At first all I heard was a hum; a sound that wasn't of this world. It ran up my legs, seemed to fill the very space surrounding me. I wanted to run but couldn't. I was glued to the spot with fear. Elan flopped around, oblivious, and from the shadows behind him, I saw Garrett emerge. I thought he was going to help him, but that hum only got louder, and what happened next was too gruesome to describe.

Right as rain, I *saw* Garrett turn. I *saw* him rip Elan to shreds. Only the stars and faraway galaxies and me were witness to that night, but I swear on Gramma's grave it's true. And Garrett saw me, only at the end, when he was shapeshifting back, in a dulled state, no strength to chase me.

I had no idea my legs could move as fast as they did.

Cassius only heard about what happened because I was talking in my sleep, and he forced me to tell him, in the only way he knows how. Of course, he doesn't believe me, claims I'm losing my mind. But if anyone's lost their mind its Cutie Pie: there's no way José he saw a real jaguar. He saw Garrett turn. That's the only explanation for why he was so lost tonight. He doesn't remember. This actually works in my favor because what he will remember is what happened between us tonight. Now that he's had the chance to experience me, there's no way that boy will back out.

The finish line is in sight. I just need to keep the cart on the horse.

Thunder rumbles deep in the sky. Thick drops of rain start to splatter on my bare arms. Storm clouds rolled in earlier, full of anger, and are about to unleash fury. I stick my tongue out and up into the dark and laugh. My last night. Cleansing rain. It's all too perfect. My spirits are up, and they haven't been up for a good long while. It's exciting to think about change, and the best part is I'll be able to say goodbye and good riddance to Addy very soon.

I've been dreaming long and hard about my new name. Names have always been important to me, and I take them seriously. A name resonates from the inside out and creates your very being. It defines a person. Mother, in her usual harebrained way, didn't have any clue about that. She decided to name all of us with the same first letter and probably thought she was being avant garde, like that screwball author Anais Nin whose diaries she was forever reading.

If I had gotten my preferred name - Veronica - instead of Vera, my story might have been different.

"Vera, Vera, can't come near ya."

My mind turned out to be like Mother's, delicate, so those taunts were more vicious than a knife in my heart.

After Daddy left us, I was saddled with looking after my sisters and Mother. I worked at the A&P and the bowling alley while Mother cried in her room and forgot all about us. There was some money, but not much, and some weeks I had to choose between buying soap or food. We couldn't afford new clothes. We were the town pariahs. The Walby girls, dumped by their father. When the boys at school started to come down on me – those cruel, awful taunts - I cried in my pillow at night. It wasn't fair. I was still desirable. It was Mother who had let herself go. It wasn't my fault Daddy left. It was *hers*.

She let the tire around her waist grow and droop. She stopped shaping her hair. Even Sunday church became a disaster, with just a smear of lipstick and not much else. I encouraged Mother to try harder (I saw all the watchful glances) but that faraway look in her eyes took up permanent residence.

I never suspected it would end the way it did. The only inkling I got was at our first church ball game of the season. It was a fine Spring day, still cool enough the potato salads could stay out, warm enough the men could play in t-shirts. I was fourteen. After using the restroom, I made my way back to the bleachers to watch Daddy pitch. Mrs. Emery and Mrs. Taylor didn't notice me sit behind them.

"You seein' what I'm seeing?" Mrs. Emery asked.

Daddy warmed up on the mound, his body long and lean as he threw.

Mrs. Taylor sighed. "Oh boy. If I had a dollar for every time I dreamed of him sliding into my home base."

They both tittered and bumped their cardigan-wrapped shoulders.

"You think the rumors are true?"

"Just because a man does business in Austin doesn't mean he'll become one of those loose Democrat types," Mrs. Taylor replied.

"Yes, but look at her," Mrs. Emery whispered, nodding towards Mother, who was down a few rows. "She's not even trying anymore. I mean, that dress."

"Henry Walby is devoted if nothing else."

Mrs. Emery clucked. "How he manages all those women is beyond me. That Vera is going to be a troublemaker with a capital T. She's already blossoming, and I've seen the boys follow her around like they're in a trance."

"She certainly was blessed with the Lord's best trimmings," Mrs. Taylor concurred, and patted her friend's knee. "But don't you worry, your Cathy's not far behind."

I slinked away, my heart hammering. At the picnic after, Mother insisted I eat, but I couldn't keep anything down. In the evening, Mother was in one of her moods so I went to bed early. Daddy came upstairs to say goodnight. He still smelled like cut grass and sunshine. Full of nerves, I asked if he had to keep working in Austin. He looked at me, the usual twinkle in his eye gone. He smiled a different smile and said Austin was how he could keep me in all my pretty dresses and didn't I want pretty dresses? I told him I was worried about Mother. He said he was worried too, but the Good Lord worked in mysterious ways. If Mother's condition was His will then it wasn't for us to question. Daddy always knew what was right and I loved him more than anything in the world so I pushed the ladies' conversation out of my head. But after that, it all started to change.

Mother got worse and Daddy's time on the road surpassed time at home. He'd come in late at night and leave early the next day. He'd lock himself in the bathroom with the phone. He had less time for me, and when we did talk it wasn't the rambling conversations we used to have about the Lord. He was short and to the point.

Something in my gut wasn't sitting right, and sure enough, on a Sunday of all days - a sticky hot, Texas afternoon - the man I loved the most in the world became the first man to let me down.

He walked out of my life forever.

"Vera, Vera, can't come near ya."

If Mother had gotten help, been the wife she was supposed to have been, Daddy wouldn't have sinned. Not in that way. If she had named me Veronica, the boys couldn't have crushed me the way they did. None of this would have happened. I wouldn't have ran away, got caught up on the streets.

Gramma saved me time and time again in those early months. The woman she shared her trailer with did shift work, and on the nights she was gone I could stay over. Gramma brushed my hair with long soothing strokes, the air minty from Menthols, my belly full of Chef Boyardee. I confessed all my troubles to her. When I was hopping between the beds of two different men just to keep a roof over my head, she reminded me I was a goddess, that I should never let a man treat me otherwise.

On my 16th Christmas, she gave me my most prized possession: a paperback about the Greek gods and goddesses. It's dog-eared now, the spine falling apart. It was with me during the dark days of Christina Melton. (Pedro smuggled it in for me. It was one of the belongings stripped off of me, like my clothes, when I first got there). It's with me here, hidden with my bible. Every name I've ever chosen comes from this book, and the names I've picked all reflect the different times of my life.

I chose Dione first, at eighteen, because she was the Goddess of Mystery and I kind of liked being mysterious. It suited me; it suited a lot of guys who gravitated to my brand of mystery. Donny loved it, because people called us D and D or D-squared, but he also loved a lot of things aside from me, including Cindy.

Isis came next.

She was worshipped as the ideal wife, and I decided I needed to be worshipped. Isis was also the friend of sinners and saints alike, and I believe we all have a little of both in each of us. (Forgive me, Good Lord, but it's true.) Isis had a long run, a good run, and it would've lasted longer if Mason hadn't fucked it up.

At Christina Melton, after Pablo was under my thumb and cooperating, enter Até, Goddess of Mischief. I had to dumb Até down to Addy, on account of retards, like Cassius, being unable to pronounce it, but I liked how it sounded fancy and French, and at the same time, perfect for a shit disturber like me. The fake ID Cassius got me in El Paso says Adelaide Louise Tremblay, and I chose Christmas Day as my birthday. (I'd never had a December birthday even though Cassius, twit, made me two years older than I really am.)

Now, with victory right around the corner, it's time for Nike, Goddess of Victory. My full name will be Nike Ambrosia Carrier (Carrier being the name on the air conditioning unit that rattled day and night outside my barred window, ambrosia my favorite dessert.)

Nike was born on January 1st, a day of new beginnings, and in her honor I've decided to cut my hair and go blonde. For the past few days I've practiced my new life in fake conversations. Nike is cultured, a woman of the world. Introducing myself with a soft handshake, I'll purr, "Hello I'm Nike Carrier,"; or, when someone offers me a glass of wine, "I prefer Lagavulin, if you have it." Nike reads the *Economist*. She has personalized stationary. Shops at Neiman Marcus. She would never be caught dead with someone like Cassius. She would never let herself get trapped here.

Thanks to Cutie Pie, I'm not going to be trapped either.

The rain starts to come down hard and I'm soaked when I finally reach the cabin. It's still dark, like I left it, and my nose twitches with the stink. Behind the bedroom door, Cassius sounds awful: his phlegmy cough, the moaning. This morning he was barfing, all delirious, and I asked him what was wrong. I don't remember much about the past couple days, only the voices, louder than ever.

After making myself a tea, I turn on the CD player and curl up on the living room couch. I was wrong about Cutie Pie. He doesn't deserve to die any more than the motel manager. Tomorrow night his arms will be around me (hopefully he'll have lasted a little longer than he did tonight) and we'll make plans for the future. It feels damn good to have a future again.

I will never, ever miss this place, although it is a shame about Garrett. If only he'd seen the light. I could've saved him from his evil ways and we would have made a great couple. Rylan is too high strung, too desperate for him. She has that permanent haunted look of a woman who has devoted her life to loving someone who won't love her back.

And she's never liked me.

If there's one thing a pretty girl doesn't like it's another pretty girl, and she's watched me like a hawk, which is all levels of ironic since she's the one who can't be trusted. But she can have this place and everyone in it. I'm done.

I turn off the lights, stretch out and drift off.

When I wake up, rain sleets against the windows.

My mind is filled with chatter, Morse code I can't decipher.

Alone, in the dark, I struggle to think because I was going somewhere, doing something, but what?

The wind is howling and it sounds close, like it's inside the house.

Like it's just down the hall.

THIRTY-ONE

DAMIEN

A VICIOUS CLAP of thunder rocks me out of a dead sleep. A scream follows. Through the cracks of the curtains lights flash and disappear then flash again. Voices. Female. Male. A car speeds away. I scramble out of bed and yank the curtains open. Rain hammers down in sheets. I can't see anything. Still in the same clothes from last night, I run to the foyer, pull on my shoes and dash outside. A massive crack of lightning turns night into day.

"Damien!"

Near the pavers on the hill, lit up like a ghost, is Rylan. She rushes towards me, her head tucked under her arm against the onslaught of rain.

"What's going on?" I ask.

"I'm not sure," she says, shivering, soaking wet in a thin bathrobe.

"Cassius is sick. Addy came here, yelling for help. Garrett just went back with her."

"Head back inside, get dry," I tell her. "I'll wait out here until they get back."

She grips my arm. "I don't like this."

"I'll find out from Garrett what's up," I say, the fear in her voice making me uneasy. "I'll come up and find you."

Her eyes dart back and forth, her platinum hair a dark helmet in the rain. She lets go of my arm and runs up the pavers. Lights blaze from their house, too many lights for this time at night. Rain smacks down like bullets and I duck back inside to grab a hoodie, huddling on the porch until shaky beams of light appear. I run into the night, waving my arms at the SUV. Garrett pulls up beside me and rolls down the window. He's soaked, hair plastered, his face a mask of concern. From the back seat come heavy, labored groans.

"Is he okay?" I ask. Cassius is curled up in the fetal position. A rancid smell fills the truck.

"I don't know," Garrett admits. "He's sick. Totally out of it. I'm taking him to emergency in Espanola."

"Where's Addy? Is she going with you?"

He shakes his head. "She's lost it. Can you get her and bring her to the house? Rylan has keys to the truck. Tell her what's going on, okay?"

"Yeah, of course."

Cassius starts coughing and convulsing on the back seat.

"Jesus, he sounds horrible. Should I come down with you?"

My hand rests on the door. He reaches for my arm. "I need you here. Can you wait until I sort this out?"

Our eyes meet. A thousand unsaid things crackle between us.

"Ok."

He digs in his jeans and hands me his phone. "I'll call you once I know more."

The taillights disappear in the rain and I can't shake the feeling something very bad is going down.

"Does he know what's wrong?" Rylan asks, handing me the keys to the truck. Her bathrobe is gone, replaced by a sweatshirt and jeans. She's ashen. Worry lines bunch on her forehead.

"No idea. But he sounded really sick."

"Do you know how to get to her cabin?"

"No."

"It's the last one. Just follow the road all the way down. It's marked with blue reflective lights. Turn right once you see those."

"Has anyone been sick like this before?"

"No," she says and then reconsiders. "I mean, sometimes after a session, the odd person feels ill, but that's normal."

Normal. What the hell does that even mean anymore?

"If you see Bola, tell him what's going on," she adds. "He should come here."

Bola. We haven't crossed paths since the meeting. I sure as hell don't want to see him now.

"There's a flashlight in between the front seats," she says, just as the lights in the house dim. "You might need it. Sometimes the electricity goes during a storm."

Driving to Addy's cabin is an exercise in frustration. The truck wipers bash full tilt and still, the road is barely visible. Giant pools of water hide the potholes and the truck bobs and creaks whenever I hit one. The common house is dark but a couple of cabins after it have lights on. After another stretch of dark road, blue reflectors finally flash in the headlights. Addy's cabin is shrouded in black and the bad feeling from earlier intensifies. I grab the flashlight and dash to the door.

"Addy!" I wait, pound on the door again. "You in there?"

Another boom of thunder rolls across the sky and the rain lashes harder. Forget about staying out here. The door is unlocked and I push it open. The stench hits me first. With my hand over my mouth, I step inside. "Addy?"

Something shatters under my sneaker and I jump out of my skin. Fumbling with the flashlight switch, the crushed remains of a light bulb gleam like shrapnel on the hard wood floor. And it doesn't end there.

"What the...?"

It's like a bomb has gone off. Everywhere the light beam lands, there's more debris: a box of Kraft Dinner, macaroni exploded out of it; a CD snapped in two; clothing still on hangers, strewn like lifeless bodies. Moving deeper into the cabin, the stench burns my eyes. It's not just sickness; it's a feral, mad smell. I cover my mouth again, gagging. In the living room, couch cushions are scattered, the floor lamp toppled over, its cocked shade hanging like a snapped neck. The hair on my arm bristles. This isn't a joke. This is serious destruction.

A muffled moan breaks the silence, and I spin around looking for the source. At the end of the hall is a closed door. Horror movie 101 is never open a closed door; not in a circumstance like this. Almost weightless with fear, I edge towards it.

Inside, she's lying face down on the bed, motionless. The room is thick with heat. "Oh my god, Addy." She turns around and squints into the light. Her face is bloated and unrecognizable. "Are you okay?" I ask.

"He's killing everyone," she whispers.

"What? What are you talking about? No one's killing anyone." I sit down on the bed and lower the flashlight. "Garrett's got Cassius. He's taking him to the hospital."

"He's going to die. *We're* going to die." Her voice rises into panic. "We need to get out of here."

"Stop saying that, okay?"I say, as she gropes for clothing piled on the bed, her movements frantic. "You're freaking me out."

"You said we were leaving. You said."

"Listen. Addy. Stop." I grab her slim shoulders and they're slick with sweat. "We're not going anywhere right now."

"But you said."

On her knees, hair falling over her shoulders; if she didn't look completely demented, if the room didn't reek like sickness, it would almost be sexy.

"Yeah, I know I did, but we can't right now. Do you understand?" It's a fair question. She's miles away from lucid. "Do you understand?" I ask again.

Her head starts to shake back and forth slow, then violently. Then she launches at me like a missile. I tumble backwards and she starts punching me. "You fucking said! You're a liar, like all the rest. A liar. A liar. A liar."

"Addy," I yell, both arms in front of my face to ward off the attack. She's surprisingly strong. "What the fuck? Calm down."

When she runs out of steam with her fists, she starts belting me with the pillow. "Get me out of here," she sobs. "You promised."

In between pillow wallops, I tuck and roll off the bed, landing on something hard. A bowl upends and stale vomit gushes onto the floor. The smell is too much. What's left in my stomach empties right on top of it.

"He's killing everyone," she says, watching me retch. "Why don't you believe me?"

I stagger to my feet, cuffing my mouth, stomach muscles sapped from all the heaving. "It's going to be okay."

"No," she whispers and her eyes are glassy, filled with pain I can't understand. "Why don't you believe me?"

"I don't know what's going on, Addy. But I won't let anything happen to you, okay? I promise." I offer her my hand. "C'mon. Can you stand?" She clamps onto my arm, bobbles and weaves climbing off the bed. "Do you have a jacket? It's pouring outside."

"By the kitchen," she says.

We move down the hall and she stares vacantly at the junk littered on the floor. At the front door, she struggles to lace up her sneakers, eventually sitting down to finish the task. From here, I can see the kitchen: dishes stacked on the counter, bags of garbage sagged against the wall. How can such a pretty girl live in such a pigsty? She stands up and teeters against me.

"Are you sick too?" I ask. "What did you eat?"

"I'm not sick," she says vehemently. "Don't ever say that. I am *not* sick."

"Okay, okay, you're not sick. Forget I asked." I nudge her towards the door. "Let's get out of here."

"Where are we going?"

"To Garrett's."

She takes a step back. "Don't leave me alone with him."

"I won't. He's gone. With Cassius. Remember?"

She looks at me, confused.

"Do you remember what he ate?" I press.

Her eyes flicker, a slow dawn of realization. Her hand tightens around mine so hard it hurts. "Poison," she says.

It's like a piece of steel jammed into my kidney. "Poison?"

"It's all Rylan's fault," she says, and her voice is small and scared, like a child's.

THIRTY-TWO

IT'S ALMOST 4 A.M. Addy is curled up on the sectional, asleep, finally, after Rylan forced her to drink NyQuil. Bola's come and gone, with instruction to get him as soon as we hear anything. I'm so tired, I'm seeing double. Rylan stands at the window, staring out into the night.

"He's got to call soon," she says. "They must know something by now."

"If you want to sleep, I can stay up," I offer again.

She turns towards me, arms crossed tight across her chest. "Something's wrong about all this."

"What do you mean?"

"Where were you the other night? Not last night, the night before."

"My house. Why?"

"'My house'," she repeats, her face stony. "Why didn't you answer when I knocked on the door?"

"I don't know," I say, but the edge in her voice makes me sit up in the chair. "I was probably sleeping."

"Garrett was almost tolerable in the past two weeks," she says, her expression cool. "He's been the worst he's ever been since the other night. Figured you might know why."

"I don't, sorry."

"You've spent all this time together and never talk?"

"Sure, we talk."

Her eyes narrow on me. Outside, the storm has died down, but there's another one brewing right here. "Did you come here looking for him?"

"You asked me that before. I had no idea about this place."

She walks over to one of the chairs flanking the sectional and rearranges pillows that are already neatly ordered. "So you just happened to get a flat right by us."

"Yeah, and then I beat myself up and asked to be brought here," I say, irritated. "Anything else?"

"Is there a reason you're getting uptight?" she asks, perching on the rolled leather armrest.

"Yes. You're grilling me."

"All I know is nothing's been the same since you got here. He won't even let me on the computer. He's protecting you. Why?"

"He's not protecting me."

"Bullshit."

"Rylan?" a voice calls from downstairs.

"Up here," she says, her eyes fixed on mine.

On the landing, Bola stops as if he's collided with the tension in the room. His hair, not in its usual braid, sprays out everywhere, like he's been zapped by electricity. "I couldn't sleep," he says. "Any news?"

"Not yet."

To me, Bola grunts, "Why you still here?"

"Garrett asked me to keep watch."

He glances at Rylan. "I've got a bad feeling about this."

"Join the club," she snorts.

Addy starts to stir on the couch, making small noises. Rylan glances over at her, lips pressed tight.

"What's with her?" Bola asks.

"She was pretty messed up," I answer.

"What a surprise," Rylan mutters.

"Give her a break, would you?" I snap. "Not everyone's an ice queen like you."

Her mouth gapes open. "Excuse me?"

"You heard me."

"You're way out of line boy," Bola threatens, taking a step towards me.

Rylan quickly backs Bola. "And you didn't like Cassius."

"What?" I ask, edging towards hostile. "You think *I* had something to do with this?"

With an innocent look she says, "I never said that."

"Yes, you are."

"Maybe it's time for you to get out of here," Bola says, pushing his glasses up with his middle finger.

"And where were you the other night?" Rylan marches on, undeterred. "You weren't at home. Cassius got sick right after that."

With this new piece of information, Bola's features darken. The room seems to shrink.

"I told you..."

Just before it gets ugly, Garrett's cell phone starts to shimmy on the coffee table. Rylan forgets all about me, dashes to pick it up.

"Hey. Yes, I'm fine. She's fine, asleep." Her eyes flick towards me. "Yes, he's here. And Bola just got here. What's going on?" The longer she listens, color drains out of her face. "Are they sure?" she asks, almost missing the chair as she sinks down. "Is he going to be alright? Okay. Okay. Yes." She gnaws on her thumbnail. "Are you going to stay? Really? Oh my god. Can they do that? Alright. I won't. I'll tell him. Yes, he's right here."

She hands me the phone with a stunned look.

At the dining room table, three cups of coffee have all gone cold. We're jittery enough. Cassius has been poisoned. Eleanor's at the hospital, making a scene, out for blood. The cops want to swing by. It's a triple header of bad news.

"It must've been her," Bola says, nodding towards Addy.

"No one here liked him," I remind him.

"We all liked him just fine," he spits back.

"Not from what I saw."

"Well, except you," he says. "You two were oil and water from the get go."

"Why do I have to keep repeating myself? I had nothing to do with this."

"Can you prove it?" he asks.

"I don't have to prove anything."

"You're going to have to prove it."

"So are you."

"I don't like you," he finally says, both hands gripping his coffee mug.

I lean back and cross my arms. "Then we're even."

Bola glares at me from across the table and right now I'm glad there's some distance.

"You're forgetting about Garrett," Rylan interjects, adding another layer to the toxic atmosphere.

"He had no reason to poison Cassius," I say.

"Why are you so sure?" Rylan asks. She's at the head of the table, where Garrett usually sits. "And what the hell do you know anyway? You're been here a month. I know, we *all* know, a lot more than you."

"Who else has access to that greenhouse?" I ask.

"No one," Bola says. "He keeps it locked."

"And no one knows where he keeps the key?" I ask, with a pointed look at Rylan.

"Right. Garrett the open book, the welcome mat out. What do you think?" she fires back.

"You're under as much suspicion as everyone else," Bola adds.

"Says who?" I ask. "You?"

Bola bangs his fist on the table and Rylan jumps in her chair. "*I'm* the one going to talk to the police when they get here. They're going to want a suspect. I think it's time we all got our stories straight, don't you think?" He glances over at Rylan and she picks up where he leaves off.

"Is there something else we should know about you before the police show up?" she asks with a bitter smile. "I'd hate for them to find your car and have the shit hit the fan."

"No. There's nothing else you need to know."

"I guess we'll find out soon enough if you're telling the truth," Bola says, the chair scraping on the floor as he stands. "I'm going home to get some sleep before the police get here." To Rylan, "Make sure you watch him."

"I'm not going anywhere," I say.

Bola leaves and Rylan fiddles with sugar packets she dumped on the table. "You better pray it isn't that prick Vandenberg showing up."

"Is he a cop?"

"He's got a hate on for Garrett, this whole place. Just like Eleanor. After last time, he swore he'd bring him down."

"They've been here before? For what?"

"You know, I left you two alone because it was a relief for me. I needed time to myself to think." She stacks the sugar packets one by one. "What did you two scheme up, huh? Tell me the truth."

"We had nothing to do with this."

"'We,'" she repeats.

"Yeah, we."

She glances up, a gleam in her eyes. "Addy seemed pretty interested in you."

"What's that supposed to mean?"

"You're a guy. She's a girl."

"She's with Cassius. I don't work that way."

After placing the last packet on the tower she pauses. "Which way *do* you work?"

"Addy told me tonight this was all your fault," I say, and hold her gaze.

"That stupid crazy cunt," she sniggers. "Of course she'd say that."

"Maybe I should talk to the cops too."

A muscle in her neck twitches. With a furious sweep of her arm, the sugar packets fly all over the table, some onto the floor. "Go ahead and talk to the cops. I'm sure they'd *love* to hear from you. Now, if you'll excuse me." She stands and gives me a withering look. "I know there's something up with you. I've known all along. If you would've been up front with me from the start, I might be more sympathetic, but it's too late now."

She disappears down the hall and slams a door.

This is turning into a nightmare.

I debate going back to the guesthouse but it doesn't matter. Sleep will be futile no matter where I am. I stretch out on the sectional and vibrate with stress. When I finally drift into sleep, another nightmare kicks in. I'm back in the kiva, that awful hum getting louder and louder. It won't stop. It eventually wakes me up. Groggy, sweaty and uncomfortable, I sit up. The living room is flooded with sun. Addy snores lightly. The sound of that hum continues. It crawls up my spine like a parade of ants. On the dining room table Garrett's phone buzzes in silent mode. I roll off the couch and stumble to answer it.

"Garrett?"

"Bola?" Cedric asks.

"No. It's me, Damien," I say, my mouth thick, full of cotton.

"Buenos Dias. You tell Bola please the police are here. I just let them in."

"Yeah, okay. I will," I say. "Thanks."

I hang up, my heart pounding. In the far corner of the living room two walls of glass meet. I'm there watching when the cops pull up. With a deep breath I head downstairs.

It's time to take matters into my own hands.

THIRTY-THREE

THE LIGHTS ARE unnecessary but I guess they want to prove a point. A heavy-set man lumbers out of the driver's side.

"Afternoon son," he says, twirling his handlebar moustache. He does a short walk around the car, taking his time, his leather boots squeaking as he surveys the surroundings. His partner, a rangy Mexican, gets out of the cruiser and gives me a curt nod.

"What's your name?" Moustache asks.

"What's yours?" I ask.

"I'm Fuentes," the Mexican says. "He's Vandenberg. We're looking for a Bola?"

"He's not around right now. You can talk to me."

Vandenberg has both fleshy hands on his hips, the left one resting on his gun. "Where is he?"

"He's asleep. Not feeling well."

"Seems to be a trend." He takes a step closer to me and pulls off his sunglasses. "We hear there's been some trouble up here. You want to fill me in?"

"You should talk to Garrett. He owns the property."

"We already did. We have a few more questions we'd like to ask."

His eyes, almost colorless, disappear as he squints. "You know he's being held down there, right?"

"Last I heard he's at the hospital."

"He was..." He pauses. Clears his throat. "But your...comrade, took a turn for the worse." He pauses again for dramatic effect. "You know anything about poisonous plants being grown up here?"

"Like I said, you probably want to talk to Garrett."

Vandenberg cracks his neck. "There was nothing but a bunch of defected Apaches up here for the longest time. When did you show up?"

"I've been here for a while."

"You a runaway?"

"No."

"How old are you?"

"Twenty-five."

"What's your name?"

"Drake."

Fuentes's boot clunks onto the front bumper. He leans on a skinny knee. "Like the rapper?"

"Eleanor Marks described you to me. You remember her?" Vandenberg asks. "You two met a few weeks ago."

"I remember her."

"She said you were looking pretty beat up, limping. Anything you want to share?"

"No."

"We're here to help," Fuentes adds.

"What sort of drugs and potions is he feeding everyone up here?" Vandenberg asks.

"I've never seen any drugs."

After a lengthy stare down he says, "We can play this a couple ways, kid. The best way works in your favor, if you cooperate."

"Am I under arrest?" I ask.

He pauses. "Not yet."

Fuentes continues in good-cop mode. "Don't feel you have to

protect him. You give us what we need, we make sure he doesn't come near you again."

"I know my rights."

"So...no drugs," Vandenberg says conversationally, trying another tack. "That's not what we heard is it?" he asks Fuentes. "What about," he waves his hand around, "these black magic powers he apparently has. They for real?"

"Did you ask him?"

Vandenberg continues, "Does he force you to do things you don't want to?"

"No one's forced to do anything."

"Except no one's allowed to leave," he fires back. "Is that right?"

"No one wants to."

"Drake..." Fuentes starts.

Vandenberg cuts him off. "Pretty tight security up here. Feels like overkill for what he claims is a bunch of people living off the land."

"It's his land. He can do what he wants."

Vandenberg laughs. "We got that impression too, from talking with him. Pretty cocky. Of course, if I was a millionaire who didn't think I had to answer to anyone, I guess I'd be pretty high on myself."

Sweat is pouring down my back. Five more minutes and there's going to be a pool around me. "If you have any specific questions, ask them. Otherwise, I'd say we're done."

They look at each other with raised eyebrows.

"'We're done,'" Vandenberg repeats with a tight smile. "Seems like I've heard that before." He pulls himself up to his full but hardly intimidating height. "Just so you know, we're far from done. Today was just a courtesy call. The warrant is getting approved and we'll be back." He reaches into his breast pocket and pulls out a card, handing it to me. "What I need from you is a list of everyone who lives here. Full names, date of birth, last known address before coming to this circus. We'll be back to interview everyone in a couple of days. I need that list by tomorrow. Can you handle that..." a pause, "...Drake?"

"Sure," I say, and make sure he sees me crumple his card before I put it in my pocket.

"You let everyone know no one leaves this property until we've done our due diligence. That means you."

"Got it."

They make no motion to leave. Vandenberg stands casually, twirls the end of his moustache again. "He looks familiar, doesn't he?" he asks Fuentes, who nods, his ice-blue eyes intense, popping against dark, pocked skin. "Be interesting to see what comes up once we have your information. Your real name better be on that list, otherwise we'll haul you in for obstruction of justice." With a smug look he takes a couple steps closer. "And you're the kind of guy that doesn't too well in jail if you know what I mean." He nods up at the house. "Where's the wife? I remember her being quite pretty."

"She's asleep."

"It's almost eleven. Why is everybody sleeping?"

"Is it a crime to sleep in?"

Fuentes bites back a smile. Vandenberg crosses his arms. "Murder has a way of keeping you awake at night, doesn't it?"

"No one's been murdered," I say, and keep my eyes locked on his.

"Apparently you don't know the history with him," he says. "You might not be so quick on the defense."

"I know about the abortions," I reply quickly, "the girl that died."

"Abortion is the least of his trouble, young man. I don't agree with it, but it's still legal in this state." He slips on his sunglasses, motions to Fuentes that it's time to go. "I don't know how you got here or what the allure is, but I'm warning you, get out while you can. You're playing with fire." He opens the cruiser door. "You get me that list. Tomorrow by five."

Fuentes slides in the front seat of the cruiser and puts his sunglasses back on.

Vandenberg, with one heavy arm draped on the door says, "Well, *Drake,* it's been a real pleasure chatting. I'm looking forward to hearing what you and everyone else have to say once we have our warrant. You all better have your IDs ready and stories straight."

The door slams shut and he guns the engine. The lights *and* siren come on as the cruiser heads down the road.

The message is loud and clear.

THIRTY-FOUR

A LAYER of tense apprehension follows me back to Garrett's house. I just lied about my name. Once they come back with a warrant and find my car they'll put two and two together. With no idea when Garrett's coming back, *if* he's coming back, and neither Bola nor Rylan in my corner, hanging around isn't an option.

In the foyer, it's eerily quiet and anxiety bubbles in my gut. The mere thought of sneaking around in his house feels wrong, but after Vandenberg's comments, whatever Garrett told me - about me being safe, himself, this place - doesn't add up. In the past three weeks I've been so fixated on forgetting everything it hasn't bothered me to be disconnected. Garrett never offered time on his computer and I never asked. It's time for the real story.

I creep up the stairs and pause at the landing. With the sun at full strength, the main floor is washed in yellow and gold. It all looks so normal, so everyday, except for Addy, doped up on NyQuil, asleep on the couch; what happened with her yesterday is miles from normal and nothing I want to experience again. Shuffling past her in socked feet, I make my way to the far side of the kitchen, to a door that leads downstairs. Garrett gave me a brief tour of the house one afternoon, but we never went down there, where his office is. Where I'm headed now. The hallway off the kitchen ends at their bedroom, several yards away, where Rylan sleeps. With my eyes peeled in that direction, I turn the door knob in small increments, like I'm cracking a safe. Slipping through the open door, I'm halfway in, halfway out when...

Thump.

I freeze.

Shit.

If I needed to backpedal from here, I could. There's a believable story.

But Addy's still asleep. There's no movement from the bedroom. When Diesel pads through the kitchen with a curious look on his face, relief floods through me.

"You," I say, his head butting against my leg. "Seriously?" He purrs as I scratch and my chest wells. It's so simple, the love of an animal. No confusion. When I get the hell out of here, wherever I end up, I'm getting a cat. "I'll be right back, buddy," I whisper, pushing him away with my foot as I close the door. "You be my watchdog, okay?"

It's only ten steps to the bottom of the stairwell yet it feels like half a mile. Compared to the main floor, down here its cool and dim, blinds drawn over the window at the far end of the hall. There's just enough light to see the double doors a few feet away from me. His office.

Damn.

A security keypad is mounted above the door handle. The average person uses stupid things, like their birthdays, as passwords but Garrett isn't average or stupid. More importantly, I don't even know when his birthday is. Now what?

Another *thump* echoes above me. The air pressure in the hall shifts. One of the double doors sinks back from the other with a sucking sound. It wasn't shut properly. I cock my head, tingling with stress. There's no believable story here. If someone comes down now,

I'm busted. Seconds drip by in slow agony. With no other sounds, convinced it was just Diesel, I push inside.

For a second, nothing makes sense.

I knew Garrett lived a different life before here, but I can't even imagine him in this room. He's so physical and raw, a man of the earth. This is command central of the Enterprise. Five computer monitors seem to float above the curved desk, mounted on metal tubes bolted to the floor. Banks of decks and componentry line an entire wall. Red lights blink and flash, the drone of sleeping electronics hanging in the air.

What is all this stuff?

A thin wireless keyboard is the only thing on the desk. It can't possibly bring the wall of equipment to life. Or can it? Pressing the "D" key, a password bar pops up on one of the monitors. It's a signal to leave, to get the hell out. One more thing about him I can't figure out. But I don't leave. Being in his private space, even this foreign one, is strangely intimate. I lower myself into the leather desk chair and rub my hands along the armrests, into the indentations created by him. Whatever soap or shampoo he uses, the scent lingers in the air. The same clean smell when he was behind me, adjusting my golf swing. It's a reminder of the past two weeks, how we have gotten closer. A little rush pulses through me.

Maybe it's not impossible. Maybe...

No.

There are too many thoughts, too many questions. I need answers. But all the cabinets are locked. Not even a pen lying around. Then I see it: a rolling chest of drawers, hidden deep under the desk. I crouch down and roll the cabinet towards me. The first drawer sticks at first before yielding with a good yank. Inside are pens and pencils organized with OCD neatness. Drawer two contains nothing but envelopes. The third drawer practically falls open, no weight inside.

Acid fills my throat. A wave of lightheadedness forces me to clutch the desk. The hardest thing I've ever had to do in my life is reach inside that drawer for my car keys. In the palm of my hand they don't even look real.

He lied. Why?

I know what it's like to feel gutted. I've been there. Many times. I don't know this feeling. I stand, stuff the keys in my pocket and back away like everything's radioactive.

"What are you doing down here?"

I spin around, reeling. Bola.

"I, uh, I was just looking for some paper."

Arms crossed, his permanent frown deepens. "How did you get in here?"

"The door was open."

"It's never open."

"It was, I swear."

He scans the room, sensing the panic pouring off me. He knows I'm guilty of something, he just doesn't know what.

"I just heard a police siren. That's why I came over. Where are they?"

"They just left. I spoke to them."

"Why didn't you come get me?"

"Rylan was asleep. I thought you might be asleep."

"*I* was supposed to talk to them," he says, his voice rising as takes a step forward. "What did you say?"

"Nothing. I mean, they asked a bunch of questions and said they wanted a list of everybody who lives here. I came down here looking for paper."

The lie rolls off my tongue too easy. Thank god the password box on the monitor has faded to black. Bola looms like a wall in front of me, his stillness deceiving. We're one wrong word away from a fistfight.

"Upstairs," he growls with a jerk of his thumb.

I slink past him, my hand flat against my pocket to stop the keys from jingling. He closes the office door, pulling it tight, and follows me back upstairs into the kitchen.

"Where's Garrett's phone?" he demands and I've barely dug it out of my pocket before he snatches it away. Any further conversation dies when Rylan shuffles down the hall towards us.

"Everything okay?" she asks, squinting in the bright sun. Dark circles hang under each eye. "Any news?"

"I just spoke with the police," I say. "Cassius is still in critical condition."

She tightens her robe and looks at Bola, confused. "Why didn't you talk to them?"

"He didn't follow orders," Bola grimaces. "What a surprise."

"They're coming back with a warrant in a couple days," I continue.

"What?" Rylan rubs her mouth, agitated. "Where the fuck is Garrett?"

Bola holds up Garrett's phone. "I'll call the hospital and see what's going on."

We both listen, Bola first getting the number from directory assistance, then navigating through the hospital labyrinth, trying to get information. After hanging up, he says, "Sounds like he left a while ago. They wouldn't give me any information on Cassius."

Rylan's hundred-yard stare out the window drifts to Addy, finally sharpening in my direction. "I want you to leave," she says. "*Now.*"

"Fine," I say and head towards the stairs, brushing past Bola who warns,

"You stay put in that house until Garrett comes back."

Without another word, I'm downstairs, and have already pulled on my shoes when the sound of an engine rumbles outside.

"It's him," I hear Rylan say. "Thank god."

Bola calls down to me. "Get back up here. We all need to talk."

When Garrett comes up the stairs, his steps are heavy and slow. He stops on the landing looking dazed, clothing rumpled, hair scraped into a messy ponytail. We're standing there like zombies, staring back at him, waiting. Finally,

"He's dead."

It's like I'm watching an entirely different person. Every word he says, every movement he makes, I second guess it all. He must sense something. His eyes keep flicking to mine, questioning. He's downloading information as fast as he can, Rylan borderline hysterical, grilling him on every detail.

"What's going to happen with his body?"

"I have to go back and make arrangements for the cremation," Garrett says.

"You have to ask Addy about next of kin. You can't just..." Her face crumples and she starts to cry.

Bola puts his arm around her awkwardly. "The police came earlier," he says to Garrett.

"I passed them on the road. How did that go?"

"Why don't you ask him," Bola says, giving me a sour look.

"You spoke to them?" Garrett asks me. "Did they ask who you were?"

Bola's eyes sharpen at the concern in Garrett's voice. "He didn't come find me like he was supposed to."

"I thought you were asleep," I say.

"Liar," Bola says.

"What did they want?" Garrett asks.

"Fuck the police," Rylan butts in. "We need to figure out who did this."

"Shhh," Garrett says.

"Don't fucking sshh me," she says, whacking his arm. "It's your plants that killed him."

"Hey, hey," Bola says. "Calm down. Now's not the time to be throwing accusations around."

"I'm so fucking sick of this place," Rylan says, slumping against the chair.

Garrett shoots her a dark look and asks me for the gist of what the cops said. When I'm done, he says to Bola, "We need to have an emergency meeting. Can you round everyone up? Seven pm. Everyone has to attend."

Rylan starts to cry again. "What's a meeting going to do? You think someone's going to stand up and..."

"Why is she crying?"

Our heads collectively spin towards Addy. She's chewing on a fingernail, her eyes widening when no one says anything. "Is he dead?" she asks, her voice barely a whisper.

"Like you even care," Rylan says, her voice acid.

Addy's face morphs into something rancid. "You are a grade A bitch. You don't deserve him."

Rylan jumps out of her chair, whizzes over and smacks Addy on the face so hard she almost tumbles to the floor. "And you do? Give me a break."

The morning was already a write off. In the blink of an eye, it turns into an episode of bad reality TV. With a cry, Addy lunges at Rylan and they crash to the ground, yelling and grabbing at each other. I've heard of catfights but never seen one and watch on the sideline, stunned. Garrett and Bola rise out of their chairs and circle around the women, waiting for the right moment to enter the line of fire. Bola lunges first and with a swift yank, pulls Addy to her feet. Garrett scoops Rylan up in a bear hug.

"Get off me," she yells, squirming in his arms. "And get her out of here. Him too," she spits at me.

Garrett tightens one arm around Rylan and fishes the SUV keys from his pocket. He throws them to me and says, "Can you take her back? I'll see you at the meeting."

Addy wrestles hard in Bola's grip. "Let me go. I want to go home."

"Outside," he says, pushing her towards the stairs. "Then I'll let you go."

"I'm not two years old," Addy shouts.

"Neither am I," Rylan says, and wrenches out of Garrett's grip. They're both breathing hard, like two boxers just finishing a round.

Rylan looks at me like I'm the plague. "What are you staring at? I told you to get out."

Garrett, face flushed, says, "We'll talk later, okay?"

I nod, mute, and head for the stairs, not sure I want to talk to him ever again.

Outside, Bola stuffs a cranky Addy into the front seat of the SUV and slams the door shut. As we pull away from Garrett's the heaviness lifts, and I can finally think. With my car keys materializing, Cassius dead and the police closing in, all the goalposts have moved.

It's time to come up with a new strategy.

THIRTY-FIVE

ADDY

MY FOCUS IS COMING BACK in the car, along with my energy. I'm still so tired. This was the longest dark period I've had and I need to sort myself out. I'm having trouble remembering and Cutie Pie won't shut up.

"Addy? Are you listening?"

"I am. I'm just thinking."

It's another one of those bright summer days, too bright for my mood.

"I'm sorry about Cassius," he says. "I know he was a jerk in some ways, but..."

"He was a jerk in every way, so don't be sorry," I interrupt.

He glances over, all cautious-like. Poor thing. Cassius was right. He is a pussy.

"Are you okay to talk?" he asks.

"About what?"

"Our plans. To leave."

Plans. What plans?

"Yeah, sure."

"Good" he says, relieved. "The police were here and they're coming back. We..."

"The police were here?"

"Yeah, a couple hours ago. That's why we need to talk. They're coming back with a warrant. They want to interview everyone."

Goddamn.

"Addy?" he asks.

"What?"

"You look...freaked out."

"It's all just a little much, right now."

"No shit. You could go to jail."

I pause, not sure I like where he's going with this. "Why would I go to jail?"

"C'mon Addy," he says, like I'm five years old. "Everyone knows how Cassius treated you."

"You think I killed him?"

"It doesn't matter what I think," he backpedals.

"It does to me."

"No," he says, after the smallest hesitation. "I don't think it was you."

"Then who do you think did it?"

"I don't know. Not for sure." But he has his suspicions. "All I know is we need to get out of here."

"How do you propose that?"

"I found my keys," he says, with emphasis.

I think that's good news.

"Oh. Do tell."

"Garrett had them the whole time."

That, I know, is bad news. I can hear it in his voice.

"I see."

He's silent the rest of the way, allowing me precious time to filter through the pieces. The other night Cassius was sick. I thought he was drunk at first and I knew what that meant. Where he was. But then he stopped talking. Or did he? And how did I get to Garrett's house? There was a storm, that's the last thing I recall.

Once we reach my cabin, Cutie Pie offers to help me inside and I shrug him away with annoyance. Does he think I can't walk? Then, as I open the door, he steps to the side, as if some boogey man is waiting for us.

Or an equivalent.

"Sweet baby Jesus. What happened here?" I ask, both the smell and the disarray in the entrance hall overwhelming.

"You don't remember?"

"Well, I course I remember," I lie. I have no recollection of any of it. "I just forgot how bad it really was."

Bad doesn't really cover it. I've never been the neatest thing on two legs yet this makes my skin crawl. It's like mother's room. I have to kick things out of the way just to carve a path to the kitchen.

"You want some tea?" I ask, keeping up appearances. "I've got peppermint or chamomile."

"Peppermint please."

I busy myself filling the kettle while he looks around like he's looking for something. His nervous energy makes me nervous.

"What's up?" I ask, putting the kettle on the stove.

"Do you remember what you guys ate the other night?"

"Regular stuff." I have no idea.

"And you feel okay?"

"I'm fine," I insist. "Just fine." Shoving dirty plates to one side, I make space for us to sit at the table. "So," I start. "Let's talk about the plan."

Galvanized with talk of action, he takes a deep breath. "I was thinking, now that I have the keys, we could just drive. At least get to the where you thought we should go."

I pause, my memory hitching. "Your car's been fixed?"

"No, it hasn't been fixed," he says and looks at me funny again. "But I have the keys now. You said you had connections. Where are they?"

"Of course," I say, my mind racing to fill in the blanks. "Colorado."

"Where in Colorado?"

Where?

"Durango." The home town of Pedro, bless his retarded wife.

"Is that close?"

"Close enough. North a couple hours."

"Okay. So all we need to do is get to the main highway. We can ditch the car, hitchhike from there."

Something about his keys flutters in the back of my mind.

"Why did Garrett have your keys?" I ask.

"It doesn't matter," he says brusquely. "I have them now. That's all that matters."

But there's real hurt on his face. He's devastated.

"It matters to me." I pause. Lean in. "Hey. What's going on?"

His big brown eyes are so lost when they find mine. "I think you might be right. About Garrett."

"About what?"

"But he's not that crazy, is he? I mean, killing someone...that's bad. And he uses those plants for the sessions, right? This could easily fall back on him. It doesn't make sense. Why would he put all of this at risk? It's his life."

Hold on. He's rambling like I'm not even here. He's rationalizing, struggling with something.

"Did you ever love Cassius?" he asks out of the blue.

"What does that have to do with anything?"

"I just wanted to know."

His misery is adorable in a sad, pathetic way, and that's when it hits me. It's the briefest of things, a speck, not even, in a dark corner of my memory. At the workshop. There was a fight. I saw something. What was it? The memory teases and fires something deep in my belly. Something old and painful. Before I can latch on to it, poof, it evaporates. My mind, always letting me down.

"Forget him," I say and put my hand on top of his. For once, he doesn't pull away. "What matters now is us. When are the police coming back?"

"They said a couple days."

"Okay, so we have time to get things together. At the meeting tonight, let's try and get as many details as we can."

He shakes his head with steeliness that surprises me. "I'm not going to the meeting."

"You think that's a good idea? We should probably act normal, like nothing's going on."

"I'll just say I'm not feeling well."

Now he looks like he's about to cry. I'd peg him to be a hundred and seventy pounds, mostly height, not weight, and he's usually so straight and rigid, but it's like he's carrying the world on those broad shoulders. Crushed. Time to suss this out. Slow and steady, I crouch down beside him and keep my voice gentle.

"I don't mind being your partner in crime, Damien, but I need to know what I'm getting into. What's going on?"

He starts to fidget distractedly with the ring on his finger and just like that, an empty space in my mind fills. The other night, how bad I wanted him. How he caved, like I knew he would. A swell of lust fires between my legs. I imagine that long finger deep inside me, making me scream in all sorts of ways. Part of me wants to fuck him right now, but I'm just not in a seducing mood.

"I've had some trouble," he finally says.

"No shit. I'm asking what kind." I search his eyes and find the fear. "You're running from something aren't you?"

He nods, barely. Bingo. I pat his knee in a motherly way. "You've heard all about my troubles," I say. "It's time for you to tell me yours."

THIRTY-SIX

DAMIEN

AFTER DROPPING Addy off at the meeting, my headspace is a strange brew. Back at the guest house, Diesel is curled up on the porch swing and jumps down to follow me inside. He watches with curious detachment as I yank all the curtains closed, dump a case of beer on the table and slump on the couch. I make quick work of six beers, my mood shifting with each bottle. First I'm pissed off, then, frustrated. I'm not sure what I feel when I crack beer seven.

Or when the front door opens and closes.

Bracing myself against the sudden chill, Garrett enters the living room, his eyes dark. They skip from me to the six empties on the table. "Party of one?" he asks.

"You're number two."

"That's a lot of beer."

"I don't have to drive."

"You missed the meeting."

I hold up the beer bottle. "I was busy."

"I wanted you to be there."

"Well, I wasn't."

He lowers himself into the armchair beside the couch. "Hey."

"What?"

"Look at me." I shift my eyes reluctantly and he leans forward, elbows on his knees. "We need to talk."

"Then talk."

After a pause, he says, "We need to sort this out."

"*This*, meaning?"

"You know what I mean," he says, an uncomfortable look on his face.

"No, I don't."

He drops his head and sighs. "Damien..."

"No. It's not *Damien*," I say, slamming the bottle onto the table. "It's not fucking Damien. It's over, okay? All of this shit." I dig the car keys out of my front pocket and rattle them in front of him. "These look familiar? We went out looking for these. You *pretended* to look for them when you had them the whole time."

He doesn't even look surprised. Instead, he pinches the skin between his eyes. "You have every right to be upset."

"Oh, thank you. Thank you for *allowing* me to be upset."

"I wanted to help you."

"Bullshit. Rylan was right. There's always a plan with you. We made a deal, but it was all lies from the start."

"I don't feel good about what I did."

"I don't think you feel *anything*. That's your problem. It's like this is all an experiment and you're the mad scientist. Sessions and drugs and powers you can't even control. This place is your own personal laboratory and you're detached from all of it. From everyone." I'm shouting, my own ferociousness unrecognizable. "Cassius is dead and you don't even care."

His head drops into his hands. After a few seconds, he slides his face up. "I do care...and there was a reason."

"Yeah? And what was that? To fuck with my head? So that you could feel better about yourself? You found someone more screwed up than you are?"

With a flash of anger, he says, "*You* told *me* you wanted to change things. You didn't want to spend the rest of your life burning shit down."

"Right. And what did that get me? I almost freaking died. Are you even aware of what's going on here? This whole goddamn place is falling apart. Cassius is dead. Dead! Someone *here* killed him."

"Don't change the subject."

"Oh right, we don't want to talk about people *dying*," I say, and throw my keys to the floor. "You're insane! What was the plan this whole time? Really. Tell me."

I cross my arms and glare at him with as much drunken bravado as I can muster. His hands clench and unclench. Finally,

"I wanted you to stay."

"Why? Or is this more of your underworld bullshit you haven't told me about?"

"Why is it all bullshit now?" he demands. "You're the one that wanted to do a session. I told you what could happen and you weren't honest with me either. I agreed because I wanted to help you."

"You know how you help? You don't lie. I'm sick of being lied to."

"Then why are you lying to yourself?"

It's just a moment, but in those few silent seconds the whole night tilts.

"Excuse me?"

"Of course it's easier to blame everyone else, isn't it?" he says, flinging his arm right to left. "Blame it on shrinks who can't figure you out. Blame me. Pretend nothing's wrong."

"Now you're trying to twist shit around? Make this my fault?"

But the dynamic has shifted, and he stands up, his voice hard. "Why *do* you light fires Damien? Tell me."

He takes a step towards me and my whole body starts to vibrate.

"What do you mean?" I ask, but I know full well what he means.

"You can't even say it," he says with disgust. "How is anyone supposed to help you?" He kicks at my keys on the floor. "And what would you have done if you *had* your keys? Drive away with no money, no plan, into the Colombian sunset? You're deluding yourself." He pulls his own keys out of his pocket and throws them onto the floor beside mine. "You think you know it all? There you go. Leave tonight and take the SUV. I'll tell Cedric to let you out."

He stalks out of the room and I'm momentarily stunned at the turn of events. I don't know what I was hoping for, but no way he's getting out of this, this easy.

"I'm delusional?" I shout, following him into the foyer. "You spent half an hour looking for keys that were in your goddamned office. You live here with jaguars and spirits and fucking unicorns running around."

"You're like everybody else," he says, yanking on his shoes. "Needy. Wanting something from me."

He tries to shoulder barge past me but I block him.

"I never asked you for anything. You asked me to trust you but you don't even trust yourself," I say, and my hands push on his chest, so hard he stumbles backwards.

"Don't," he warns.

"Don't what? I'm not one of your sheep. You can't tell me what to do."

I push him again, harder, but this time he's prepared, resists against me.

"I said don't."

"You're going to die here lonely and miserable with people you don't give a shit about," I yell, jabbing my finger on his chest in angry bursts. "The king of nothing. The truth is *you're* too fucking scared to change."

He grabs my hand, crushing it, and yanks me towards him. Tears swell in my eyes, and I know he can see them, he's that close, and I hate it.

"Go ahead," I say, ready for the hit. "What are you waiting for?"

"No..." he whispers, his whole body shaking. "I never wanted to hurt you."

Maybe it's the beer or the stress, I can't tell, but the hallway starts to compress and there's a pause that seems to go on forever and I want to sound brave and bold and sure of myself but I'm not sure of anything anymore so instead my voice sounds far away, not even part of me when I yank my hand out of his and tell him, "Too fucking late."

And as soon as I say that his eyes flare huge, like he's come face to face with some unimaginable thing, and the next few seconds are impossible, except they're not, because they happen.

He shoves me against the wall with something like fury, except it's deeper, scarier, and the drywall cracks beneath my spine, and his mouth presses against mine as he forces himself inside, his taste sweet, earthy, nothing like I imagined, and a million pulses of energy are crashing into me, his fingers rough, pushing down the front of my jeans, and in another lifetime only fire could bring me to my knees but his touch is like a bullet ripping through me and my legs buckle, I'm falling, and he catches me, pulls me up, and we stumble down the hall, an awkward dance of tangled legs and arms as we crash through the door onto the bed. Shirts, pants, everything is ripped off and we crack heads in the process, don't even care or slow down, and he's on top of me, kissing me, mauling me, out of control, and cool air ripples over my exposed skin but his hand is hot groping between my legs and even though I want him as much as he wants me I can't stop my body from tensing.

His hand pulls away and all I can hear is ragged breathing, mine or his, maybe both, and I want to tell him so many things, things I've never told anyone, but nothing comes out, only a strangled sound, and his lips brush against my forehead, his voice barely a whisper when he says he isn't going to hurt me, and he doesn't mean it *that* way, he means it the way I need it to be, and because of that, I submit, and the bed melts away into a dark ocean of rhythm and swells, riptides pulling me under and I'm sinking, dissolving, like salt in water, I can't tell which way is up, and if I didn't know how to swim, I swear, this is what it must feel like to drown.

THIRTY-SEVEN

"HOW OLD ARE YOU?" Andrew asks.

"Ten."

"Have you ever done it?"

"No."

"You can still do it at ten," he says and hands me a canning jar filled with gin he swiped from downstairs. "If you wanted to."

We're in the third-floor attic bedroom, my room, sitting on the floor. His face is red and shiny, like mine. Under the sloped roof, two skylights are cranked wide and offer no relief. The air conditioning in the villa conked out two days ago and Dad kept going on about useless wops, until mom, with a nervous look at Andrew's parents, Ezra and Marion, corrected him, and said Italians, sweetheart, Italians. This trip is for Dad and Ezra to spend time together because Ezra has contacts in Asia. Contacts Dad wants.

I take a sip of the gin and cringe. "Have you done it?"

"Of course," he says. "Lots. The girls in New Jersey are all sluts." He shrugs with indifference. Andrew is fourteen and can speak Hebrew; wants to be a dentist. "Kind of takes all the fun out of it."

"How is it?"

"Amazing." He smiles at some memory and leans back against the bed. "But I'm tired of trying to figure out girls. Too much work."

His girlfriend, Ella, called last week and it sounded like they were fighting. After, we played in the shed at the back of the yard. We burnt ants with an old magnifying glass, carved bad words - fuck, shit, tits - into a rotten patch of the wall, laughed ourselves into bellyaches when Andrew peed on a spider. We didn't touch the container of gasoline in the corner. Maybe it was the flash of red my brain silently registered. Filed for the future.

"It's way too hot in here, man," he says, and pulls off his t-shirt, tossing it into the corner. His skin is brown and smooth. He drapes an arm around my shoulder, draws lazy circles on my skin with his finger. "That's better, right?"

"What are you doing?" I ask with a nervous laugh.

"C'mon, Damien," he says, dropping his head closer to mine. "I saw you watching me."

I tried not to watch. How his wet shorts clung to him when he came out of the pool. He takes my hand and moves it between his legs, holds it when I try and pull away. "It's okay," he whispers. "I'm just like you."

I want to be like him: tanned, confident. Not beat up in gym class or after school because I was looking where I shouldn't.

"Relax," he says. "Just close your eyes."

His mouth skims over mine and I start to shake. He pulls back, crystal-clear blue eyes peeking out from under blonde bangs. "Did you like that?"

"Yeah..." I say, trying to swallow.

"Are you scared?"

"No," I lie.

He kisses me again and his tongue is strange and wet, searching in my mouth. He starts to fumble with the waistband of my shorts. Beneath my hand, he's swollen and it's like everything in my brain stops working, until Marion's drunken laughter drifts up from the pool.

"Wait. Wait," I say, pushing him away. "Lock the door."

"Don't worry. They're all downstairs." He shoves me onto the rug with a wicked smile. "They can't hear us if we're quiet."

With slow, small tugs, he pulls my shorts off and stares at me for so long, I cover myself, embarrassed.

"No, don't." He pulls my hand away and runs his finger down my chest. It circles around my belly button then drifts lower. "I wanted you since the day I got here. Do you want me?"

I won't remember saying yes, or him pulling off his shorts, lying on top of me, or my head banging against the night table, the crash of the lamp as it falls. All I'll remember is Andrew wrenched off me and Ezra yelling, "What the fuck is going on?"

Skittering up against the bed, Andrew, pale, no longer confident says, "It was his idea. He wanted to try."

"That's not true," I say, scrambling to sit. "I didn't start it."

Ezra's eyes are thin little blades cutting into me. "You're saying my son is a homosexual? He's got a girlfriend, don't you, Andrew?" Andrew nods like a bobble head. "Go to your room," Ezra barks. "Now!"

Andrew grabs his shorts and bolts out the door. I'll never see him again.

Ezra yanks the blanket off the bed and tosses it at me with disgust. "Cover yourself for Christ's sake."

"But...he wanted to."

He crouches down, the six pointed star on his necklace tangled in chest hair. "Let me tell you something, kid," he starts, then notices the overturned jar. He picks it up, sniffs it and shakes his head. "Drinking at ten? Well, that seems to be the least of your problems, you faggot." He jabs a finger on my chest, his breath dirty from cigars. "If you say one word about this to anyone I'm going to chop your dink off. Do you understand?"

Petrified, I just nod.

He stands up and wobbles, his fake hair slipping to one side. "Your dad was right, you know. There's something wrong with you."

The door slams behind him and from downstairs a spray of voices rises; falls. Mom comes up and knocks on the locked door, asks me to let her in. I tell her to go away. At 2 am, when all the noise stops, I sneak to the bathroom, pee, and race back, forgetting to lock the door.

I've just drifted into sleep when the door squeaks open. It's Mom, I think, at first. I don't want to talk to her. She never helps. But the floorboards creak in a different way. I can smell gin, cigars. The mattress sinks and groans with the weight of another body. My muscles lock up. If I don't breathe, maybe he'll go away. Maybe...

A hand gropes under the covers, flips me over and pushes my face deep into the pillow. I try to scream but the hand pushes harder on the back of my head. A knee forces my leg apart.

"Shut up you little bastard. Don't make this worse."

The next morning I forget about the puddle of green beside the bed. My foot squishes into it and I almost throw up again. Using a t-shirt to wipe up the mess, all I can think about is getting out of here. After a long shower, I stare out the bathroom window, looking down at the pool. If I could jump I would.

Downstairs, Mom and Dad are at the kitchen table drinking coffee from tiny cups. Mom perks up when she sees me. "Morning sleepyhead."

Dad flips through the newspaper in front of him and I can tell he's not reading anything. He's like a black hole sucking all the light out of the morning. The villa is quiet; too quiet.

"Where is everyone?" I ask.

"Andrew and his parents left early this morning," Mom says carefully. "They had a family emergency."

"Are they coming back?"

"I don't think so, honeybun."

Flies buzz around a bowl of spoiled fruit on the table. Leaning against it is a package of Ezra's cigars. A matchbook with blue lettering - La Nazione - is tucked in front. Mom nudges Dad under the table with her leg. He folds the paper in half, pressing hard on the crease.

"Mr. Ballantine was very important for my business," he says in his calm voice; the one that means he isn't happy. "The whole reason we came here was so we could get to know each other. They were quite upset."

"Were they upset because of their emergency?"

In the sunlight, the skin around Mom's eye is red, starting to swell. She stands up slowly and gives me a kiss on the cheek. "It's alright honeybun. You come out to the pool after breakfast, okay? This afternoon we'll do whatever you want." Before she leaves, she squeezes Dad's arm. "Franklin. Don't be too hard on him."

When the sound of her high heels fades, Dad pats the table. "Come here, Damien."

"Am I in trouble?"

"Do you think you should be in trouble?"

"I dunno."

"I think you do know."

He crooks his finger and wiggles it towards him. I inch forward, but it's like I'm looking at him through the wrong end of a telescope. He's smaller, far away. Or maybe it's my imagination.

"The Ballantine's left because of you," he says. "Millions of dollars down the drain because of you. Do you deserve to be punished?"

"Yes?"

"That's right," he says and grabs both of my arms, yanking me towards him. "And millions of dollars is worth how much punishment?"

"A lot?"

His manicured fingers dig deeper, cutting off the blood in my arms. "You're a little bastard aren't you?"

"I, I don't know what you mean."

"Trust me, you're a little bastard. Say it."

"Why?" I ask, blinking back tears.

"Because you are one." He shakes me hard, like I'm covered in dust and he wants to get rid of it. "Say it."

"I don't want to."

"Say it!" he shouts.

My chin trembles, tears spilling down in streams. "I'm a little bastard."

"For Christ's sake, don't cry like a baby," he says, flinging my arms away with disgust. "If you want things to be better, you take your punishment like a man. You don't go to Mom, you don't tell anyone. Not this time, or the next time. Do you understand?"

"Yes," I say, the memory of my shower this morning vivid, the hot water running cold and still not feeling clean.

His dark eyes flash and he grabs Ezra's cigars. "Here," he says, forcing them into my hand. "Keep these as a memento." He unfolds the newspaper and flattens it out. Raising his coffee cup, he takes a sip, waves his other hand and says, "Go find your mother."

"Jesus Christ," Dad yells. "What the hell are you doing?"

The cypress tree, one of ten lining the driveway, is a giant orange matchstick. He yanks frantically on a hose and starts to spray the tree. "You little shit. How am I going to explain a goddamned burnt tree?"

Mom comes running out the front door in her bathing suit, a towel wrapped around her. I'm sprawled on the gravel, the red jerry can and Ezra's matches beside me. She rushes over and kneels beside me. "Are you ok?"

"Go back inside Gwen," Dad says.

Her eyes dart back and forth between the fire and me. She squints at the pile of fabric smoldering at the base of the tree. When she realizes it's my bed sheet, the color drains out of her face. She covers her mouth like she's about to be sick. He keeps spraying. Doesn't even look at her.

"I said get inside Gwen."

THIRTY-EIGHT

I DUMP the rest of my coffee in the sink, not hungry, not thirsty. From the kitchen window, I can see his house, the empty slot where his truck should be. Empty, like the bed this morning. I knew he was gone, even before I reached over. There's a certain sound to a room when you're the only person in it.

Diesel meows and winds between my legs, a welcome distraction.

"C'mon, buddy," I say, and scoop him up. "I got nothing. You need to eat."

His warm fur is comforting and I hug him tight, thinking how I got it all wrong last night. How my heart sank when little tremors shook the bed after. That I couldn't believe Garrett was laughing, of all things, and I couldn't even talk, just lay there, my mind blank and full of a million things, all at the same time, and I didn't resist when he pushed me onto my side, rolled me like a log, happy for the dark room, because anything was better than seeing regret in his eyes.

I waited for him to say it was all a mistake, I was a mistake, and I wanted to scream, to run and get away, but there was nowhere to go and I almost forgot how to breathe until he slipped behind me and his arm draped over top. He pulled me close and buried his head in my back. Only when his hot tears slid onto my skin, his body shuddering against mine, did I realize my mistake. He wasn't laughing at all.

When his body finally stilled, I wrapped my arm tentatively over his. We lay in the dark, both of us silent, me trying to understand how it was possible to feel so alive yet so exposed. When I finally drifted into sleep, I couldn't tell the difference between his heartbeat and mine.

Today, of all mornings, I don't want to be alone.

Out on the porch, it's muggy. The hot sun bakes the wetness from the rains out of the ground. Diesel's pink nose sniffs the air and I scratch his belly. "What do you smell, huh?"

"So he stayed with you last night."

I spin around, startled, and Diesel wiggles out of my grip, bolts down the stairs.

"I was wondering what happened to him," Rylan says, pushing the porch bench back and forth with a sandaled foot.

"Hi," I say. "I was about to come up."

"You're too late. Garrett's gone."

"Gone where?"

"To town."

I clear my throat. "You want a cup of coffee or something?"

"Really," she laughs. "And what on earth would we talk about? The weather?" She continues, as if she didn't expect a reply. "You weren't at the meeting last night."

"I wasn't feeling well."

"Interesting," she says. "And Garrett didn't get in until three a.m."

"I..."

"Shut up." Her foot slams down, the bench coming to an abrupt halt. "Bola said he caught you sneaking around downstairs yesterday. What were you looking for?"

"A piece of paper. The police wanted a list of names and..."

"Who put you in charge anyway?" she interrupts.

"I was only trying to help."

"Don't," she says, her voice gritty. "Just don't."

"Don't what?"

"Stupid doesn't suit you, Damien, so don't pretend you don't know what I'm talking about. You think you can just waltz in here and everything changes?"

"I'm not..."

"What do you think is really going on?"

"I don't understand."

"Bringing you here, all this," she says, with an irritated wave of her hand. "You think this is all going to be a happy ending? Sorry to burst your bubble sweetheart. He's just using you."

"You're wrong."

"You believe what you want to believe."

"If he's such a bad person, why have you hung around?"

"Fuck you."

My hands clench in my pockets. "He doesn't love you."

"God, you're pathetic," she says, laughing rudely. "I've known Garrett for ten years, a hell of a lot longer than you. He's always two steps ahead of everyone, trust me. Why do you think he killed Cassius?"

"Why do you keep saying he did it? Why would Garrett kill him? He saved his life."

"Saved?" she asks, standing up. "Why do you think he let that slut and Cassius in here in the first place? Because he has a heart of gold? Cassius was a guinea pig. A test. Garrett was bored and that's what you don't understand. You're so fucking desperate you can't see. He doesn't love you. He can't love anybody. He doesn't know how. All he wants is to be able to do what he wants, when he wants, and not answer to anybody. Why do you think he's even here? Because he loves the Apaches? No, he's here because he has something no else has, and for a megalomaniac who thinks he's God it's a fucking wet dream."

"They wouldn't have all moved here if they thought he was a scam," I say, not quite sure of my own words.

"Of course not. They believed he would use it the way it should be used. He *promised* them. But he's a liar."

"Addy had the most motive," I say. "Everyone knows how Cassius treated her. And I saw her in the greenhouse, in Garrett's greenhouse. She was cutting plants."

"When?" she asks, crossing her arms.

"When I first got here."

"You're full of it."

"I did. I swear."

Her eyes are narrow, ringed in red. "I don't owe you any favors, in fact, I don't owe you shit, but I know you had nothing to do with this and neither did Addy. This is all Garrett. But Bola wants to string you up and if you stay here, I can't guarantee what the outcome will be."

"You just want me to leave."

"Yeah, I do actually, but not for...."

Rylan clutches her stomach and a little groan escapes. Eyes wide, she brings her hand to her mouth, stumbles over to the railing, leans over and pukes.

"Jesus." I rush over. "Are you okay?"

She pushes me away with surprising force, catches her breath.

"We need to get you to the hospital," I say, the wave of uncertainty nothing compared to the tsunami that's about to hit. "What if you've been poisoned too?"

"I haven't been poisoned you idiot," she says. "I'm pregnant."

THIRTY-NINE

AFTER RYLAN LEAVES, I second-guess everything. Third-guess if that's even an option. Every conversation I imagine doesn't end well. I skip the shop and JD pops by with some lunch. She's worried and refuses to leave until I talk to her.

"I don't know what to believe right now," she says. Both of our sandwiches sit on the porch bench, half eaten. "Garrett was acting funny before you showed up, but so was Rylan."

"What about Addy?" I ask.

"Well, you saw in the short time. Cassius was such a turd. They were mismatched from the get go. I just can't see Addy being a killer, though. She's troubled, I don't deny that. Who wouldn't be with Cassius? But she's too sweet in my books." She glances over, a guilty look on her face. "I'll be honest with you only because I know I can be. I don't mind that he's gone, not one bit."

"Does every woman here need to follow the rules, about the abortions?"

Her brow crinkles. "Where did that come from?"

"Just wondering. Everyone's been together for so long. Mistakes happen," I say, as if I know.

"You know I don't agree with the abortions, but mistake or not, it's the one thing he's never compromised on."

"So even Rylan would need to get one."

She cocks her head. "Is there something you're not telling me?"

"No. I just never really knew what the deal was."

"It's Addy, right?" she asks, after a beat. "You have your eye on her."

"No, no, no. It's nothing like that. Forget it. I don't know why I asked."

"Drat," she says, and smiles. "Well, I won't lie. I was kind of hoping if you were in that way, it would've been with me." She laughs and it's enough, barely, to put us in a mood good enough to finish our sandwiches.

But its still hours until he shows up. Night has started to fall. I'm crashed in a deck chair on the back patio when the sliding glass door opens.

"Hi," I say, sitting up. Christ, just seeing him...

"Hi."

He has a few days' growth on his face and I like him better with it. After an awkward few seconds, I ask, "How'd it go?"

He nods his head towards the house. "Let's talk inside."

It's still a hundred degrees in the living room, a wall of heat. He sits on the couch, leaving a cautious distance between us.

"I had to deal with some things this morning," he finally says.

"I get it."

"I didn't want to leave."

"I get it."

He breaks off my glance and looks into space. "They've confirmed it was belladonna."

"Is that one of your plants?"

"Unfortunately."

"What are we going to do?"

"The police will be here in a couple of days with the warrant." His hands knit together in a tight grip. "You can't be here."

I sit taller. "Where will I be?"

"Take the truck," he says, like he's already thought this through. "I'll give you a bunch of cash. You'll have to try and make it on your own."

"What? You can't stay," I say, my voice rising. "You can't trust her. She thinks you did it. She...."

"Woah, woah, woah," he interrupts, hands up. "Whose she?"

"You haven't talked to Rylan yet?"

"No. Why?" he asks, immediately alert. "What happened?"

"She knows," I say, and pause. "About us."

"What did you say?"

"Nothing. But she said you killed Cassius." I swallow hard. "And she said she's pregnant."

The total silence almost kills me. Then he shrugs, matter-of-fact.

"You know?" I ask.

"Of course."

"You don't care?"

"Maybe I would if it was mine."

I'm momentarily confused, before it all hits me. "Cassius?"

"Yep."

"You're sure?"

"You can't make a baby without sex."

"But, I mean, if you knew..." I pause, the energy in the room different...layered. "That's motive."

He looks at me in a strange, calm way. "Do you think I killed him?"

"No. But if it's one of your plants, and the baby..." I stand up so quick I get a head rush. "You could go to jail."

"I know," he says, suddenly terse. "That's why if you're gone at least you have a chance. I'll take the plates off your car, scrape off the VIN..." He lists all these things off on his fingers.

"No," I say, my voice thick. Yesterday I couldn't leave here fast enough, alone. After last night, everything is different. "We need to go together."

In the coiled silence he drops his head back and stares at the ceiling. "I can't leave here," he finally says. "Like this."

"Like how?" I ask and the swell in my throat is like a hundred bee stings. "Like how? Tell me."

He raises his head and looks right at me. "With loose ends."

By the way he says it I can feel something tighten in my chest. A ripple of understanding passes between us.

"I need to know I can trust you," he says.

"You can trust me."

"For sure?"

"I mean it. I swear."

"So you believe me?"

He was willing to sacrifice himself to save me. That says it all. What was I even thinking that he had anything to do with this? It's Rylan trying to deceive, to get me out of here. Addy: pouncing on my weaknesses, to save herself.

And as if on cue, we hear a voice shouting outside.

"Damien!"

Garrett rises from the couch with a questioning look.

"I know you're in there," Addy says, banging on the front door. "I can see lights on."

"What's she doing here?" he whispers.

"C'mon," she urges, rattling the doorknob. "Do I need to break down the door?"

"You have to let her in," he says.

"Are you nuts?"

"Go," he says, nudging me. "I'll stay in the bedroom."

"Hold on," I call out, trying to think straight. Of all the bad scenarios I could have envisioned, this is number one. We edge down the hall and I motion for Garrett to lock the bedroom door behind him. Once he's inside I run my hands through my hair.

Calm down. Breathe.

I open the door just a sliver. "What's up?"

"Well, hello to you too." She nudges the door with the toe of her sneaker, narrows her eyes at the resistance. "Are you going to let me in?"

"What do you want?"

"Are you on crack? Why do you think I'm here?"

Her voice echoes loudly in the hall. Too loud. I glance back at the bedroom. At that moment, she shoves the door open and pushes past me, twists out of my reach when I try to nab her.

"Hey," I say. "You can't just barge in." I grab her wrist and she yanks out of my grip.

"Simmer down. No one saw me come here."

"Are you sure?"

"Yes, I'm sure. What do you think this is, amateur hour?"

I would pay a million dollars right now for her to leave. Maybe two. It must show on my face.

"You're acting strange. Why?"

"I'm fine. Well, maybe I'm nervous."

"Relax," she says. "I have some good news."

"What?"

"Last night, I couldn't sleep. I went down to the security gate, early, like at 4 a.m. He kept telling us there's someone there twenty-four hours, but this morning..." She grins. "No one was there."

"Uh huh," I say.

"Don't sound so excited," she says, dryly.

"I mean, it's great, it's good," I say, a bit desperate. I motion again for us to move into the kitchen but she shuffles down only a couple of inches. "But, uh, how do you know it's not a one-off?"

"I thought of that, obviously, so I'm going to check again tonight. If it's the same deal, that only helps our cause."

"Okay."

She cocks her head. "Why are you whispering?"

"I'm not."

"Yes, you are. What's going on with you? It's like we've never had this conversation."

"Sorry...I'm just...stressed."

She smiles, like she was waiting for that answer. "I know you. All worked up. No place to go." She walks me right up against the wall. "How about we do it on a bed this time? Linger a while."

"I don't think that's a good idea right now."

"Why not?"

She pushes closer and I put my hands up between us. "Addy, c'mon."

"What?" she asks, laughing. "If I recall, you enjoyed yourself the other night. It was a world's record in enjoyment."

Her hand slips under my shirt and my reaction is the same as it was that warm March night in Griffith Park, when Lorelei insisted we could see the stars. I dozed off on the grass, sleepy after the movie. She knew better, or I thought she did. After, she cried, her body a tight ball in the dark. The bruise on her arm lingered for over two weeks. The thought of being just like *him* has never left. It makes me sick.

"Ow! What the hell?"

"I'm sorry," I say. "I just need you to...I just need to be by myself right now."

She inspects her arm for damage, a hurt look on her face. "You said you'd never hit a girl."

"I didn't hit you."

"You grabbed me. Violently."

"I didn't mean to. I didn't mean to hurt you. I'm just...a little edgy."

"Yeah, well, so am I," she says with a pout. "I'm trying to find ways to take the edge *off*."

"I know you are, Addy. It's crazy what's going on and I'm sorry for hurting you. Really." And I am.

"I accept your apology only because I know you're out of sorts."

"Thank you," I say, and squeeze her hand just to be safe. "Let's go into the kitchen. I need some water."

Finally she moves. In the kitchen, I gulp down two glasses of water and wipe my mouth. "So, what's the plan?"

"The plan is we bash that fucking gate down. I mean, we're dumping your car anyway so who cares right?"

"You think the car is strong enough?"

"If not, we take out the hut. Cedric is collateral damage."

"But we're not going to kill him."

"Only if we have to."

I can feel the color drain out of my face. "I don't want to kill anyone."

"Don't be such a pussy, Damien. It's him or us. Survival of the fittest."

"Okay," I say, surprised at how tough she sounds.

"You sure?" she asks, skeptically.

"Positive."

"How much money you have now?"

"Around $2,500."

"So we have about $3,500 in total. That should be enough. If you're ready, we could do it this morning."

"Uh...I don't think I'm ready."

"What do you have to do? Pack?" She laughs at her own joke. "I'm not quite ready either, but you better find your resolve quick, because after tomorrow is the next day and that's when we go for sure."

"I'll be ready. I promise. But I should get some sleep. Can we, uh, call it a night?"

"You are one strange boy, Damien," she says. "I know you need me and keep putting me off. It's not healthy, you know? A man has to have release or he gets squirrelly."

Shut up. Please.

"It'll happen. Once we're out of here, I'll feel better."

She smiles. "A lady should never say these things, but I'm looking *very* forward to our next encounter." Parting my hair to one side, she says, "Get your beauty rest, okay? I'll come by tomorrow with news about the gate."

On our way back to the front door, it's impossible to concentrate.

We're almost there when she turns and says, "Oh, one more thing..." before stumbling and pitching.

"You alright?" I ask, steadying her with my arm.

We both look down and in the dim light nothings clear, except the bright orange of Garrett's shoelaces. My blood curdles. Addy's head whips around to scan the hall. She lingers on the bedroom door. It's now open, just a crack. "We're still doing this, right?" she asks, her voice different, slower.

"Of course," I say, and pretend all my insides aren't pooling onto the floor.

"Why did you lock your front door?"

"LA habit, I guess."

I can feel her mind racing; see the uncertainty in her eyes. She unlocks the door slowly and steps outside. Moths bash around the coiled light bulb overhead. She turns to face me and the light casts an ominous green glow on half of her face.

"Don't let me down, Damien. You don't want to see me when I'm mad."

When she's gone, I collapse against the door, the worst taste in my mouth. Walking down the hall to the bedroom is like walking to my own execution. Garrett sits on the edge of the bed, barefoot. His hands are pressed down hard against the mattress, triceps ripped. When he finally looks up, out of his curtain of hair, his face is creased with anger and something else.

Hurt.

"What the fuck was that all about?"

I tell him everything.

When I get to what happened in the bathroom, his expression is pained. I tell him that it was after the session, that I didn't know what was going on, that I was drunk. When he points out that I was drunk yesterday too, his eyes are flat and bewildered. "You just told me I could trust you."

"You can," I say, frustrated at him for not understanding, and at myself, for screwing things up. "I'll prove it. I'll just tell her I changed my mind." Then, desperate for any solution, "Or why not let her leave? That would solve everything."

"Because you told her why you're here. She won't keep quiet." He leans back and swoops an agitated hand through his hair. "Fuck, now I have to rethink this. We don't have a lot of time."

When he says 'we', the smallest sliver of hope creeps back in. The session blew us both up like a 5,000-piece puzzle dumped on the floor, and maybe he realizes this, because the flash of his anger disappears when I tell him I'm sorry. But the silence is long and tense before he speaks again. "I have an idea but I need to know for sure I can trust you."

"You can," I tell him. "I promise."

"You're not going to like it."

"Why not?" I ask, the pressure at the back of my head roaring back, after it had just disappeared.

The next few minutes are torture. The only way I can process what he's telling me is to pretend it's not real, that it won't involve me.

The mood after is somber and requires beer. It requires eighty shooters of vodka. We've moved to the kitchen and four empties are on the table between us; about the same number of words we've said to each other. Both of us are so lost in thought, when the front door bangs open we jump in our chairs. Rylan storms in and glances at Garrett's bare feet, then mine, as if being sockless was some kind of crime.

"Sorry to spoil the party," she says with a tight smile.

"What's up?" Garrett asks, like he was expecting her.

"You've been gone all day."

"I just got back."

"Bullshit. You've been here for more than an hour."

"You're spying on me now?"

"Right," she scoffs. "Of course you think it's all about you." Her tone shifts into accusation. "I saw Addy come over. Since when are you two pals?"

"We're not. She wanted to talk to Damien."

Rylan shoots me a dirty look. "Really? About what?"

I start to edge out of my chair, but Garrett grabs my arm. "You're not leaving."

"Do you think I *deserve* to know what's going on?" Rylan asks Garrett. "Or wait, I forgot. Caring is beyond your comprehension, isn't it? Unless it benefits you."

"Are we really going to have a discussion about caring?"

"I was stupid enough to care. To think *you* might care, one day."

"Is that why you fucked Cassius?" he asks with disdain. "To get me to care?"

Rylan's face reddens, all her features sinking.

"What?" He laughs and leans back in the chair, his arm draped casually over top. "You didn't think I knew?"

"I never wanted it that way," she says.

"What way did you want it? And when did you plan to tell me about..." he nods at her stomach, "that thing? You know the rules."

"Rules?" She bristles. "Give me a break. They're your own fucking traumas you force on everyone else. Mommy aborted the brother you wanted, so..."

"Enough," he says, holding up his hand.

"No, it's not 'enough', it's not 'we're done'. You can't cope, so you spread the misery. That's always been your way. I'm not giving this one up." Fired up, she turns to me and unleashes. "Did he tell you about his dad? How he screwed investors, my family, his own family. Then Mommy turns on both of them. But you had a way of getting back didn't you?" she asks, her attention back on Garrett. "The chickens come home..."

"Enough!" he yells, so loud, the can of instant coffee rattles on the countertop.

Rylan gazes in my direction without really looking at me. "I *always* knew," she finally says, her voice wavering.

"Don't," he warns and stands.

"Suicide my ass. She had immunity. You got away with it. I *lied* for you."

I glance nervously at Garrett. His hands have tightened into fists.

"I was cleared of any charges," he says with a weird tone.

"On paper."

"Paper is what matters."

"I told him this was all you," she continues, gesturing at me. "I'm sure you've tried to convince him otherwise."

"Hey. I don't know..." I start.

"What's there to convince?" Garrett asks, cutting me off. "Cassius beat Addy, cheated on her. You know she's not quite alright up here," he says, tapping his head. "I'd say it doesn't look good for her."

"You're going to let an innocent person take the fall?"

"She's not so innocent."

"Just because your parents screwed you over doesn't mean you have to follow in their footsteps."

He inhales sharply, and Rylan backs up towards me, as if I'm some kind of protection.

"You knew what was going on. That's why you killed him. That's how you deal with shit you can't handle. You destroy it. Like us." The way she looks at Garrett, if a live grenade were thrown in the room right now it might almost be better. "We can't go back after this and you know it, so just tell me the truth. Was my testimony worth it? Worth all this?"

"It was for me," he says after an uneasy silence.

A single tear spills down her cheek. "Fuck you," she whispers.

"You came here for news, right?" he continues, brutal, efficient. "The police will be here with the warrant tomorrow at six. That's the news."

She hesitates. "And you told Addy this?"

"I'm telling everyone tomorrow. There's a meeting at five. He'll be gone before then."

Rylan's eyes skip back and forth between Garrett and me as if she senses something's not right. "After all this, he's just going to leave," she states.

"Isn't that what you wanted?"

"You never cared about what I wanted."

A small line creases his forehead. He stares at her, unblinking. Finally he says, "Let's go." And as he passes me, "I'll find you tomorrow."

The front door slams and Rylan slumps against the wall. The air is thick with defeat. My mind is reeling as her eyes skirt the kitchen, like she's trying to recall memories. Of the meals she cooked in here, the times they shared. There was a surreal-ness to the discussion Garrett and I had earlier, like it was an idea for a movie or TV show we'd never make. Now, seeing Rylan's broken frame, the fragility of her, with the enormity of what's going to happen, is like a punch to the gut.

Her eyes are dead, no emotion when they find mine. "He liked boys even back at Princeton," she says. "He was just too chicken shit to do anything about it. Don't think you're anything special."

"I'm sorry Rylan," is all I can say.

She pushes off the wall with a look of disgust. "No, you're not. Neither is he."

FORTY

ADDY

BETRAYAL IS the worst kind of wrongdoing. It's sneaky and dishonest. Worst of all, you never see it coming.

Why I thought Cutie Pie was going to be any different I don't know, but I can only blame myself. At some point I have to live up to my own flaws and see why I've made the same mistakes over and over. Why my luck with men always runs out. I've spent the past hour thinking long and hard about this. Some might call this 'seeing the light'. For me, it's pure redemption. Recognizing my sins. With the Good Lord as my witness today, here on and forever after, I will never trust another man as long as I live.

The trouble is, I have always believed that as a woman you stand by your man. You do everything in your power, especially with the female powers, to keep your man happy. If you keep him satisfied, he will stay. He will treat you kindly. But what I learned years ago, on that fateful Sunday, what I've just re-learned, is that you can have every power under the sun as a woman and it might not be enough.

On the Sunday before Daddy left for good, I didn't suspect a thing. We attended church and headed to the diner for our usual burgers, fries and milkshakes. (Veronica and Violet had stopped coming to church months before. They flat out told me their souls didn't need saving, but I knew what it really was: a line in the sand. I was on Daddy's side; they were on Mother's. Daddy didn't seem to mind. I was always his favorite.)

As we sipped our milkshakes, he asked me about the sermon we'd just heard. He knew I was smart and always wanted to hear what I liked about a sermon or what I thought the message was. I was never wrong in my answers. But the sermon that day was tricky.

"What did you think of his advice, that you can't stop a bird from landing on your head, but you can stop it from nesting?" he asked me.

"Well, I'm not sure I understood the example," I said honestly.

"I'll tell you little V." (Little V was his nickname for me.) "It means you have the power to control your life. A bird may land on your head, but if you don't want it there, you can shoo it away before it makes a nest."

"So if I let a bird make a nest on my head, I'm letting the bird be in control?"

"That's right," he said. "Now that's always easier said than done, and we don't always have control. Or we think we do, but when a bird lands, we might decide we like it and let it stay, and then we change. Now we have a nest."

"Oh, I get it now," I said, just as the busboy came to take our plates away.

He was probably sixteen, a fierce rage of acne masking his decent looks. His nametag said Arnold. After stacking our plates into his bus tub, Arnold wiped our table with determination. I picked up my milkshake glass so he could clean underneath it, and his eyes fell on the top part of my dress, where I was nice and developed. He looked away when I caught his eye and glanced nervously over at Daddy, who kept his hands very still in his lap, like he was praying.

Just before he left, Daddy reached out and grabbed his arm. It was an uncomfortable moment: Daddy's hand clamped on a stranger in the diner, where every Tom Fool could see. Arnold looked worried, like he was going to be reprimanded. Daddy fished out a neatly folded ten-dollar bill from his wallet and tucked it into Arnold's hand, wrapping his own around it.

"You're doing a good job."

I could tell Arnold had never seen that much money in his life. Hell, we never had an allowance worth that much. I was shocked Daddy would be so cavalier with money he always told me to be so careful with. When he winked at me, I didn't understand. Not trusting the moment, thinking that Daddy might change his mind, Arnold pocketed the bill, smiled at both of us.

"Thanks mister," he said and hustled back to the kitchen with his good fortune.

This was the moment when it all changed.

Everyone thinks its patterns in behavior that help predict what people will do, when it's the unpredictable actions, the one-offs, that let you see their true weaknesses.

Daddy's eyes were no longer on me. He was watching the departing derriere of Arnold all the way down the aisle, a dreamy but strained look on his face. That's when I knew. I heard stories of men and women cavorting with their own kind, and the thought had always repulsed me. The Good Lord said it wasn't right. It's not how we were designed. But when Daddy looked back at me, I knew. And he knew I knew. The ceiling fan chugged above us, spreading the hot air, the thick smell of bacon grease. He got up to pay the bill and never said goodbye. I never saw him again.

Whenever I dream of Daddy, it's always that day in the diner. The day he broke my heart. The look in his eyes. The look of betrayal.

And now, in my kitchen, it hits me like a ton of bricks.

The mug slips out of my hand and shatters on the floor.

How did I ever miss it?

The workshop. The fight. Cutie Pie with his shirt off. The strain on Garrett's face; the *restraint.* Just like Daddy's.

Like a hot flash, I burn from the inside out.

Cutie Pie is not only a sinner like Daddy was; he's a double-crossing motherfucker. He isn't going to leave with me. He's been corrupted. The thought of Garrett and him together makes me ill.

Numb with anger, I sweep up the remains of the mug and dump the broken crockery into the garbage. Instead of falling heavy, the pieces tinkle merrily on something solid. Underneath the coffee grounds and remains of lettuce, there's an empty wine bottle. I pull it out, my mind spooling. I never developed a taste for wine. It clings to the sides of my throat like a virus. But I know wine. Syrah is thick and red, like blood. This bottle is expensive and can only mean one thing. Little Ms. Fancy Pants, that wine-drinking bitch. Did they have the nerve to drink and cavort in here?

Dear Lord, give me strength. Right now, I don't know who I hate the most. I only know one thing: Garrett's an abomination. There is no absolution for his kind of evil. He needs to be stopped.

A knock at the front door almost brings on a seizure. Who the hell is this? I toss the bottle back into the garbage and edge the microwave forward. My fingers cup the worn handle of the shank, as lovingly as a mother touching her child.

When I open the door, I'm shocked, but smart enough to hide it. They ask to come in and I say sure, because this has got to be good.

FORTY-ONE

DAMIEN

FORGET ABOUT SLEEP. The next morning, I'm a wreck and it doesn't help when Garrett discovers that Rylan has disappeared with his handgun.

"What?" I ask, as he paces back and forth. "I thought you only had rifles?"

"I had it since I came here. Before she arrived. I didn't think she knew about it."

"Jesus. Would she..."

"She's not that kind of person," he insists.

But is it possible to spend years with someone and still not know him or her?

"You won't find her," I say, certain, even though he hasn't looked everywhere. "And maybe you don't want to if she has a gun." He sinks onto the couch, deflated. My hands wring together. "It's because of the conversation last night, right?"

"Yes," he finally says, then, "I don't know. Maybe." His head drops into his hands. "I'll find her though. Don't worry. Nothing's changed."

"It has for her."

There's another raw silence. The morning sun blazes outside, the living room already distressingly warm.

"She said she lied for you."

He slides his head out of his hands, just enough to see the furrow on his brow. "It was a long time ago."

"I need to know Garrett."

His eyes shift to meet mine. "Now?"

"Yes," I say and sit down next to him. "Now."

The air conditioner cranks in the truck, but when I knock on the door of Addy's cabin the back of my t-shirt is soaked in sweat.

"What are you doing here?" she asks, her eyeball the only thing visible in the crack of the door.

"Can I come in?"

"Not right now."

"Can we talk outside then? There's a little adjustment to our plan I need to discuss."

"An adjustment?" She slips out the door and shuts it tight behind her, but not before the smell escapes.

"We have to leave this afternoon."

"Why?"

"The police got their warrant. They're coming here today."

Her eyes widen. "Are you shitting me?"

"No, Garrett found out yesterday. Last night, when you came over, he was there." I look at her guiltily. "That's why I was a little panicky."

"He was there when I was there?"

"He was out the back. I told him there was too much heat with the police coming and he agreed. He said I should leave before they got here. He seemed really worried."

"So he told you all this last night," she states, like she's reading it from a book.

"Yeah."

"And when are they coming?"

"Six p.m. Garrett wants everyone to meet in advance, at five. If everyone's in there, distracted, it's your best chance to slip out."

She bites her nail, looks off in the distance.

"Addy?"

"What?"

"Are you in?"

Her look says *almost*. "Run me through this step by step. I need to make sure you've thought of everything."

"Uh, well, everyone will be at the meeting at five. I'll stay behind at the shop and get my car."

"You have the keys?"

"Yeah."

"And you can drive it out no problem?"

"Yup."

She leans back, surprised. "You already tried?"

"Yup. I mean I started it," I correct. "Even with the spare, we can make it."

"What if the cops are early?"

"Why would they be?"

"You seem pretty sure about that," she says, crossing her arms.

"It's our only chance, Addy," I say, beads of sweat popping on my forehead. "You have any other ideas?"

"I know enough about Garrett he'd throw his own mother under the bus," she says with unsettling grimness. "If he's worried about exposure with you, why risk you leaving so late? You should be gone by now."

"I wanted to say goodbye to everyone."

She scuffs at weeds growing through the porch boards with her sneaker. "Manners to the end, huh? I guess you were raised right in some way. Too bad we never crossed paths earlier."

"Better late than never right?"

A ghost of a smile appears. "So true," she says. In the lengthy pause after, she seems to be weighing something in her mind. "Where will you be with the car when I come out?"

"By the side entrance. Where the gangway is."

"And Cedric?"

"What about him?"

"You're ready to fight fire with fire?" She stops, smiles. "So to speak."

"We'll do what it takes, right?"

Her eyes drift over me. "You seem way more confident than last night."

"Garrett was there, you came by. I had to sort out all this stuff on my own."

"Uh-huh."

"We're cool then? Do we need to talk about anything else?"

"Sure, we're cool."

She's still so pretty, even without makeup. I squeeze her arm with a shy smile. "I promised I wouldn't leave without you."

"Yeah, you did," she says and puts her hand over mine. "You're a man of your word. That's nice to know."

We stand awkwardly in the hot sun, neither one of us wanting to be the first to break the connection. In the flowerbeds on either side of the porch, demoralized plants are shrivelled and brown. The windows of the cabin are streaked with grime.

"So...then," I prompt.

"Yeah, well, it's almost eleven. I better get ready," she says, her hand falling off mine. "Don't worry, I'll pack light."

FORTY-TWO

IT'S A LIE, of course.

How many more lies can there be? I don't know. Take a number.

The police aren't coming today. They're coming tomorrow. It's part of our plan and our plan is coming to a head.

It's 4:03 p.m. The air in the bedroom is sluggish with heat.

Lying on the bed, my stomach grinds. Sunlight streams in through the bay window, catching the crystals, a reminder of my first morning here. Back then, this room, this place, was strange and unknown. Now it's jammed with memories. Some, I hope to forget.

In the shop this morning, after visiting Addy, I tried to keep busy. I put another coat of stain on the new bench, the one we're never going to use. On the back, we carved *Built by D.H. & G.K.* and with my mind elsewhere, I let excess stain gum up in the letters. Talking to JD at lunch was torture. When she asked me where Garrett was, I froze. Garrett and I agreed to stay apart today. He was busy this morning, doing what he needed to do. When I brought up Rylan, JD said she hadn't seen her all day. Shortly after, I puked in the bathroom.

Now, it takes supreme effort to peel myself off the bed. My mind still swirls with everything Garrett told me earlier.

He explained his father got indicted for fraud because he was running an illegal fund, a pyramid scheme. When his mother agreed to testify against him, his father hung himself in jail. The investigation stalled. The Securities and Exchange Commission wanted a scalp, so Garrett was the next target. The prosecutors sweetened the pot for his mother in hopes she'd testify Garrett was also involved. When she buckled, Garrett turned to Rylan. They'd been broken up for over a year but Garrett promised to pay back her parents all the money they lost in his dad's fund, if she'd be his alibi, swear he wasn't involved. He told her they could try again, to try and make it work, out here, if she helped him.

This made my heart seize up.

"She came out here because she loved you," I said, my voice hollow. "But you didn't love her."

"I was wrong to do that," he said. "It was a mistake from the start. But she was my only chance."

I was about to ask why she had stayed this whole time then didn't. Hope can be cruel when it's all a person has. When that's taken away, when there is no going back like Rylan said, what did that translate into? I was spared, temporarily, from dwelling on that question, as Garrett continued his story.

During Garrett's trial, his mother died; killed herself. Perhaps out of guilt for framing her son. Garrett came out here shortly after, Rylan a couple months later. It took Garrett's lawyer seven years to find all the offshore money his father had hidden: almost a billion dollars. All the money Garrett has been using here has been traceable. And there isn't much left. After a few big trading losses, he's up against a wall.

"With this offshore money," he said, "We can disappear forever. I signed for it when I was in New York. It's all there. Numbered accounts."

"But..." I paused. An alarm bell went off in my brain. "Were you planning to leave here? Before me?"

"Yes," he admitted, but quickly added, "I didn't know when or how."

The room seemed to darken. "Am I the how?"

His hands were warm when they cradled my face, and I'd forgotten, or did I ever know, what it felt like to have someone look at me the way he did then. "You're the *why,* Damien, the most important part. I've waited my whole life for you."

There was a dumb silence, a tug in my chest. I just nodded, mute, and not because I couldn't speak. Sometimes there's nothing left to say. Falling in love isn't a decision, it's a recognition, and right then, seeing the vulnerability in his eyes, I knew I'd do anything, as long as we could be us.

Back in the bedroom, I wish it were already over.

It sucks what's happening.

It sucks big time.

With heavy steps, I walk out of the guest house one last time. Six minutes later, I've parked Garrett's truck far enough away from the common house and now slink towards it, walking duck-like through the dry grasses. At the rear of the meeting room, there they are: soldiers waiting for their general.

The jerry cans are five gallons, bigger than I normally use. Two gallons fit nicer in the Lexus, but in this instance, size doesn't matter. I've lit enough fires. I can burn a house down with a match and three copies of *LA Weekly*.

But that was then.

Now, the brass Zippo Garrett gave me is a like a boulder in my pocket. Kneeling in the grass, I struggle to unscrew the cap off one jerry can. It's impossible to keep my hands steady, let alone concentrate. I sit back on my heels and take a deep breath.

That's when hard metal pushes against my spine.

"I knew he was a sick fuck, but this takes the cake," she hisses. "And you were going to let me burn, weren't you?"

"No," I manage to choke out. "It's not what you think, Addy."

"Don't you dare Addy me," she warns. "'Not what I think', my ass. Get up. Slow. Hands in front. You run and you're dead." She drives the gun barrel deeper into my skin as I fumble upright. "Against the wall. Face me." Under the baseball cap, her eyes are sheened with madness. "Oh, Cutie Pie. I never imagined you to be this way. What a waste. I can understand his corruption. He's been under the sway of the devil." She strokes one of my cheeks then the other with the barrel. "But *you*."

A thick scent of sweat fills the air. Mine. She lowers the gun and studies me.

"You have nothing to say? After catching you red handed?"

"Please..."

The butt of the gun slams into my skull, pain ricocheting like a pin ball gone berserk. "Fuuuuck. Addy. No."

"Stop snivelling like the coward you are. You tell me how this is all playing out. What was your big plan?"

"There wasn't one."

The gun explodes beside my head. Aftershock shatters in my ears.

"Jesus Christ," I yell, shrivelling into a ball. "Don't shoot me."

Inside the meeting room, screams, a swell of voices. Addy jams the hot barrel under my chin. "I asked you a question."

"Oh god," I say, my eyes clenched tight. "Colombia. We were going to Colombia."

"South America?" she asks in disbelief. When I nod, she cackles. "Oh, how romantic. You two gallivanting and holding hands on another continent." Tsking with disgust, "You men think you're so fucking smart. Your stupid little speech this morning. You think I believed you for one minute? I went in with both eyes wide open and guess what I saw? I always thought Garrett was smart, but turns out he's even dumber than you. He's wearing a bloody watch. He never wears a watch. That means he's keeping track of the time, and what for? To cue something up....with someone," she adds, significantly. "And who said to me they were going to be late?"

"I'm sorry," I say, as if an apology could somehow stop this crazy train. "Honest."

"It's too late for apologies, Damien. I debated sparing you, but you're both sinners that can't be saved." She yanks the gun off my chin and shoves it against my temple. Her other hand slips down and starts to rub my crotch.

"Don't..." I plead. "Please..."

"Oh, but you like that, don't you? I remember. You wanted it soooo bad." She gyrates up against me and whispers in my ear. "You better not get hard, you pervert."

On the other side of the meeting room wall, chaos has erupted. The roar of voices grows hysterical.

"What the hell is going on in there?" she demands. "Answer me!" Wedging the gun between my legs she unloads a bullet into the ground. The recoil slams the gun into my balls.

"Stop. Please," I gasp, the whole world gone black. "He's coming out. He's locked them in."

Her hand pats around the only hardness in my pocket. "And what do we have here?" she asks, pulling out Garrett's truck keys. "The getaway car?" She stuffs them into her pocket and shoves me off the wall. "Let's go meet lover boy, shall we? Just remember, I'm not a pussy like you. I've got four bullets left and am not shy to use them." With one hand gripped on my shoulder, she pushes me forward, her other hand pressing the gun against the back of my head. "That's right," she mutters. "Nice and slow."

With each halting step forward, the prospects get bleaker. I'm trying desperately to think of a way out of this when Garrett peels around the corner. He skids to a halt when he sees us. Addy yanks her arm around my neck, points the gun at him. "Hands up, fuck face."

The brief flash of anguish on his face disappears and he raises his hands up. "Put the gun down, Addy."

"Nice try. Your little run has come to an end. You and lover boy here. I just don't know the best way to go about this. I can shoot you both or I can herd you back in there, tell them all what you were about to do, and watch them shred you alive."

"Let him go and I'll do whatever you want."

"Uh-uh. Cutie Pie had his chances to make things right and he failed," she says, and jerks on my neck. "Didn't you?"

"It's not about him," Garrett says. "It's me you want."

"I don't make deals with the devil."

"You already did," he reminds her.

"Our deal's come and gone. Long gone."

He takes a cautious step forward. "Where's Rylan?"

"Wouldn't you like to know," she says, edging back with me.

"Where is she?" he demands again.

"Why do you care all of a sudden, huh? You're the reason she fucked Cassius. The reason *he's* here, the reason why you never looked at me. You're disgusting. You both are." She yanks hard on my neck again.

"Addy, c'mon," I plead, the whole situation slipping away, "don't do this."

Garrett's motionless, but I can tell every cog in his brain is spinning. "You've got another twenty years to serve, Isis Aurora. If you do anything to him, you're never going to see freedom again."

Everything about her, even her body chemistry, changes. I can smell it.

"It's amazing what comes out of people's mouths just before they die," he continues, his voice smooth and gentle, like he's reading a story to a kid. "You're a murderer."

"It was self-defense," she says, her body now rigid behind mine. "Unlike you, killing for fun."

"Why don't we come to an understanding," Garrett says, moving forward a step.

The gun cocks on my temple. "Don't you even think of coming closer," she warns. "You're evil, pure evil."

Garrett stills. I'm completely confused with their conversation.

"Don't do it, Isis," he says.

A hissing sound rumbles from deep inside her. "I'm not going back. It ends here for you, not for me."

It's impossible to describe: a gun against my brain, a lunatic in charge, every option a fail. Garrett's poised like a cat, waiting to pounce, but it's me that makes the first move when the sound of smashing glass distracts us all. Addy's grip loosens just enough and survival instinct kicks in. I swivel and tackle her, both of us landing hard on the ground. The gun flies out of her hand. I scramble on top of her.

"Fuck you," Addy screams and starts to buck wildly.

Garrett bolts to the gun, grabs it and pushes me off Addy. In one fluid motion, he pins her arms above her head and throws me the gun.

"Get ready," he says.

More glass crashes, the windows of the meeting room disintegrating as chairs are thrown against them from within.

Addy continues to buck violently under Garrett. "Get off of me."

"Where's Rylan?" he demands.

"Let me go and I'll tell you," she says.

His other hand clamps around her face. "Where is she?"

"She came to me last night, like we were long lost friends. Asking for my forgiveness. Saying we needed to work together. She wanted you dead. The only thing we had in common. Poor thing. You should have heard her cry." She spits in his face and laughs. "I love it when they beg."

He punches her so hard, her face wedges deep into the dirt. Blood spurts out of her nose.

"Garrett," I say, my stomach lurching, "don't."

"You're sick," he says to her. "I knew it the minute I met you."

"I'm sick? You're about to barbecue thirty-six people. And for what? So you could have a big, fat cock in your mouth?"

"Shut up," he yells, his arm muscles bulging as he squeezes her wrists.

"Oh, I had it too. Before you. You should have heard *him* beg. He was dying something awful."

"Shut up!"

He starts to pummel her with vicious strokes and I drop the gun, try to pull him off her, but it's like trying to grab an avalanche thundering down a mountain. He's in full, deadly motion. "Garrett. Please. Stop."

He swivels towards me. Dirt and blood streak his face. He's panting hard, fever in his eyes. "Shoot her then."

"No," I say, backing up. "No, I can't."

"Cutie Pie can't kill shit," Addy croaks, her face a pulpy mess. "He's weak."

"Shoot her," Garrett yells at me. "In the head!"

"You're not like him Cutie Pie. You never will be."

The sun disappears as dark clouds swirl in the sky. The air starts to hum in a way I've felt before. Garrett looks up, alarmed. "Damien. Give me the gun. Quick. Now!"

Cold wind starts to whip and thunder rumbles overhead. Something worse than fear erupts inside me. "What's going on?"

"Give it to me," he yells again and this time his eyes are afraid, looking past me.

I turn around and everything comes to a standstill. "Jesus."

The animals are lined up like an army about to attack. In front of them, the jaguar paces back and forth. The sky is completely black.

"Damien..." Garrett says, his voice disappearing as his back arches in a whipping crunch, like he's been tasered. His shirt starts to bulge, seams ripping as he expands. His scream is tortured agony.

"Run!" Addy yells. "He's turning."

But I can't move.

Garrett jerks and contorts like a puppet pulled on a string. His body arcs forward into a half circle, his spine splitting through the skin on his back. Tendons snap. White bone glistens with blood. Thunder rumbles overhead. What's left of his clothing falls to the ground as his limbs expand and contort.

I collapse onto my knees, my hand over my mouth. "Holy shit."

The hum is full throttle. The entire ground shakes. The darkest sounds pour out of Garrett's mouth, his head deforming in slow motion. A thick coat of black fur starts to sprout all over. Beneath him, Addy writhes helplessly. The parts of her touching Garrett start to smolder, the smell of burning hair and flesh filling the air.

"I told you," she moans and it's the last thing she'll say.

The metamorphosis ends with the stench of rotting flesh. Garrett no longer exists. Saliva drips out of the jaguar's mouth, the same one I came face to face with in the pit. Long, yellow teeth jut from its jaws. It flings its head back and growls, an old, galactic sound. With preternatural speed it rips Addy's throat out with a savage pull. A spray of warm human debris splatters over me and I'm on all fours, hyperventilating and puking at the same time, everything going the wrong way. Out of the corner of my eye, the animals and jaguar continue to storm towards us. Panicked, I dig through the grass.

The gun. Where's the gun?

I yank it out of a tangle of weeds, the weight a reminder of its deadliness. Sitting up, one knee cocked, I remember what Garrett told me with the rifle. Aim, breathe in, and then shoot while exhaling. But my elbow slips off my knee as I try to steady myself. *C'mon. Focus.* I lean hard, my elbow digging deep into my thigh. With the world spinning, my eye line bounces along the gun sights. The jaguar bounds in and out of them. Inhale. Exhale.

The kick is ferocious, like being punched and I tumble backwards. The jaguar keeps barreling towards us. With the sound of the gunshot, the creature that was Garrett howls. It swipes a heavy paw in my direction, but it's a dopey movement and just misses my shoulder as I roll left. Only yards away, the real jaguar locks eyes on mine. Flipping over to lie prone, I steady the gun and line the sights up.

"Fuck you," I whisper.

The last four bullets explode out of the gun. A prehistoric shriek deafens the afternoon. The jaguar crashes to the ground, its unearthly sounds fading as it dissolves and sinks into the earth. One by one, the other animals evaporate in a cloud of matter, thin trails rising to disappear in the wind. Lightning cracks on the cliffs and rocks explode, shattered remains raining down. Beside me, there's a thump, a strangled sound.

I throw the gun to the ground and run.

"Garrett!"

FORTY-THREE

HE STARTS TO CONVULSE, rivulets of slime hanging out of his mouth.

There's a grotesque squishing noise, like pieces of wet meat being handled. Fur starts to fall off him in chunks, burning as they hit the ground. His limbs stutter back, reforming arms, legs. I watch the transformation back, horrified, until it's just him, naked on the ground.

"Garrett. Can you hear me?"

My skin sizzles touching his shoulder. I yank my hand away. He's burning up. Ripping my shirt off, I wave it over him, frantic. "C'mon, c'mon, c'mon. You can make it." Finally, his eyes flutter open. Tears of relief blur my eyes. "Oh my god. Are you okay?"

He looks around, dazed. "What happened?"

"It doesn't matter," I tell him. "C'mon. Can you get up?"

He raises himself up on his elbows, awkward and slow, reflexively covers himself with one hand. "You didn't shoot it, did you?"

"I think so. It's gone. They're all gone."

His eyes widen. "You shouldn't have."

"Whatever, I did. Here," I say, standing up to undo my jeans. "Put these on. We have to get out of here."

"You're not safe," he insists, his words slurred.

"We'll figure it out. I don't care. Just get up," I plead. "Please, we need to go." He lets me pull him up, but he's unsteady, weaving back and forth. "Hold on to me," I order, and maneuver his legs, one at a time, into my jeans. They barely fit him. I can't even do up the zipper.

"But..." he starts.

"You're delirious. We're fine. We're leaving, remember? Far away. Like you need."

He stares at my underwear, bewildered. "What are you going to wear?"

"It doesn't matter. I'll find something." I bump against the shredded mess that was Addy and it makes me sick all over again. We can't leave her out here. "Can you pick her up? I can't carry her myself."

He looks down at her body with an ill expression. "You don't understand. I made a mistake."

"Shut up! I don't care," I yell, my nerves frayed. I've never seen him like this: lost, a deer in the headlights. "We've both made mistakes. Lots of them."

Focus. Don't lose it now.

I force myself to take a deep breath. "Yes, I care. Of course I care," I say, and clamp both hands on his shoulders, give him a shake. "But, we'll talk about it later, ok? C'mon, please. We're so close."

"Okay. Okay."

"You get her shoulders. I'll grab her ankles."

With the awkward load, we shuffle slowly. She's heavy and her skin is still warm. Tendons visible in her throat tense and release as her head lolls side to side. Every step is a battle to not puke or collapse. Close to the meeting room, the shouts and pounding continue, and maybe it's hearing them that make Garrett finally seem lucid, back from wherever he was.

"I'll pull her inside," he tells me, setting her down on the gangway stairs. "You start."

"I need the lighter. It's in your front pocket." He fishes it out and tosses it to me. "And grab the truck keys from her pocket," I say, pointing at Addy. "She took them from me."

He nods grimly and I break into a run.

The sun starts to cut through the clouds and the afternoon light is perfect, what photographers call the magic hour, except there's no magic going on here. At the back of the meeting room, voices spiral out of the broken windows and with determined focus summoned from who knows where, I pretend they're not real. What we're doing isn't right; it will never be right, it will be a shadow hanging over me that will only get smaller with time. But I've been on the other side. Lived through too many wrongs. Those shadows will never go away either.

Lorelei once asked me about commitment, and back then, I didn't know any better. But this is what commitment is. It means doing things I'd never do because of the promise of something better. And I deserve better, even if it means this.

Working quickly, I splash gasoline up the sides, along the back perimeter of the building; I'll do the front next so the fire is even. As the jerry can empties and fumes surround me, it suddenly hits. There is no seduction, no rush. No agonized moment, my body about to explode. I've waited a long time for this, and I pause, not quite believing it. From now on, fire will be like an old friend I think of once in a while. We've shared things I'll never share with anyone. Things I'm now going to share with him.

With the last jerry can in hand, I run back to the gangway, weightless, but any levity evaporates seeing Garrett's somber face. He's sitting on the steps, arms resting on his legs, hands knitted in front.

"You alright?" I ask.

"Yes," he says, although his voice is strange and disconnected.

Unable to read him, guessing, "I'm sorry. About Rylan."

"It's not your fault. None of this is."

His gaze shifts behind me, and I look back too, at the truck in the distance.

"You got the keys, right?"

"Yeah."

With a reluctant glance at the meeting room, I swallow hard. "Let's get this over with."

I'm halfway up the stairs when he grabs my leg. "Wait."

He stands and takes the jerry can out of my hand. His kiss comes out of nowhere, and in those dreamy seconds I lose myself in him, almost forget it all. When we pull apart, his hand clamps on the back of my head, pushing our foreheads to touch.

"We made it," I remind him, because he looks unsure. "We're doing this."

"I know."

"Get the truck ready," I say and head up the stairs. "I'll only be a minute."

In the coat room, Addy's body is slumped against the far wall. A dark brown stain spreads around her. The meeting room door is barricaded with the wooden braces Garrett installed early this morning. Through the walls, the screams are a grisly reminder of what I've agreed to do.

JD's voice cuts through suddenly, as if she's right behind me. "Sammy," she moans, "I'm so sorry. Please forgive me."

Oh god. I need to get out of here.

My arms are leaden pouring gasoline on the walls, the floor, over Addy. When its empty, I toss the jerry can into the corner, turn around and freeze.

It's in the way his 6'4 frame blocks the door.

His eyes flash, like a shutter opening. I don't want to think they're closing.

I take a step forward and he holds up his hand. "No," is all that comes out. Then, trying to contain my panic, "Garrett. What the fuck."

"You weren't listening," he says. "It's trapped inside me now. It can't go back. I'll be like this forever. That's why I never shot it."

"It doesn't matter," I tell him. "We'll figure it out. Somehow."

He shakes his head, gutted. "I should have told you. I did the session to try and help you but I also wanted to get rid of this. For *you*. I didn't want you to ever think you wouldn't be safe with me."

Behind me, the barricades on the door flex and crack. Desperate bodies flung, trying to escape.

His hand opens like a flower. "Give me the lighter."

"No," I say, the worst fear bubbling in my throat. "No way."

"Damien," he pleads. "It's too late. Please."

Time, space, everything warps. The future that was there, seconds before – *I can still fucking taste him* - is gone, changed forever. A feeling I don't even have a name for tightens around me. "But you said we'd go together."

"I can't control it now," he says and glances at Addy's body, agonized. "It can't end like that for you. For me. I could never live with myself."

Beneath me, gasoline spreads under the soles of my sneakers. I start to tremble uncontrollably. "Garrett..."

"This is the only way," he says. "For me and you. You know it's true."

But is it? He said I was the *why*, the most important part, but if I'm the *how*, it means something I can't, won't, *refuse* to comprehend. My mind reels then blanks. A strange wash of dizziness rushes through me. "Then say it, if it's true. You know what I mean."

"Please," he says, his hand reaching, the bang of bodies against the door growing louder, the screaming more intense. "You know."

"Then just SAY IT!" I yell. "Just fucking say it okay?"

And he's there, in the doorway, wearing my too-small jeans, looking ridiculous and frightened beyond belief, and when he says he loves me, it's like he can't even understand what he just said and that's how I know it's true. Then somewhere, in a place beyond comprehension, my own truth takes a bloody form: if I can't be with him, I don't want to be at all.

My throat swells with grief, with the inevitable.

I toss the lighter to him and his face crumples with devastation.

"Then do what you have to do."

The space between us turns blinding white.

There is no more sound, just the memories of a hundred fires raging clear and bright.

Too many fires.

Too many pieces of me.

I've been holding on tight for so long and can't do it anymore.

Love was something I never understood. It was a word, a concept with too many variables, something else I couldn't control. Now I understand it, but whoever said love is grand is a freaking liar, because love is brutal, because how can I be so close to it yet so far away?

I close my eyes. It's getting impossible to breathe. I fight the nerves and anticipation and the last thing I think about is this:

Garrett's floating in the river, eyes closed, arms and legs spread like a starfish, the water around him tiny diamonds sparkling in the sun. And that's how I'll always remember him: at peace, both of us at peace, on a hot sunny afternoon, when I finally felt like I belonged in this world.

And like ashes dusted in the breeze, my fears and doubts start to drift away, something unknown takes over, and it comes to me at the worst possible moment, when there's sweet fuck all I can do about it.

This is what it feels like to let go.

FORTY-FOUR

REMAINS OF CULT MEMBERS RECOVERED

Reuters – Newswire

TODAY, the remains of thirty-seven people were removed from a remote property in New Mexico, north of Abiquiu. Fire fighters were called to the property on the evening of August 1st, when smoke was reported in the area. Due to the remote location authorities were unable to attend in time to save anyone. All but one of the bodies was found in a single building and its speculated they were locked in when the fire was set. The contentious property was recently under attack for a series of abortions and alleged deaths of several members of the cult living there.

Damien Hester, the alleged arsonist responsible for the fire that destroyed the Pacific Palisades, CA housing development of Virginia Hills, is widely speculated to be among the remains. His vehicle was found on the property, although it is unclear what connection, if any, he had to the cult. Damien's father, real estate tycoon Franklin

Hester, whose development firm, Hester Real Estate Corp, was behind the Virginia Hills complex, was unavailable for comment.

Thirty-two-year-old cult leader Garrett Sawyer Kaller, son of disgraced Wall Street trader Mitchell Kaller, was not one of the identified victims. Mitchell Kaller, who had an estimated fortune of four billion when he died, became synonymous with Wall Street greed, after he bilked millions of dollars out of investors with a Ponzi-like scheme. When his wife, socialite Heather Braun-Kaller, was granted immunity to testify against him, Mr. Kaller took his own life in jail. Garrett was also alleged to be involved in the Ponzi scheme, but was eventually found innocent. Ms. Braun died during Garrett's trial, and her death was deemed a suicide, despite traces of a rare poison found during the autopsy.

Garrett moved from New York City to the New Mexico property seven years ago and became the leader of the secretive group, which was reported to have demonic leanings. The Native American members, defected from the nearby Jicarilla Apache Nation, believed Mr. Kaller to be a powerful shaman, although Eleanor Marks, a nurse who previously treated one of the deceased cult members at a hospital in Espanola, New Mexico, claimed Mr. Kaller was using concoctions of drugs and poisonous plants to subdue and brainwash the members. The rare Brugmansia shrub, native to tropical South America, was found on the property, along with several other toxic and rare plants. The Brugmansia genus contains the alkaloid scopolamine, a powerful hallucinogen whose effects include memory loss.

The entire property is now part of a more detailed investigation and remains under heavy security.

Garrett Kaller is believed to be alive, still at large and identifiable by the rare condition of Heterchromia iridum, which results in two different colored eyes. Local authorities are working closely with the FBI in this investigation, and they have created an anonymous hotline for any leads on the whereabouts of Mr. Kaller.

Anyone with information is encouraged to call.

PART THREE

FORTY-FIVE

GARRETT

LAST NIGHT I had the same dream.

I'm in the back seat of the truck. Cassius is driving, too fast, and I yell at him to slow down. In my lap is the most delicate creature I have ever seen. Dark waves of hair. Pale and fragile. His life, literally in my hands. The swell inside me is urgent, frenzied, and all I know is he has a story, a life, somewhere, and the desire to know it, to shape it, to steer him away from it, towards me, is as strong as the desire for his slim, smooth body to press against mine.

He's right there, so close.

I brush my lips against his, but he's cold. Frozen solid.

His eyes snap open and they're black and lidless, like a demon.

He starts to burn and I wake up screaming.

I forgot how it works so close to the equator: the tropical sun maddeningly in the sky for twelve hours, before twelve hours of night. During the day I can pretend he's about to come around the corner and smile. I'll touch his skin. Feel his heart beat.

But I can't pretend at night.

From Mexico, I went through Guatemala, El Salvador, Costa Rica only at night. In Panama, the fisherman, surprised at my Spanish, pocketed the wad of bills without asking questions and told me to stay below deck. The sky was flushed with the last light of dusk when he dropped me close to Jurado: a tiny strip of buildings hugging the Colombian coast. At his beach house, there was no discussion of rates or length of stay and his lined face, salted from sun and sea, only nodded when I handed over more bills.

The house is half a mile away from the village, perched close to the ocean in a protected bay. Behind me, the jungle is alive with sounds I can't place. From my hammock, the waves of the Pacific crash only a few yards away. The west coast of Colombia is beautiful, like he said it would be. He was right in so many ways.

Ways I can't bring back.

This morning, a bank of clouds hangs behind the jungle, dark and sinister. Waiting. Carola, the fisherman's sturdy daughter, hovers over me, brown eyes wide with worry. Gringo's in the hammock again. Unwashed. Same clothes. Every few days she drops off food and water, but I'm sick, not eating. The house smells like sweat and vomit, rotting food. Ants march silently along the baseboards, up the walls. Carola offers fruit, tells me to eat, and I wave listlessly.

Go away, before you end up like the two villagers, mangled, their throats ripped out.

The storm has crested, moving west to east. The night air is heavy with salt. Waves thunder on the beach, the ocean black and full of fury. Sand dissolves beneath my feet as the back rush of the tide pulls me in. Pulls me deeper.

Sartre was right, after all.

We come into this world with the ability to do anything, and in the end, are defined by our choices. Haunted by the wrong ones. I can't expect anything good in this lifetime, not after the things I've done, so the only thing left is hope. Goddamned hope. Hope is what *I* gave other people. And now, every day, it gnaws on me, like a disease with no cure. Hope that maybe there is an afterlife and maybe, just maybe, that's where I'll see him again.

The sand has disappeared and I'm floating.

This time, I don't fight the riptide and drift further than I've ever been.

The lights on the shore slip out of sight.

In the moonless night, I can't tell where the ocean stops and the sky starts.

I can hear him calling my name, or maybe it's just the wind.

ABOUT THE AUTHOR

Andréa Fehsenfeld lives in Vancouver, Canada. When she's not writing, she's either taking photographs, standing stage left at a concert or dreaming of sunshine and the smell of coconuts.

Her mailing list fans get top priority: exclusive content, giveaways and contests are all part of the fun. Join the tribe:
Andrea's Newsletter

If you enjoyed *Completion*, please consider leaving a review on Amazon or Goodreads.

Please connect with Andréa on social media or via email. She'd love to hear from you.
Email Andréa

AFTERWORD

Completion is a work of fiction. Although the area north of Abiquiu, New Mexico is famous for its spectacular red rocks, open spaces and mystical energy and there are many side roads spilling off of Highway 84, the 'spider's web' of roads described in the story, along with the cult compound and all the characters, are creations of my imagination.

ACKNOWLEDGMENTS

Writing is a solo experience but it takes a tribe to bring a book into the world. Without the support, effort and inspiration from the following people and places, my creative journey wouldn't have been nearly so satisfying.

Daniel Burgess edited the manuscript and it was a long three months waiting for his feedback. When his positive notes came back it was a blast of confidence. The few suggestions he had were spot on and reworking those elements made the story richer. Muchos Gracias.

Thank you to Gordon Thomas for reading my samples and being a supportive and thoughtful professional.

Writers Digest offers great services to all levels of writers. Through one of their seminars, my first ten pages (early stages) were critiqued and the subsequent advice provided was invaluable.

The Vancouver Public Library continues to be my make shift writers cave. Being able to write uninterrupted is paramount and I'm grateful for their free spaces. Their fantastic resources proved invaluable for everything from research to strengthening my writing skills.

Off the beaten path in Cerrillos, New Mexico, I found the perfect muse for this story. Matt and Sarah Brown are owners of a magical house in the middle of nowhere and the days spent wandering in their home and the surrounding property while writing this book infused the story as much as anything.

Vernon Petago, Heritage Specialist for the Jicarilla Apache Nation in Dulce, New Mexico provided valuable insight into Tribal structure, customs and language. It was a special afternoon visiting this remote area and hearing your stories about Shamans.

What else can I say about New Mexico other than there's something about that place! She lured me into her lair years ago and the mystical experience I had during my inaugural trip was so unforgettable it became the inspiration for Garrett's back story.

Originally, the three parts of the book were introduced by lyrics. Unfortunately there were clearance issues so they were removed. While disappointed, I'd like to give a shout out to the following musicians whose songs will forever remind me of this story: Willa, Phosphorescent and PJ Harvey.

My friends and beta readers offered incredible feedback during the entire process. Their time and encouragement was greatly appreciated. A special shout out to Jennifer Rainnie and Samantha Gill.

My sister, Corine Masich, reads everything I write and has an uncanny nose for sniffing out adverbs. You're the best sister and proof reader.

To my nieces and nephews Sylvia, Olivia, Lily and Michael: you remind me why I love life.

My parents instilled wanderlust in me and never once held me back from pursuing my dreams. Without their many positive influences, I wouldn't be the person I am today. I love you guys.

Lastly, Jeremy. You're my biggest fan. Without your support and love this book would not exist. Thank you. Smooches. XO.

Made in the USA
San Bernardino, CA
22 July 2018